Forever Inn Love

ERIN BRANSCOM

Forever Inn Love

Freedom Valley Series

Copyright © 2023 by Erin Branscom

Erin Branscom
www.erinbranscom.com

ISBN: 979-8-88662-018-4 (ebook)
ISBN: 979-8-88662-017-7 (paperback)

Editor: Emerald Edits and Editing 4 Indies
Cover Design and formatting: Yummy Book Covers

For my Dad.

SENSITIVE CONTENT WARNING

Hi, readers. I'm always careful not to upset anyone by not giving warnings about my stories. I love to write deep characters with real life issues. In this book it talks about anxiety and PTSD from a combat veteran, child neglect and abandonment from a parent, and loss of a friend (not on the page).

I graduated from high school in a small town. And that town wasn't very kind to me at times. There's always going to be a Hamilton in your town. Don't let them win. Always be kind to others. The high road is the best road. The best revenge is success.

When I started writing, I wrote to escape real life that felt really freaking hard. And I wanted to write real life struggles and issues so that I wouldn't feel as alone and others wouldn't as well. I love to make up new small towns that I would actually want to live in. I hope you love Freedom Valley as much as I do.

I love you all and want you to be kind to yourselves,

Erin

Forever Inn Love

CHAPTER 1

Callie

THEN

Senior year...

"Did you know that when otters fall asleep, they hold hands so that they won't drift apart in the water?" SJ murmurs as his hand finds mine. He leans forward, his forehead resting on mine.

"No." I kiss him. "I did not know that," I say softly to the boy who has become so much more than just my best friend.

He threads his fingers through mine, our knees touching as our legs swing off the cliff of our favorite overlook spot just outside town. "You're my otter, Callie."

"You're my otter, too, SJ," I murmur, looking at the boy I call mine. I love him so much. Statistically, some people never find their soulmate, and I found mine in the seventh grade. He's my best friend and my forever.

"Did you get the rest of your applications turned in? I know those were bugging you," he says, breaking my thoughts.

At the mention of college applications, I close my eyes and feel my body tense. I know I should be excited about college and finally leaving Freedom Valley and getting away with SJ, but my parents are making things hard. They made me apply to every Ivy League school. Even though I've repeatedly told them where I want to go, they aren't listening. I did it anyway just to humor them, but I know what I want. SJ and I are going to NYU, and that's that. We're getting out of here as soon as we can and starting our new life together. Then I will hopefully get into a med school on the East Coast. We have a plan. I want to be an ER doctor. SJ is still undecided on what he wants to do, but we're doing it together. He knows he has my full support for whatever he wants to do. Sometimes he talks about business, and sometimes he wants to be a mechanic.

"Yes. Now the waiting game begins." I sigh, relieved to be done with it all. What I want doesn't matter. They don't even see me or hear me. I suspect they just want me to get accepted to a bunch of different colleges so they can brag about it to their friends at the country club. Ever since I was little, probably as far back as preschool, my parents have told me that I'll become

a doctor. Luckily, I happen to love science and want that, too. But I have a suspicion that even if I didn't, I wouldn't have had a choice. Not without an epic meltdown and battle. My parents are relentless and very controlling. My dad's favorite topic is telling everyone that he's going to put me through medical school and have a daughter who's a doctor. Gag.

They have no problem showing off my achievements, but they don't even really know me. I'm invisible otherwise. They don't care to know who my friends are, what I want to do or who I am as a person. I'm a commodity, an asset, nothing more. The disconnect here with them makes me feel so lonely.

His body heaves a deep sigh next to me. "What's the sigh for?" I look over at him.

"We've been talking about leaving Freedom Valley for so long. Now that it's finally happening, I'm just nervous about everything. How it'll all work out." SJ overthinks everything and always has to have a plan. And the fact that he doesn't seem to have a plan yet worries me.

He stares longingly at me with warm, whiskey-brown eyes that I've gotten lost in for the past five years. At times, we can have entire conversations with our eyes and no words spoken. "What do you want to do?" I ask.

"What do you mean?" He picks up a pebble and rolls it between his fingers.

My fingers circle the stack of braided friendship bracelets around my wrist as I twist them out of habit. "You know, college?"

"I don't know." He shrugs. "I feel like I'm supposed to know. I'll figure it out."

"Do you still want to play football?"

He looks out and tosses the pebble over the cliff, and we both watch it drop into the ravine. "I thought I did. It doesn't make me happy anymore like it used to. I like playing for the Eagles, but I feel like I might want to do something different in college."

"You can do anything you want to do, SJ. And you don't have to know right now." It feels overwhelming and exciting to have everything in front of us. I know what I want, and while I wish SJ did, too, it will all work out. I know it.

"It seems like here in Freedom Valley, football is my identity. It's the only way I fit in. I want to figure out who I am away from here where I'm not judged for my family."

Sadness fills me when he talks about being judged in Freedom Valley. I want to remind him about how great he is when he feels this way.

"You have a great dad," I remind him. He looks over at me and nods in agreement, but I can tell he's still sad. His expression is defeated. He's lucky to have a dad like Sam. We both know it. SJ's dad, Sam, has been more of a parent to me than my own parents.

"What makes you happy?" I press, watching as the sun sets in front of us. I shiver since the warmth of the sun is almost gone.

His eyes scan the horizon, and he says softly, "I don't know. But whatever it is, it's going to be with you. College, med school, residency, I'll be there with you. We'll figure it out together."

"Together," I agree. "Pinky promise?"

"Pinky promise." He leans closer and kisses me.

NOW

12 years later...

I can't remember a time when I didn't love SJ. He was Samuel Michael Reid Jr. officially, but his close friends called him SJ when I knew him. I wonder what his friends call him now. I grit my teeth as I think about how I wouldn't know what he's called now because we're no longer friends. We're no longer anything. I know a few choice words I'd *like* to call him.

My shoulders sag with defeat, and I lean back against my couch, trying to will my brain to think of anyone or anything but SJ. It's impossible at this point.

I gaze out the window at dusk and watch the leaves falling from the trees in front of my cottage. Porch lights and streetlights illuminate the street, and it's getting darker earlier now. Fall is my favorite time of year, and I haven't even slowed down to enjoy it.

I'll never admit it to anyone, but I do still love him. It's hard to just stop loving someone who was supposed to be my forever. I just wish he'd been a better man. Someone who means it when he says he loves someone and makes plans.

I feel like I used to know everything about him, and now I feel like I've lived an entire lifetime since we've been apart. I feel like it's been broken up into three parts. There was the beginning when we were awkward thirteen-year-olds on a seventh-grade field trip and then became inseparable friends who didn't care what anyone else thought about our unusual friendship. Then there was the middle when we were in high school, and we became soulmates. I couldn't have imagined living life without my best friend. My SJ. Then there was the after without him. That wasn't the way it was supposed to go, but I had no say in it. And now he's back in Freedom Valley after twelve years of us being apart, and I don't know how I feel about that. I haven't seen him yet, but just knowing he's right here sends my stomach into nervous knots. I start to think about how I can continue to avoid him. Maybe I'll just keep working myself into the ground by continuing to take on every available extra shift at the hospital. That's been working out so far as to not see him, but as for thinking about him? Yeah, I haven't figured that part out yet. He's probably at his dad's auto body shop working, pretending I don't exist anymore anyway. He's good at that. And despite being mad, sadness and concern fill me when I think of the rumor that he doesn't go anywhere and has been a recluse since he moved back. Then I heard another rumor that he might be working at the high school. But I've tried not to listen to any rumors since hearing about him fills me with so many mixed emotions. Freedom Valley loves to gossip, so I don't take any of it seriously. A part of me wants to go to Sam's shop and confront him and finally get answers. And a part of me wants to kick his ass. *I could do both*, I muse with a shrug. He deserves it. *It's justified*, I reason.

It's hard to heal when you don't know what caused the hurt. It contradicts everything about me as a physician. I'm a healer. And when I can't figure out what's hurting a patient, it bothers me. I've never been able to figure out what hurt SJ enough to leave me. Instead, I've been full of so many mixed emotions of love, hurt, anxiety, and anger over a wound I haven't been able to heal.

I take a deep breath and remind myself I'm a doctor. A professional. An upstanding grown-up citizen of Freedom Valley now. I'm supposed to be cool, calm, and collected, not going around fantasizing about kicking someone's ass. Although it was a nice ass.

And if he wanted to talk to me, he would. He could come and find me as well. When it comes to SJ, all bets are off. He *was* my person. And now he's not. It's been twelve years since we broke up, and he broke me. And I think I did a good job trying not to think of him for years. But now I can't seem to stop, especially since he's just a few miles away. I purposely avoid Main Street, where Sam's Auto Body Shop is, and take the roads around it. In fact, I'm severely overdue on my oil change, and my engine light has been on for longer than I care to admit. *I need to go to the next town over and get it checked out on my next day off,* I make a mental note.

My mind wanders, and I take in my tiny light blue cottage that I rent from Mrs. Winters. It sits just behind her cozy house. It's sparse and not decorated since I'm usually working or sleeping. But it's home and the closest place to a home I've ever had. I bought a couch and bed, and that's about it. I keep reminding myself that I need to get around to decorating and making it feel more like a home. But lately, I feel like I'm on the outside looking in on my life. Being back in Freedom Valley stirred up more feelings than I thought it would. Maybe on my next day off, I'll pick up a few things to make it feel cozier in here. Throw blankets, a fall-scented candle, and maybe even a few pumpkins for my porch.

Mrs. Winters a.k.a. Goldie, short for Marigold, is our beloved retired town librarian and the woman who has been like a mother to me. She's my favorite person on the planet. The only anchor I have in life right now. She's a spitfire, always has been and has been the backbone of our community, championing kids and being an advocate for anyone who needs it. Her husband, Rex, passed away when we were in high school, and she's been my best friend and family when mine hasn't been there for me.

Growing up here, the town library always felt safe, warm, and welcoming. Goldie made this a haven for all of us kids.

Located in an old historic Victorian home on the edge of town, the library is impressive. It felt more like a cozy home. I still can't smell oranges or wood furniture polish without being taken back to the feeling of being at the library. She still does a lot for this town and is heavily involved even though she's officially retired now. She seems to have even more time on her hands now to take care of everyone. I like staying here with her because I like taking care of her, too. I'm not here much, but when I am, I check in on her and make sure she's doing okay. A hard knock on my front door startles me out of my daydream, and I shake myself back into reality, exhausted from my long day.

I open the door and hold it open for Goldie. She steps in wearing her usual signature large black-rimmed glasses, her stylish dyed blond bob and bright pink lipstick with her wide contagious smile. She's always been active and walks daily and works out in her garden. She's pushing seventy but doesn't look a day over fifty-five. When I'm older, I hope I have the energy and stamina of Goldie. I smile, thinking about how not much has changed about her in the past few decades. She has a few more wrinkles, but she's still the same.

"Hey, how's it going?" I yawn and run my hand through my messy hair. It's pulled up in a ponytail that desperately needs to be washed. We're on day six of dry shampoo, and my hair is protesting loudly.

Her smile widens, then dims to a pout. "Honey, my car won't start. Can you give me a ride to the football game?" She'll be disappointed if I say no. And she knows I won't say no. I suspect her car is running just fine. She just wants me to go with her. And how can I say no? I haven't seen her in days even though we eat dinner or have coffee together here on the porch every moment that I do get while the weather is still nice.

I look down at my smelly, sweaty scrubs, exhausted from an intense sixteen-hour emergency room shift at the hospital. Then I look back up at her pleading eyes. I look up at the ceiling in defeat and sigh with a small smile. "Can you give me fifteen minutes to get ready?" Fifteen minutes is going to be the bare minimum that I'll need to pull my hot-mess self together into something acceptable. I close my eyes as I remember that I don't have clean clothes now, and these are my last pair of scrubs. It looks like my quiet night at home doing laundry, taking an extremely long, hot shower, ordering a Freedom Pie pepperoni pizza, and binge-watching the *Gilmore Girls* on Netflix won't be happening now.

Her eyes widen in triumph, and her smile grows even bigger with the notion that she's gotten me to go. "Of course, I brought my book." She taps her oversized purse. "I'll just read while you get ready." She clasps her hands together. "Oh, we're going to have so much fun. And it's the first game of the season."

"Wait, I thought you just wanted a ride?" I let out a choked laugh, teasing.

"Well, yes, dear," she feigns innocence. "A ride there *and* a ride home, of course. Hurry along. I'll buy you a hot dog, too." She gives me a look like this is supposed to all be common sense for me.

Well played, Goldie, well played.

I trudge to my tiny bathroom, strip off my smelly scrubs, and toss them in the overflowing hamper in the corner. This is not my idea of… wait, what day is today? It's game night, so it must be Friday. I yawn. I'm going to need coffee for this. A lot of coffee, I think as I turn the hot water on full blast and step in, hoping it'll wake me up.

Surprisingly, I feel slightly more human after my hot shower, and I reach for my soft and worn Eagles T-shirt that was once SJ's. The one thing I let myself keep all these years. I reason that it's more mine than his. He has no claim to a football team. It's threadbare from wear. You can barely read his name on the back or make out his number now from sleeping in it and countless late-night study sessions. I've probably washed it hundreds of times. But it's my comfort shirt and one of the only reasonably clean articles of clothing that I can scrounge up.

I guess I could use a night out with Goldie after what

has been too many back-to-back hospital shifts that never seemed to end, only overlapping into each other. I've lost track. I throw my long blond hair back and put it in a quick braid down my shoulder. I brush my teeth, put a little mascara on my long dark lashes, hoping to brighten my tired blue eyes, and head out. I should put more effort into it, but this is the best I've got. My mother would be horrified if she saw me out like this. I don't think I've ever seen my mother without a full face of makeup and a perfectly ironed designer outfit. Even her pajamas match and are fancy.

I sleep and eat mostly at the hospital these days, only making it home to shower and change clothes. It's no wonder Goldie cornered me when she could. She probably misses me. Guilt fills me, and I make a mental note to come home more. Sometimes it's just easier to bury myself in work. After all, this is what I've worked my butt off for. To be a doctor. I made it, and I couldn't have done it without Goldie's support and encouragement. And while things are rocky with my parents, she's the only person I can rely on now. Even though I've almost achieved everything I wanted, something still seems missing. I feel lost. For twelve years, my identity has been wrapped up in becoming a doctor. And now? I've made it, but I don't know what to do with myself besides work. It's like I lost my identity somewhere along the way, and I'm trying to find myself now that I'm back home.

"Hurry, we don't want to miss the kickoff!" Goldie calls,

snapping me from my identity crisis thoughts.

I nab my keys and purse. "I'm ready, but I'll need coffee."

She reaches over and puts a hand to my cheek, and I can't help but lean into her cool and gentle touch. "You work too hard, honey. You need a night off and some fun." I don't miss the twinkle in her eyes. She's up to something. And honestly, I'm too tired to question her right now. I'll be lucky if I'm able to stay awake for the game. I've been known to nap anywhere and at any time. My car, the storage closet at the hospital, anywhere I can. After finishing four years of college, four years of medical school both in New York, and an intense Boston emergency room residency that was physically and mentally grueling, sometimes I think I'm still tired from it all, even now that I've been working as an official physician for months now. A temporary physician, but still, a physician. I can't wait for Freedom Valley Memorial to make it official with a contract and hire me full time. I'm looking forward to starting my new life back here in Freedom Valley.

Goldie updates me on everything going on in town as we make the short drive to the Freedom Valley High School stadium. We park, and I lean my head down to look up through the windshield. "Huh, it looks bigger."

"Oh, it got remodeled a few years ago after we won state again. Football is even bigger now than when you were in school. I love seeing all you kids grown up and coming to games with families of your own."

I can't imagine being responsible for anyone but myself right now. It's been strange being back in Freedom Valley and seeing some of my friends around town who are now married and with kids. Sometimes I feel like time has flown by, and we can't possibly be old enough to have families of our own.

We get up to the ticket booth, and I reach for my wallet, and a young man leans out. "Mrs. Winters, go on." He waves us in cheerfully as the game has already begun and music plays as they announce the players. I shake my head and laugh about how she's still a local celebrity even though she's retired. I don't know a single soul who doesn't adore her, and if anyone said anything bad about Goldie, I'd never believe them. Besides my parents, maybe, but they don't count. They're mean to everyone. You'll never find a woman with a bigger heart than Goldie.

"Hurry, we have to get to our seats," she calls as she hurries into the crowded stadium where it looks like there are no seats left. This doesn't seem to deter her, as she makes her way to the middle of the stadium underneath the announcer's booth. She pushes through, waving and smiling to everyone. I hear someone call, "Mrs. Winters is here!" and I kid you not, the crowd parts for us, like the sea parting in waves. What. In. The. World. Like I said, local celebrity. Being with her has some perks.

She hugs a few random people I vaguely recognize. I look around and take in the bright stadium lights and the smell of popcorn and hot dogs. This is my first game since high school and the season's first game. The excitement in the stadium is contagious. I realize I'm not as tired anymore, and she nudges me. "Are you excited?"

It does feel good to be out and about. "Thank you for coercing me into joining you," I add dryly with a smile.

She laughs and playfully nudges me with her hip as she claps as the team runs onto the field. She's wearing a Freedom Valley jersey with a cheetah pattern, glitter lettering, black slacks, and cheetah-patterned ballet flats. So very Goldie. The back of her bedazzled jersey says, "Mrs. Winters." I'm sure someone made it for her.

I wasn't sure how I'd feel being back here where all the memories of SJ have stolen pieces of my heart and that familiar melancholy creeps back in that I've worked hard to push down and try to forget over the years. The ghosts of memories haunt me daily being back here and it's been harder than I imagined it would be. But I'm determined to make a new life here with Goldie. Figure out who I am and what my new life looks like now.

As I'm getting settled in my seat, someone taps on my shoulder, and when I turn, it's a woman who looks around my age, but I don't recognize her. "Hey, is that Coach Reid's old number?" She nods with a grin down at my shirt. "Still a big fan?"

"What do you mean?" I ask, confused. How can she even read that to know that and what does she mean by "Coach."

"Wait, Allie?" I stare at her, shocked. Her familiar green eyes, playful grin, and dark wavy hair remind me of someone. Then it dawns on me. She's Allie Harper, Evan's younger sister, and she's all grown up now. I have so many childhood memories with Evan and Allie and their family's Golden Gable Inn.

She grins at me. "Yep, it's me. It's so good to see you again, Callie." She reaches over and gives me a hug, smiling.

"How are you?" I look over and see a little boy with her who looks about five.

"I'm good, this is my son, Caleb. I just opened my own bakery. Baked Inn Love." She smiles, and it feels good to see a familiar friendly face.

"Hi, Caleb," I say to her little boy, and he gives me a little wave. He's wearing a bright blue Freedom Valley hooded sweatshirt and an Eagles ballcap that is big on him. So cute.

"Dad's here!" the little boy shrieks excitedly as a tall good-looking man joins them and puts his arm around Allie and kisses her. He bends down and scoops up the little boy and hugs him, too.

"Callie, this is my husband, Logan. Honey, this is Callie. Evan and I grew up with her. She just moved back, and she's a doctor here now."

Like I thought to myself earlier. Small town, everyone knows everything about everyone. I muse. I hold back a grin, a warm feeling filling me being back in a place where people know me and remember me. Something that didn't often happen in big cities going to college and school. I was lost in the crowd and often just another face. It was lonely, and ironically, it feels less lonely being back in a place where people know me. I've missed this.

Logan shakes my hand. "Nice to meet you."

"It's crazy we haven't run into each other yet," she says. "But I've seen you around."

"Well, to be honest, I practically live at the hospital, so unless you come there, I probably wouldn't see you. I haven't been very good at getting out," I admit.

"Well, you must come see the bakery. We also have a book club that meets on Wednesdays, and we'd love to have you."

"Count me in," I say as I take in their cute family. This is why I moved back to Freedom Valley. Facing my past and all the pain that happened here made it way more of a challenge than I had anticipated. But it's still home. Where Goldie lives, where my friends are. And even though coming home has been hard, it's something I needed to do.

I realize I need something more than the hospital. And while Goldie has been great, I need friends. I will make time for this.

I think back to what she first said. "What did you mean

when you said *Coach* Reid? Is SJ's dad, Sam, coaching?" I ask, confused.

"No, SJ," she says confused like I should know this. "Are you not in touch with him?"

My face scrunches up, and l whip my head over to look at Goldie. She looks straight ahead like a deer in the headlights and won't look at me. *Oh my God.* What has she done?

I turn back to Allie for answers. "What do you mean, *SJ*?" My hands tremble, my breath catches in my lungs, and a feeling of nausea rolls through me. I can hear the blood whooshing through my ears to the frantic beat of my erratic pulse.

Is he really a coach here? My eyes are wide, and I stare at her almost silently begging her to tell me this isn't happening. Suddenly self-conscious, my arms cross over my chest to cover up his number, but REID is still across the back. Even though it's worn down and you can barely make it out, it's there. *Why did I wear this shirt? Oh God.*

Allie says nothing over the crowd's noise but points down at the field. My eyes follow her and land on him. I freeze. My hand goes to my mouth, my eyes wide. The noisy stadium is gone. I'm frozen in time watching him, just like I did from this very same spot over a dozen years ago. My body buzzes with nerves like someone just shocked me with defibrillator paddles. I always wondered what it would be like to see him again, and now, I know. *There he is.* My stomach clenches, my face still buzzing. Is it hot out here? It feels so hot all of a sudden. I pull my shirt and fan myself with it nervously, taking a deep breath, struggling to remember to breathe.

It's strange to see him at thirty. In my mind, he's still the eighteen-year-old boy who left me behind and never looked back. Not even a note, text, or email. Yet here he is just casually standing on the field talking to players in a bright blue polo shirt whose tanned massive biceps bulge out from the sleeves. Tattoos curl around his arms, peeking out of the sleeves that weren't there before—the muscles *and* the tattoos. I wonder what those tattoos mean. My fingers itch to trace over them and figure out their patterns. He's wearing a blue Eagle's hat pulled low, so I can't see his eyes. But if I could, I know they'd be the same whiskey-brown eyes I used to get lost in. I can tell you every gold and green fleck and speck that colors those whiskey-brown eyes. They used to be mine. I used to be his. He's like a walking hottie coach McHotterson down there, and I can't take my eyes off him. My body and mind feel like they're in separate places right now. My heart is beating fast.

As if he can feel my eyes on him, he turns and looks up into the stadium. His eyes wander the crowd until they finally land on me. I know the moment that it happens because his body stills. He looks right at me while I stare back down at him.

I know he's looking straight at me even though the bill

of his cap shields his face. I feel it in every molecule of my body, but he just stands there with a poker face—something he never used to have with me. I used to be able to read him so easily. Another reminder of how things have changed forever between us.

It's like there's no one else here in the stadium. Just him and me, locked in an intense time tunnel that neither of us looks away from.

Time may have passed. Every day went by. But right now, it all comes to a screeching halt as we lock eyes in this crowded stadium.

I want to look away. A few tears prick my eyes. *Why did you leave me?* I want to go down there and grab him by the collar and scream. I want him to hurt like he hurt me. I want him to miss me like I missed him. But most of all, I want him to tell me *why*. Why I didn't matter to him anymore. And that's what hurt me the most.

What feels like minutes but probably just seconds later, he finally looks back down and curls the bill of his ballcap with his fist, something he used to do when he was nervous back in high school. And there he is. The boy turned man. The one I never fathomed who could just throw me away like he did.

He looks nervous as he paces back and forth on the field with his hands on his hips, eyes on his players now. Well, good. I hope I make him nervous. I hope he feels like the jerk that he is. I look over at Goldie, and she's watching me closely, looking anxious.

I shake my head at her. "A warning would have been nice," I mumble.

"And miss that emotional explosion with your SJ? Not on your life, kiddo. This entire town has been invested in watching this reunion take place. You're both back, and we needed this. *You* needed this. This is like a real-life episode of *Friday Night Lights*. And I'm here for all of it," she says with a proud grin that's hard to be mad at. She loved SJ as much as she loves me, and without her being our rock back in high school, I'm not sure either of us would have made it out of here. I can't be mad at her when I know she means well deep down.

Yet as much as she means well, she needs to understand that this isn't happening. This nosy town that's invested in this? They all need to understand. "This? This isn't happening. And he is *not* my SJ."

"Mrs. Winters, do you want anything?" a man next to her asks, interrupting our sparring.

"Ty, honey, will you be a dear and bring me two Cokes, two dogs with everything... oh, and nachos?" She smiles and hands him cash. Normally, I'd fuss and not let her pay, but I don't even have it in me. I still feel like I'm coming down off an adrenaline rush, and exhaustion is settling back in. Like I just got thrown off an emotional roller coaster and hit every bump on the way down.

"You got it. Be right back," he calls over his shoulder with a curious look at me and down to the field where SJ stands. *Great.* Like I said, nosy town.

When he's gone, Goldie leans over and says, "That handsome fella is Ty, and he works with your SJ at the shop."

"He's not *my* SJ," I groan. "Don't think this is over. You did me dirty," I remind her, twisting my braid nervously over my shoulder.

She pushes her glasses up on her face. "Just in case you're wondering, he's looked up here three more times since you both incinerated the stadium with those smoldering stares," she shares with delight.

I groan again. "I wasn't wondering." But I was. I really was wondering. Why is he looking at me? What is he thinking?

I sneak a look back down at him and see him lean over to say something to a player, then clap him on the back as the player runs onto the field. On the back of his polo shirt, it says Coach Reid. And his butt in those jeans? Jesus. The years have been good to him. Too good.

No staring at his butt, Callie.

I will admit he does look good. Thirty looks good on him. He looks sexy and mysterious, but he's a stranger to me now. A pang of sadness fills me when that thought hits me. And that feels so wrong. We used to know everything about each other. Now? I'm just another woman in this crowded stadium to him. It's like what we had never mattered.

A million questions burn through my head. When did he become a coach? What happened to him in the past twelve years? And most importantly, why did he just up and leave?

~

CHAPTER 2

NOW

"Coach, I don't know if I can..."

"Tripp, you *do* know. Now get out there and run the ball just like we practiced. You've got this," I clip, eyes locked on the young player in front of me. Tripp is one of our rising star players who has a lot of talent and a whole lot of self-doubt. He reminds me of myself at his age, and that's why I'm tough on him. I know he has talent. I just need him to realize it.

"Yes, Coach." He takes a fast swig of water and jogs back out onto the field.

We need this win. The team has been struggling with Coach Murphy's retirement announcement, and the unknown of who will officially take his place weighed heavy on everyone's minds. I want to build trust with the team and get the full-time coaching job I've been working toward. I've been a volunteer coach this season. I care about these kids and look forward to coaching them every single day.

I'm nervous because I don't want to let these kids down. I work hard to keep my poker face in place so they don't see me slip. It's been over twelve years since I carried the ball down this same field. It's not lost on me that for part of the past year, I was an absolute wreck when I got out of the Army. Now here I am trying to prove to myself, these kids, and the town that I can be their coach. I close my eyes as self-doubt tries to sneak in. Nope. Not thinking that way. Just like Tripp, self-doubt has no place here.

And who would have thought that I needed these kids just as much as they needed me? It has been good here, and I can't mess it up.

The buzzer sounds, and they're off to a great start. They're good, and they have the potential to take state again. We're going to work our butts off and make this happen.

I pace the field and watch closely. I hear cheering and look up to see the stadium buzzing and full of excitement. It's a mass of blue and white, face paint with players numbers on cheeks, and cheering. It feels good to be back here. It feels strange to be back here without her. Almost every memory I have here in Freedom Valley includes Callie in some way. She always cheered me on and waited for me after every game. I could always count on Callie to be there for me.

I used to look up at these same stands and look for her. And she'd be wearing my number forty-four, smiling, and cheering me on with our friends. But she's not mine anymore. I ruined that, and the damage is done.

As my eyes survey the crowd one more time, a nervous energy builds within me; something I can't shake loose. Something not pertaining to the game. My gaze slows, narrowing on the seats, the people in them, cheering and laughing. Hairs stand up on the back of my neck, a buzz filling my body before my eyes finally land on hers. An oasis of calm and stillness in a sea of noise and movement. *No way. She's here.* I knew we'd run into each other eventually. It would be impossible not to run into her in our small town. I can't look away. I can't stop. It's been twelve years and leaving her felt like torture. I never stopped missing her or thinking about her. Like a coward, I'm relieved that she's up there and I'm down here so we don't have to talk. Her eyes lock on me, and she looks as surprised as I am.

My breath catches in my chest. She's even more beautiful now, and I never thought that possible. Her light blond hair is longer and pulled back in a long braid down her shoulder. Her wide, bright blue eyes are familiar and etched in anger and betrayal. I can feel it radiating down here onto the field. Callie and I used to always be in tune. I could usually feel if she was upset and vice versa.

Some people would call us soulmates. And maybe we were, once. Just two lost and lonely kids constantly drawn to one another. Until I made damn sure neither of us believed in the idea anymore. But seeing her here? It's like something has ignited in me, and my body is on fire. Adrenaline races through my veins, and I try to remain calm.

Panic engulfs me, and I look down and realize that I forgot how to breathe. I remind myself to breathe and start to count to ten. I look for something I can see and smell. I focus on the here and now just like my therapist at the VA taught me. No panic attacks tonight. I'm trying to get this town to trust and respect me as a coach. *I won't fall part again*, I remind myself.

Honestly, I don't remember much of the rest of the game. The kids played, and I stood on the sidelines alternating trying not to look up at her, pretending to know what was happening on the field, and avoiding a panic attack of finally facing her. I couldn't stop looking up there. She sat with Goldie and kept her head down most of the game. But what's with wearing my old shirt? Faded and worn, but still mine. I recognized it instantly. What is she doing? What does this mean? Did she come here to see me? I thought for sure she would never forgive me, but maybe I have a chance at even being friends with her again.

I take a deep breath and rub my chest with my knuckles. Ten, nine, eight, seven. . .

The final buzzer sounds, and we won. The Freedom Valley Eagles won their first game of the season. I pat the players on the back as they walk by. "Great game, guys!" I'm too out of it to even think about celebrating, but I will try to put on a congratulatory face for the team. A few players give me questioning looks as they walk by, so I desperately try to pull it together.

"Yoo-hoo, SJ, over here," someone says over my shoulder, and I freeze at that familiar voice. I turn slowly, and there she is. Goldie. Growing up without grandparents or a mother, Mrs. Winters meant so much to me. Still does. I kept in touch with her, but I should have done a better job of it. My dad visited me over the eleven years I was gone, but I couldn't bring myself to come back to Freedom Valley after everything that happened. And over the past year, I did a lot of healing and soul-searching, and kept to myself.

I close the space to the bleachers and pull her in for a big bear hug. I inhale as I hug her, and she still smells the same. She smells like home.

"I've missed you, sweet boy," she murmurs into my chest. Heat fills my chest hearing this and fills me with a good feeling.

"I missed you too, Mrs. Winters." I continue to hug her

tight. Over the years, she's written me countless letters and emails, filling me in on all the town's happenings. That's part of why I've felt like I didn't miss out on as much when I came back. I read everything she sent to me. I treasured every email, note, care package, and the occasional phone call.

"Call me Goldie, honey," she reminds me. "Why haven't you come over to see me yet?" She pulls back and asks with a slight frown and tears in her eyes as she looks up at me.

"I'm sorry..." Regret fills me as she reaches to hold my arms, staring up at me with genuine happiness. Not the same reaction I got from Callie up in the stands. I look around, wondering where Callie went.

"Nonsense. I want to catch up with you soon. You come by and see me, you hear?" she says firmly, laying a reassuring hand on my cheek.

I look down, and my breath hitches. I didn't realize how much I'd missed her. I regret not going to see her when I got back. But to be honest, I wasn't fit to see anyone when I first came home. I have a lot of people to catch up with, including Callie if that's even an option.

"You're doing such a good job with these boys," she says, filling me with pride.

I nod and pull the bill of my cap lower. It feels good to hear this. I have been working hard with them, and I'm glad they're off to a good start with their first win. Despite me almost losing my shit after seeing Callie for the first time tonight, I think we did great for the first game of the season with me as a first-time coach.

"I'm glad to see you're doing better. I was worried about you." She searches my eyes. Clearly, the rumors did get around our small town. I hate that people knew my business and knew I struggled.

"I'm okay." And I am. I've been working hard on myself. I'm not the same person I was when I first came home. It's been a hell of a year.

"Yes, you are." She squeezes my forearm gently. "Also, you know you can't hide from her forever," she says with a wink, disappearing into the crowd, not waiting for a response.

I sigh. No, I can't. I knew I'd see her eventually. I've wanted to see her more than anything. I've paid attention to what she's been up to on her social media, but I needed to get myself healthy and squared away before I take on the mess I made. Ready or not, I'm here for it. It's time to make things right.

The music is loud in the shop, and I don't even realize my dad has joined me until he lowers the volume on the speaker and my head swivels over. I nod, and he sits on a stool and slides over near me. "Good first game last night."

"Thanks," I say as I pull off a tire, set it aside, and reach for the next one.

"Tell me, why are you working on a Saturday night?" He takes a pull on his beer. "You should be out having fun."

"I like the quiet." Mainly, I like not dealing with customers. I like getting lost in my work and not having to stop and deal with small talk and mindless chatter.

"I don't mind you working at night as long as you're not isolating like you were." He leans back in his chair, his quiet tone letting me know he's serious.

"I'm not," I assure him. "Been handling my stuff." I put the lug nuts on and tighten them, the noise radiating throughout the shop.

He nods thoughtfully and adds, "It'll do you some good to get out there and start meeting new people."

"Dad, we live in Freedom Valley," I add dryly. Even after being gone, not much has changed. Most people still know everyone here. Besides, there's only one person I'd want to see. And she probably still hates me.

He takes another pull of his beer. "I'm telling you that you need to get out and meet women."

I roll my eyes at that. "Nobody wants someone who likes to stay home, watch football, and not make ridiculous small talk."

"Callie would," he says. "She's back, you know."

Way to just jump right into that, Dad.

I don't get a chance to respond because, luckily, his phone

rings, and he pulls it from his pocket to answer, "Sam's Auto Body." I take the opportunity to finish up as he takes his call, relieved to avoid the conversation.

I already knew she was back. But she was off-limits. Callie used to be the brightest, happiest person I ever knew. I wanted to become a man she'd be proud of when I returned. She always believed in me and encouraged me, and I wanted to prove her right. I still feel like I'm working on that. I wanted to have my cabin ready, have a job as a coach, and be someone she could be proud of so she'd forgive me for what I did. I always thought I'd see her again when I had it together, and I'd beg her for a second chance. And in my dreams, she would say yes, and we would be together. But now that it's happening, I'm starting to panic. What if she hates me?

Dad listens to the call, and his eyes meet mine and narrow, letting me know we're not done with his conversation. "Yeah. What's the address? We'll get out there. Thanks." He ends the call and slides the phone back into his pocket.

"Well, you're in luck. We have a tow at the hospital. Ramie, one of the nurses, called it in. Best be getting out there since you like the quiet night shift, and all." He smirks like he knows something I don't.

"Got it," I grumble as I grab the keys and head out.

CHAPTER 3

Callie

THEN

"Did you see her shoes? I mean, who wears neon green Converse shoes? They look like booger shoes. And what's up with the weird boxes drawn on them? It looks so dumb," someone says loudly from the seat behind me. I know everyone can hear what she's saying about me.

I slide farther down in my seat and try to tune out Kayla making fun of me. Okay, yes, my shoes have the periodic table drawn on them, but so what? What's it to her? I happen to like science. I've always been the odd kid who loves school. I've never had many friends, and it's not that I don't want them. I just *have a hard time making them as an extreme and unapologetic nerd. Not very many people want to be friends with me unless they're copying my homework or mocking me.*

Kayla snickers again and leans forward to look down at me. She laughs louder as she leans back and whispers obnoxiously loud, "She saw me."

I roll my eyes and ignore her. I hate middle school. I open my book and begin to read, wishing we were there already. I hate field trips. But the science museum is the only trip I've been excited about. I've looked forward to this for months, so I'm not letting anyone ruin this for me.

The bus halts in front of the museum, and our teacher makes a few announcements. When we stand to get off the bus, Kayla slides out quickly behind me and bumps into me. "Hurry up, nerd," she says loudly as she kicks the back of my shoes.

I hop off the bus quickly and move over to the side of the line, staring down, trying to avoid the stares and snickers from the kids mocking me. I concentrate on my shoes and try to ignore the laughter.

Two big Nikes come to a stop in front of me. I look up to see the kindest brown eyes staring back at me. His gaze drops down to my shoes. He turns and says loudly, "Green Converse, huh? Cool." He smiles at me, and I can tell it's sincere by the way it reaches his eyes. He takes my hand and tugs me along toward his group of friends. "Come on, green shoes. You're with us now."

I look back in dismay at what just happened, and Kayla's jaw has dropped, her mouth hanging open in disbelief as she stares back at us.

And I can't blame her. Because SJ Reid, the cutest and coolest guy in school, just told me my shoes were cool and pulled me along with him and his cool friends. Oh. My. God.

And if you had told me that SJ would become my very best friend from this day forward, I never would have believed you. But he was.

NOW

"Okay, Three-zero-five is done, and all the other patients are up to date. I'm finally heading out. I've been here too long," I call over to one of my favorite nurses, Ramie, who is charting on her own computer on wheels near the pit in the center of the busy and understaffed emergency room that has become my second home.

"You look exhausted." She looks over at me with concern in her eyes.

"Gee, thanks." She's not wrong. Tired has been taken to a whole new level today. What little sleep I would have gotten this week has been filled with thoughts of SJ and lingering questions about him being back. After the game the other night, I made a beeline to my car. After waiting for Goldie to make her rounds of endless goodbyes, I got her home and crashed into a deep sleep. She chatted the whole way home, and I avoided the elephant in the room, too tired to take on that subject. SJ at the game. I know she was dying to bring it up, but I didn't want to talk about it and kept changing the subject as I always have whenever she has brought him up in the past. It's been the only way I can protect myself from the hurt. Just don't think about it. Bury myself in school and now work and press on. It's the only way I could survive it all.

"You know what I mean." Ramie gives me a look. "You take *every* available shift and never take a day off. You've been here for what... how many days straight?"

I don't correct her because it's true. I've slept in the on-call room and worked far too many hours. The hospital isn't exactly running up to par these days. We need an overhaul of the administration. We're short nurses, and they still haven't offered me a full-time contract yet. All the board needs to do is meet, vote, etc. I still take every shift. This is what I've worked for, what I love. That and the many zeros on my high six-figure student loans to go away.

But right now, what I want more than anything is to go home, shower, put on clean, comfy clothes, crawl under my covers, and sleep until I'm finally rested, which will probably take a week at this point. Tomorrow is my first day off, and I won't be setting any alarms. This one day off is what got me through today. I gather up my bag and jacket.

"Get some good sleep." Ramie waves as she heads off to

respond to a call light.

"I will. Bye," I call as I step outside into the dark night. Breathing in the crisp fresh fall air, I take a deep breath. I slide into my driver's seat and lean my head back, exhausted. I turn the key to start the car and nothing. Dead. *No.* I groan. I do not have time for this today. I lay my head in defeat on my steering wheel. My trusty thirteen-year-old Honda might finally be crapping out on me. I've avoided Sam's shop as he's the only trustworthy auto body shop that I know. I can't keep getting by with duct tape and rubber bands, so to speak. I sigh. Why today?

I text Thad, a fellow doctor.

Me: Hey, my car won't start. Can you give me a ride?

I almost fall asleep for a few minutes while I wait for his response. My phone buzzes, and I look down at it. I close my eyes. Unbelievable.

Thad: Too tired. Worked all day. Call a tow.

My parents have been trying to set me up with him, but something about Thad rubs me the wrong way. When I first moved back, I went to a few dinners with my parents, and he was there, too. After interacting with him a few times, I knew I had no intention or desire to ever be romantically linked to him. I can't seem to figure out how he doesn't feel the lack of connection, too. We have nothing in common other than our jobs, which he is terrible at. My parents see him as a doctor, who comes from the "right" family, has money, and would be just perfect for their daughter. Never mind what I want and don't want.

Callie: Seriously?

I wait for him to maybe change his mind and say he's coming after all, but who am I kidding? Of course he doesn't respond. I don't even know why I bothered to reach out to him in the first place. I figured since he had just gotten off his shift, it wouldn't be a big deal for him to give me a ride.

Also, why would I date someone who doesn't care if I'm stranded? And what's worse is he keeps hinting about us getting serious. If he can't be bothered to even give me a ride, why would I even consider being with someone like that? No, thanks. I've learned over the past several years to take care of myself.

I can't call my parents and wouldn't bother anyway. I can never be too sure if either of them would be sober enough to come and get me this late at night. And I can't call Goldie this late. And even though I'm only a few miles from my cottage, I'm too tired to walk, and it's dark out. I'd probably fall asleep in a ditch on the way.

I text Ramie my dilemma, and she comes in clutch.

Ramie: I'll call you a tow. Just sit tight until they get there.

I lean back and begin to drift off as I wait.

A light knock on my window startles me, and I jerk upright and wipe some drool off my chin from my deep sleep nap. Nice, Callie.

I rub the sleep out of my eyes, exhausted, my vision a little obscured from wiping my hand over my face at the lights from the tow truck reflecting in my mirrors, disorienting me. Only when I get out of the car do I realize SJ stands in front of me and not his dad, Sam.

This day has gone to hell in a handbasket.

Holy crap. I swallow, unsure what to do with my hands. My knees are shaking so badly that holding the door is the only thing keeping me standing.

"I thought you were Sam," I manage to say. *Lame, Callie.* That's the first thing I can think of to say to the man who I haven't spoken to in twelve years.

My breath hitches, and my heart pounds. The boy who was my best friend. The boy who could calm me by just being in my presence or holding my hand, and who could read my emotions like a book and communicate with only eye contact stands right here. Now he stands before me with his hands in his pockets, so casual, looking like a delicious walking sin. And I'm feeling particularly unholy toward him at the moment. And I hate that I feel like this. I want to be so mad at him, not attracted to him. He doesn't deserve me being nice to him.

"Hi," he says casually with a smile.

Hearing his gruff, manly tone after over a decade of silence makes my heart race a bit, and I feel confused.

He's standing so close to me that I can smell him. He smells like crisp autumn in the woods, and his warm whiskey eyes are on me. He seems taller but still has one to two inches on me, so that probably puts him at just over six feet. He's wearing navy coveralls with Sam's Auto Body on the shoulder just like his dad wears. That's why I thought it was him at first. He looks like his dad did when we were younger. His Sam's Auto Body ball cap is pulled low, and he looks stupidly hot. I don't know which version is hotter—the coach version or the walking blue-collar hottie dream version.

I feel like I'm having a nightmare, only I literally just woke up. This is real. He's real and finally right here in front of me. This is not how I pictured this to go. I pictured our first meetup many times over the years, yet this is not the one that I wanted.

My favorite scenario was that I would be dressed up, have makeup on, and look like a million bucks when he bumped into me somewhere and saw what he missed out on.

Another was that I would confront him and tell him exactly how he obliterated my heart. How I have put myself back together again, and I'm now better than ever after he took the coward's way out of everything. Instead, I'm standing here, mute. My mind is in chaos—too many thoughts, wants, and needs are at war within me. I want to shake him and demand answers. I want to never see him again to punish him. I want to kiss him and see if he still kisses me the same. But in the end, I can't pick anything to say, so I simply say nothing.

"You...okay?" he says softly, crossing his massive arms corded with muscles, the sleeves of the coveralls rolled up.

It hurts the way his voice is so familiar and comforting, yet painful to hear again at the same time. It's like a stab to my heart.

I swallow and look at him, tension and hesitation pulsing through me. Then anger fills me. *Am. I. Okay?* I shake my head. He can ask me that so casually like the past twelve years didn't just happen without an explanation from him.

A little time passes, and we continue to stare at each other. I can't form actual words to say out loud, but so many thoughts race through my head. Thoughts I can't bring my mouth to say right now. It's like I'm frozen.

His gaze softens, and finally, he says, "Okay, I'll just get you hooked up if you want to wait off to the side." He turns and walks back to his truck. I watch the way his arms flex as he works. I remember those hands that used to hold me and the mouth that used to kiss me. Goose bumps appear on my arms, and I shiver, rubbing my arms as I move.

I spin toward my car, then take a deep breath and look up at the sky in frustration. I do not have the energy for this. I'm so mentally and physically drained that my emotions are dangerously close to the surface. I cannot afford to let SJ see he's the cause of most of it right now. I don't want to sit in the same truck as him and act like nothing happened. And how can he?

He gets out and comes around to my side to open the door for me. I stare at him, anger bubbling up in me. I shake my head in disbelief at his nonchalance.

"Get in, Callie." He nods to the cab of the truck. His tone has changed. He seems irritated, and I wonder what he must be irritated about. That I'm back in Freedom Valley, too? This isn't his town. It's mine, too. And I'm not the one who broke us. I'm the one with the right to be mad.

The emotions from the day I found out he left wash over me. And it hurts even more than it did that day. Because he's back and acting like none of it even happened.

"Just get in," he repeats, scrubbing a hand over his face in frustration.

I slide into the seat, then press myself up against the door and snap my seat belt on.

SJ's indifference pricks and needles at me, burrowing under my skin until it burns. A feeling I'm all too aware of from my parents, but to experience it from SJ is another type of pain entirely. I feel the telltale sting in my nose, eyes watering, my nails digging into my palms to halt the tears from falling, but I'm too tired from work and from this confrontation to stop them from falling.

I turn and face the passenger window so he can't see my face, but I'm shaking. I'm trying to compose myself before he slides into the driver's seat next to me.

The engine hums while rock music from the radio plays softly in the background. The truck smells even more like him—like a cozy warm flannel, cedar, juniper, and black pepper—causing my chest to ache. I lean against the window, seeking comfort from the cool glass and wishing this ride and this evening were over.

He looks over at me and says quietly, "I'm *so* sorry, Cal."

I look over at him, and his face looks pained when he sees mine. I don't know why, but that makes me feel even worse. Because I realize that I missed him and still love him. I can't just turn it off. I never could like he did. I want to hug him. I want to kiss him and tell him everything that's happened. But I can't.

I sniff angrily through tears and try my best to act like I don't care and shrug. "What are you sorry for?"

"Everything."

There's nothing he can say. He can be sorry all he wants. It won't change things.

He lets out a deep sigh and puts the truck in gear. I sneak a look at his profile, and he's got a five-o'clock shadow going on that he's never had before. Seeing him up close again is surreal. He's filled out, and he's a man now. Gone is the tall, lean boy. This version of SJ looks like the man I imagined he would be. Strong, solid, and safe. Only he's not safe. He broke my heart and can't be trusted anymore. He's on the no-fly list now.

"What are you thinking about?" he asks, his eyes finally looking over at me.

"What am *I* thinking?" I repeat back to him and begin to cackle like a maniac. "You want to know what *I'm* thinking?" I say as I laugh and cry at the same time.

"Yeah, I do." He looks over at me with concern and probably fear as I'm crying and laughing like a complete lunatic when he's just asked me a simple question. A question twelve years too late.

"Oh, *now* you want to know what I'm thinking?" I laugh even harder now, wiping my eyes because my manic laughing makes my eyes water even more. He looks even more confused.

At a red light, he stares over at me. And I think about making him wait for another twelve years for an answer like he's done to me.

I just glare at him, shaking my head.

"I'm worried about you, Callie."

"You shouldn't be worried about me, SJ. In fact, you should be happy to know that I'm someone else's problem now. I'm living the dream. My life is fantastic. I'm totally fine," I bite out bitterly.

He looks at me carefully, then says, "Okay." It's almost like he doesn't believe me. Well, he shouldn't because it's a lie. Thad and I aren't officially dating, and we never will. But SJ doesn't need to know that.

"Just, okay? You couldn't care less about me, right?" I say sarcastically.

Ignoring my last comment, he asks, "Okay, but where is he?"

"Who?" I shake my head, confused.

"Your boyfriend." His eyes meet mine, and he waits.

"That's... none of your business. He's Dr. Douchet," I say without thinking, but now I regret it. It feels so gross even pretending to date Thad.

"Why didn't he come get you?" He pushes.

"He's busy," I retort, looking down at my phone to see if he's bothered to text back to check on me. He hasn't. And I don't even know why I thought he would. Frustrated, I look back out the window.

"I see."

"Oh, what do you see?" I say sarcastically, turning to look at him.

"Callie. . ." He sighs, frustrated as he pulls into the auto body shop and puts the truck in park.

I glare at him and then open my door and get out. After

slamming it closed, I turn and realize I have no idea how I'll get home. I put my face in my hands and groan. This day just can't get any worse.

He comes around and stands next to me. Digging into his pocket, he pulls out and hands me a set of keys.

I reach to take the keys, and when our hands touch, I feel the warmth of his hands. My fingertips inadvertently feel his calluses from working. I wonder what they would feel like touching me. Touching him after all these years feels like coming home. He says nothing. He just stares at me, watching my face, like he's looking for clues. I glance down, not wanting to look back at him. Then I realize he's still holding the keys in my hand, and our hands are still together. I pull my hand back quickly. I want so badly to run into the arms of the SJ from before. I don't know this version of him anymore. And he's not mine. Maybe he never really was. Now I'm questioning everything. Was it even real?

"You can use the Prius over there as a loaner until we can get you fixed up," he politely offers.

"Why?" I ask him, and he knows I'm not asking about the car.

He takes off his hat and runs his hand through his messy dark hair. "Does it matter? You seem like you're all set with Dr. Douche."

"It's Douchet!" I yell, putting my hands on my hips.

"Doesn't matter, Cal," he says, his eyes still on mine. "I'll still be the one you think about twenty years from now. He's not the guy, and you know it."

Are you freaking kidding me? The cockiness in this guy. Who does he think he is? Also, why is that overt confidence so damn hot? He's confusing me and making me question everything. I long for my SJ, the one with quiet confidence. But I can't deny that I'm not intrigued by this newer, darker version of him.

I'm already in crisis mode, not sure of who I am anymore. Add in this tumultuous reunion, and it's safe to say my heart, mind, and lady parts are at total war with each other. Why couldn't he have come back a little less handsome and more washed up? Why do we still have this insane chemistry that flares from a mere look? There are too many questions, and I'm too damn tired to figure any of them out.

"What makes you think he's not the guy for me?" I question. "You don't even know him."

He crosses his arms and smirks at me. "Because he's the type of guy who leaves you stranded after you just got done working a long shift." He tilts his head and stares at me like he's challenging me. The old SJ never would have left me there stranded. We both know it. But this SJ? No, he just kept me waiting for *twelve years.*

I narrow my eyes. His audacity makes me livid.

"You don't get to do that!" I yell. "No. Just no." I swivel around and stalk toward him. He doesn't move, and his eyes don't leave mine. He just braces and swallows, his sexy wide jaw tightening, ready for whatever blow I'm about to deliver to him. He's ready to take whatever I have to dish out. I can feel it.

"Was it easy for you all those years?" I challenge, getting in his space. "Was your life better without me? Did all your dreams come true without me there to drag you down?" I lean into him and push an index finger into his chest accusingly. And it's solid. Even though I'm so mad, I still wonder what it would be like to run my palm over his chest. I hate that I still miss him.

His jaw flexes, but he doesn't move. He's still, his eyes continue staring into mine. They hold the weight of the world in them. They're duller now, like life stole away his happiness, replacing it with this heavy sadness. Thirty-year-old SJ has the saddest whiskey eyes I've ever seen. His eighteen-year-old whiskey eyes were full of hope and happiness. I don't know these eyes and what they've seen. And this is when I know I can't hate him. Because when I fell in love with SJ, I fell in love with those kind eyes. And he might have changed over the years, but those eyes and mine have seen and been through so many things together.

He turns away from me and stalks angrily toward the shop. I can feel his anger pulsing through both of us. Good. I want him to feel what I've felt. It must be nice to just be so calm when he's made me feel so lonely and worthless.

"Oh no, you don't get to walk away *again…*" I start to say. He abruptly stops and turns and comes back toward me like a charging bull.

I back up until my back hits the truck, and I can't move any farther. I know he won't hurt me. But he's *so* close. His jaw tenses, his eyes blazing, his brow lowered. His shoulders are tense like one stone thrown at him would crack and dismantle him. His hands shake, and his eyes hold so much pain in them it leaves me breathless, like I've been gutted.

"No!" he yells. "I missed you every single day. Every single second, Callie. You have no idea what I did for you and for us." His voice cracks. "You'll probably never know," he bites out.

"You left me when I needed you. You left me with them," I sob. "You knew how horrible they were, and you left me!"

Memories flood me of my parents abandoning me and barely speaking to me while I was at college. Goldie stepped up and helped me get through it all. Then I moved back to Freedom Valley and tried to reconnect with them, hoping they'd changed, but they haven't. Deep down, I know that. I can't forget the times they made me feel so small, so lonely, and repeatedly hurt me. The one person I thought would be my best friend and soulmate left me. At least my parents were here all along. I just had to reach out to them. I had no way to reach out to SJ. No idea how he was or what had happened.

"You don't know what happened," he pleads, pain etched across his face.

"You're right, I don't know. Because you just left!" I shriek. "No explanation, no note, nothing!"

He looks down, shaking his head. "That's not true. But I am *so* sorry, Callie. I can't go back and change what happened. But I can explain. We can fix this."

Devastation fills his eyes as he stares at me, and I know he's sorry. I can feel it. But it can't erase the twelve years of hurt. Someone who was my whole world just up and left me when we had plans and dreams.

He steps toward me and cages me in against the truck, his arms on either side of me. I think he's about to kiss me, and my breath hitches. Instead, he leans into me, his nose brushing along mine, and he rests his forehead on mine. My lips tremble.

He breathes me in, and his eyes close. My frazzled nerves feel like they finally slow down as he comforts me. He kisses my forehead, and somehow it feels achingly final to me. Like a goodbye kiss.

He pulls back slowly, eyes still on me. "Give me a chance."

"A chance for what?" I say, breathless and confused.

"To explain."

I straighten my shoulders, taking a deep breath. "What's there to explain?"

"There's a lot to explain," he practically growls.

"No." I shake my head.

"No?" he asks and raises a brow.

While I want to hear his explanation, I also am not sure I'm ready to hear it. I'm also not sure my heart can handle any more today. He doesn't get to swoop back into my life whenever he wants and turn everything upside down.

I storm toward the Prius then stop and turn and look back at him. "No. You had twelve years to explain. You know they say when you meet the love of your life, a part of your heart will always be with them. Well, I'm taking it back, SJ. You no longer get it. I loved you *so* much. But you broke me."

He shakes his head. "I don't believe that, and I know you don't either. You felt that!" He points at me, frustration on his face.

"Consider that your goodbye kiss. The one I never got," I say, and his eyes narrow.

My heart continues to race as I turn and hurry to the Prius. I won't be broken again. Not by someone supposed to love me. No one loved me like SJ did. And no one ever will. Not even him.

I used to wonder if SJ would want the thirty-year-old me if he ever saw me again. I don't have to worry about that. He does. I could see it in his face. And what scares me is that this is not how I thought this reunion would go. This feels out of control. Because SJ didn't just light up my world. No. He powered the sun. He's back and nothing is the same.

~

CHAPTER 4

THEN

I can't tell you how I got lucky enough to have Callie as my best friend, but somehow, I did. Not a lot of people in this town take me seriously or trust me. I'm the son of a single father who is also a local motorcycle club leader in a small town that looks down on him for that. And Callie's the daughter of a banker and comes from an entirely different world than mine. She loves science. She always has a science dad joke for me, which always makes me laugh, no matter how terrible they are. I noticed some of our classmates had bullied her, and I could never understand why. Callie McGraw is the coolest chick I've ever met. She's just

who she is, unapologetically. She loves to color in her anatomy coloring book and has the entire skeletal system memorized. I've never met anyone like her. I decided that was done. No one would ever bully her ever again. While some look down on me in this town, no one messes with the biker kid's son. I've made it my mission to show everyone that from now on, if they mess with her, they mess with me. She's my best friend now.

"Hey, knock, knock," she says as she taps me on the shoulder and pulls me out of my thoughts.

"Who's there?" I play her game.

"Element."

I shake my head and snort. "Element, who?"

"Element of surprise, I just discovered a new element!" She laughs like it's the funniest joke ever.

I shake my head and snort. "Callie, that was terrible."

She knocks me in the forearm and sits next to me. "What are you doing today after school?"

"Just practice, then helping my dad at the shop."

"Can I come over?" she asks, pushing her tortoise-framed glasses up on her nose.

"You want to come to my dad's shop?" I ask, surprised that she would want to do that. There are usually bikers everywhere, and it's dirty.

"Of course, I do. Let's hang out," she says excitedly.

"Oh. . .okay." I shrug. "You do realize my dad always has a bunch of bikers hanging around, right?" I remind her

skeptically.

"Bikers? Oh no, so scary," she says in a teasing voice, putting her hand to her chest.

"Callie..." I roll my eyes but can't help but smile. "See you after school."

"See you later, alligator," she chirps as she heads off, her backpack swinging behind her.

I take a deep breath. Something about being with Callie makes me feel like a normal kid. She doesn't treat me like it's weird that my dad owns an auto body shop that is usually full of bikers hanging out. She wants to be around me. And I want to be around her. Two kids from different sides of the tracks becoming best friends. Who knew?

NOW

"Are you ready for another box?" Evan calls from the doorway. He wipes sweat from his brow with the back of his hand. It's late afternoon. We've been working on the cabin all day, and we're starving.

Evan's been helping me lay vinyl wood flooring throughout my cabin, and I'm grateful for his assistance because we're getting it done a lot faster than if I was doing it by myself. Working on my new cabin has been my favorite thing to do besides coaching. It has kept my mind off Callie. Well, not really. But I'm trying. It hasn't been easy when I have been building it in the very spot where we fell in love, had our first kiss, first everything. Our lookout spot on the outskirts of town was always a special place. Now, it's where I'm putting down roots in my hometown. I wasn't sure I'd ever come back here, but now I know this is where I'm supposed to be.

"Let's take a break," I call. "Ty's bringing the pizza." I stand and wipe my hands on my jeans.

I look at our progress. We only have one room left. I built a four-bedroom cabin that is everything we dreamed up as kids. I grew up living above my dad's shop, and while I had a great dad and he took good care of me, I dreamed of having a home with traditions and maybe even one day a family of my own.

"Good, I'm starving," Evan says, reaching for a bottle of water on the counter.

Ty comes in the back door. "Did someone order pizza and two future Eagles?" he calls as he carries in three boxes from Freedom Pie. His little boy and Evan's nephew, Caleb, follow him, grinning at being called Eagles. Cute kids.

"Hey, guys," I call, and I notice one of them is missing a front tooth.

"Hi, Uncle Evan. Hi, Coach," they call as they look around at the place.

"Hey, what happened to your teeth?" I tease.

"Lost 'em. Tooth fairy gave me twenty bucks," he says.

I look over at Ty, who smiles and shrugs.

"Dang. Inflation works in your favor, kid." I give him a fist bump, and the kid looks like he has no idea what I'm talking about but smiles anyway.

Evan reaches over and tousles their hair. "What have you boys been up to?"

"Ty said we can help bring the pizza." Caleb shrugs as he looks at my tools laid out on the counter.

"I'm glad you came, buddy. You guys can help after we eat."

Evan sets the boys up at the counter with pizza. And I wash up in the sink while I think about how cool it feels to have friends over. I want to be able to share this space even more when it's finally done. I look around at the big kitchen and living room space and imagine a family living here. I can see it full of kids, laughter, barbecues, and traditions with friends and family. I want it all.

I always pictured it with Callie, and then that picture grew dimmer every year we were apart. Callie and I grew up in two very different worlds, yet endured so much pain in both our families. And I always dreamed of making a family for us that no one could take away or destroy. Ours. I don't care how long it takes; I want to build that. Subconsciously, I think that's what I've been building toward for the past several years. It just hasn't gone the way I thought it would.

I reach into the fridge and grab sodas. I hold them out, and they each snag one. "Thanks for your help today," I say as I snap my soda open and take a swig.

"It's really shaping up." Evan nods in appreciation as he looks around.

"It's been a lot of work, but it beats living above the shop."

"I bet. Quieter, too."

I look out the large picture windows of the cabin and stare off at the mountain and tree line. "It's definitely peaceful and quieter out here." For years, when I was on deployment, the thought of coming back here and building this cabin got me through. Dreaming of this view and a life here is what gave me hope.

"The boys and I had fun watching the game last week," Ty says, interrupting my thoughts.

Caleb is Evan's nephew, his sister Allie's kid, and Kase is Ty's stepson. They are all close friends and live on the Golden Gable Inn property. Kase's mom is the head housekeeper at the inn and new to Freedom Valley since I've been back.

It's wild to think that so many people I went to high school with now have families. I used to think about what it would be like to have a family. I didn't grow up with a mom or anyone other than my dad, the motorcycle club he belongs to, and Goldie. I didn't have the classic childhood like the Harpers had. I don't even know if I would know how to be a dad, but mine was pretty great. My parents had me when they were fifteen. My mom took off with my little sister a few years after that and never came back for me. I don't think my dad knew how to be a dad, but he did the best he could. I'm thirty, and he's forty-five now. We're still close. As for my mom and sister? We don't have a relationship, and I have two core memories with my mom. Both were disappointing. I've just realized that these are the family cards I've been dealt. And I play with the small hand that I have. I hold the cards that matter closest to me. The ones that don't? I discard, just like my mother discarded me all those years ago. She no longer matters.

Evan looks over. "The boys haven't stopped talking about how they're going to play for the Eagles someday. I don't have the heart to tell them it's going to be at least a good decade before they're old enough. But you might still be coaching then," Evan jokes.

"Next time you come to a game, bring them down to the field so they can meet the players. I'm really proud of the team and how they're playing this season," I add as I reach for a piece of pizza. I look over at the boys, lost in conversation with each other as they stare at Ty's phone. They're quietly watching some show while eating. They seem like great kids.

"They'd love that," Ty says, opening the second pizza box.

"Hey, did you know that this is the last week Molly and Frank are running Freedom Pie? They sold it, and the new owner takes over next week," Ty says. "I'll be sad to see them go."

"Yeah, their daughter Holly is staying in the loft at the garden shed right now at the inn. She lost her home and her job when they suddenly decided to sell. It was a surprise to her. She's working a temp job right now as she tries to figure things out."

"That's too bad," I say, surprised to hear this news.

"I know. But I hope things stay the same at Freedom Pie. I love that place," Evan says.

"I think my dad and I lived on their pizzas growing up," I say with a laugh.

"When are they finally going to make you coach? After all the speculation, I hear it's official that Coach Murphy is retiring. It must be a dream come true for him to get you in there to replace him," Evan remarks.

I hesitate with his kind words, but I still sometimes feel like an impostor. I appreciate hearing Evan's thoughts on this. I've been wondering what the rest of the town thinks of me now. In high school, I was a starting player for Freedom Valley. But off the field, I wasn't as accepted. As the son of a biker, some people thought of me as the town trash. Now, all these years later, I wonder how they see me. Am I still just the trashy son of a biker? The broken guy who came back from the Army? I've been trying to figure out how I fit in a town that never accepted me. Sometimes being back feels like high school 2.0, and I don't want to go through that again. Once was enough, thank you very much.

I take a bite of pizza and chew before I respond, thinking about what to say.

"No clue, I've been waiting for months. I'm a volunteer coach as of now. They know I'm interested, and Coach Murphy says he's brought me up at every meeting. I guess I'm just waiting to hear whether it's a go or not."

"It would be ridiculous for them not to hire you, especially after you've already done so much for the team," Evan points out.

"Seems like a natural fit to me," Ty adds as he hands each boy a napkin.

"We'll see." I don't say it, but I'm worried it won't happen. I'm already volunteering. Why would they buy the cow if they're already getting the milk for free? But it's not about the money. Sure, I would love the job, but I have my doubts at this point.

"How are things with Mellie and Kase?" I change the subject. Ty's worked at my dad's shop for a while now, and he's a good mechanic. He's around my age and has become a good friend.

"Good," he says with a stupid grin. "I can't imagine life without either of them now," he says, looking over at Kase.

"He's got it bad," Evan ribs him.

Ty shrugs with a grin. "When you know, you know."

I've seen the way Mellie and Ty look at each other. You can tell they love each other. Mellie brings Ty lunch at the shop. And I've seen them around town holding hands and out to dinner as a family. A weird sensation comes over me when I think about having my own family. I want that. I think I always have, but I've shoved it down and tried not to think about it. I had a few long-term relationships when I was in the military, but nothing serious beyond that. There was no one I could see myself marrying except for the one woman I ruined everything with. Callie.

She was my person.

"Speaking of," Evan hedges, "what about you? Maybe we can put you on a dating app or something. That's the only way we're going to get you out there since you rarely get out."

I roll my eyes and groan. "Have you been talking to my dad?"

"No." He laughs. "Just want you to be happy, man. Have what we have."

"The thought of dating right now is exhausting." I take a swig of my soda. "Plus, a dating app in small-town Freedom Valley is like flipping through a yearbook. Everyone knows everyone. No thanks." I shudder at the thought of dating someone's sister or, God forbid, their mom.

"No kidding." Evan grimaces. "I'm glad dating's over for me. That does sound awful."

I lean back against the counter and cross my arms. "The next woman I meet who's a keeper can just have the key to my house. Dinner's ready for her at six, left side of the bed is hers, and we're just going to skip the dating and go straight to the good part," I joke, picking my pizza up and taking a bite. But deep down, I know I only want that with one woman.

Ty laughs. "That's pretty much what Mellie and I did. We just became a family, and that was that."

"And that's also what Beth and I did." Evan nods in agreement.

Lucky. "Football season is not the time to try to date anyone. I'm too busy with the team and the shop."

"What are you going to do with the shop when you coach full time?" Evan asks.

"Same thing I do now. Dad and Ty have it handled during the day. I'll still work at night and on weekends."

"He pretty much only works nights now to hide out anyway," Ty adds.

"Why are you hiding out?" Evan frowns.

I know he's asking out of concern for me. When I first moved back, I'll admit I was in bad shape. I rarely left the house, I let my beard grow too long, and I was unkempt. I spent days building the cabin and nights working at the shop. I rarely spoke to anyone. It's what I needed then, but it got out of hand. Evan dragged me out of my dark place and got me into counseling at the VA and among the land of the living again. I will be forever grateful to him for that. I'm sure my dad is too. I know he was worried about me, as well.

"I just prefer nights. I like to focus on work around the cabin and coaching during the day. Nights at the shop."

Evan nods, but his eyes stay on me. I nod back. He's got my back.

Ty leans in and says jokingly, "It's hard to meet someone if you're working all the time."

"I don't need a woman." I roll my eyes.

"He used to have one," Evan says smugly.

I shoot him a dirty look.

He puts his hands up. "Well, you did."

"What happened with that?" Ty asks.

I sigh. "I messed it up."

"Can you un-mess it up?" Ty asks.

I say nothing, not wanting to give them any more ammo to fuel the Callie fire. It's already burning big and bright for me. The truth is, I know exactly what I want. It's always been Callie. And while I can't go back and change what I did, I'll fight for her now. I have no idea how, but I know deep down she's supposed to be with me.

"I heard she's back," Evan says evenly.

"I gave her a tow the other night." I shrug like it's no big deal and hasn't consumed every single thought since it happened.

"Is that code word for hooking up?" Evan jokes as he looks at me carefully.

"No, dipshit." I chuckle. "I literally towed her car." I busy myself in the kitchen, hoping they'll let up and go onto another topic. Doesn't seem like this will be happening.

Evan leans in. "And?" He's clearly not falling for my nonchalance.

"She's still really pissed at me." I pause, allowing images of her devastated blue eyes to bombard my mind. My head bows; gaze catching on an imperfection on the wood floor. "I really hurt her." The words are low and gruff, almost like I'm ashamed to admit them out loud to these guys. But it's the truth. Callie isn't just pissed at me; I broke her heart and ruined us.

"Well, you did just up and dip. No one knew where you were for months until your dad finally told everyone that you'd joined up," Evan adds. "I didn't find out until I came back on leave. But you never came back."

"I know," I say with defeat. "I had my reasons."

"Yeah, but does she know the reasons?" Evan asks, raising his eyebrows.

I shake my head. "She wouldn't let me explain."

"Give it time. Maybe she'll come around," Ty encourages.

"Do you know Callie?" Evan asks Ty. "She's the new doctor in town. SJ and her were together all through high school. They've been on a twelve-year hiatus."

"It doesn't look like she'll come around. Apparently, she's with someone now," I bite out.

I was livid the other night when she informed me that she

was with him. The fact that he left Callie stranded tells me everything I need to know about how he treats her. I don't want Callie to be with anyone. Anyone but me.

Evan turns to me. "Who?"

"Thad Douche from the hospital," I grit out as I rip open a new box of flooring.

Evan chokes on his soda as he takes a sip. "That dude? I know who you're talking about."

"What do you know about him?"

"He's a tool. She's too good for him," Evan hedges.

"Is Callie the hot blonde from the game the other night that you exchanged smoldering stares with?" Ty asks.

I give him a look that clearly says I don't like him calling her hot.

He puts his hands up. "The boys call her Elsa and says she looks like a princess from the movie *Frozen*."

Relief fills me hearing that Evan agrees the guy is not good enough but still knowing that she's with that Dr. Dick Douche does not make me feel better.

"Sounds like she still means something to you," Ty muses.

"A lot of history there." I shrug. "But...history means the past."

"Can't rewrite history. But you know what you can do?" Ty says.

"What?"

"Fight for your future with her." He smirks.

I think about how I felt seeing her wearing my old shirt at the game. It hugged her curves, the worn material a little thinner than it used to be, clinging to Callie in all the right places. Seeing my number and name on her after all this time. To know that she still hung onto it and obviously wore it often, given how threadbare it looked.

For a minute, I thought maybe she missed me, and I might have a chance at her forgiving me. But when I picked her up at the hospital, I realized she's far from forgiving me.

The spark is still there with Callie. Because she wouldn't hate me if she felt nothing. She only hates me because she cares, which means I can do everything I can to get her back. Even half a football field away, I can feel she's still mine. There's no denying that.

"After seeing her again, it did make me feel something. Something I haven't felt in a long time."

"What's that?" Evan asks.

"Alive."

CHAPTER 5

Callie

THEN

"What are the types of chemical bonds?" He quizzes me, holding the flashcard so I can't see it.

I'm thinking and trying to remember my notes, but he smells so good, and the muscles on his tanned forearms distract me.

"Come on, you get it right, I kiss you," he encourages.

I laugh and lean into him, knowing he'll kiss me anyway.

We both startle when someone says, "Are you doing more kissing or studying?"

SJ leans back in his chair and shuffles my flashcards for AP chemistry with a guilty grin. "Studying, Mrs. Winters."

Mrs. Winters smirks and squeezes our shoulders before she moves on to shelving books. The library has become a second home for SJ and me to study and hang out. The shop is usually too noisy, and the apartment above it is usually so messy because neither SJ nor his dad keeps it tidy. My house is completely out because my parents aren't fans of SJ or his dad being affiliated with a biker gang, as they call it, but it's really a motorcycle club. The library is home most days to both of us. And Mrs. Winters has been known to sneak us snacks and water when we've been here a long time. Once, she even gave me a heads-up when she saw my mom coming, and SJ hid back in her office until Mom was gone. If my parents knew I met him here, I wouldn't be able to come back, and I would miss Mrs. Winters and have no way to spend time with SJ. Mrs. Winters loves SJ and has never been bothered by the fact that his dad is a member of the Eastern Bones motorcycle club. She's always treated both of us with kindness like we are her own kids.

SJ glances down at his phone. "You probably need to go anyway, Cal. It's almost five. You have that country club thing tonight, right?"

I groan. "I wish you could go with me. It would be more fun if you were there."

He wrinkles his nose. "No, thanks. Also, your parents would not go for that," he remarks with a frown.

I look over at him and tease him, "Hey, you know what? Both of our parents belong to clubs," I tease.

SJ snorts. "I don't think they're the same type of clubs. One club wears leather cuts and rides motorcycles, and the other wears hideous sweaters and rides golf carts."

"I'd rather hang out at your dad's club." I shudder.

"Me, too," he says as he gathers his books and stuffs them in his backpack.

"You think you'll join the Eastern Bones when you're older?" I ask.

He shrugs. "Probably. They're my family. When I can ride, I will. Dad won't let me until I finish the basic rider class. But we've been building my bike together for a while now."

"You'd look pretty hot on a bike." I smirk.

"You'd look pretty hot on the back of my bike," he returns with a grin.

"My parents would lose their shit," I mumble.

"Your parents lose their shit over everything."

"Isn't it sad how they think they're better than Sam? My parents are the freaking worst. Sam is an angel compared to them."

"My dad's no angel. But he doesn't treat me the way your parents treat you," SJ says firmly, pressing his mouth together. "It isn't right, Callie."

I know he doesn't like my parents. We have a secret plan to get out of here when we graduate. Freedom Valley will be behind us, and we'll have a new life together in college.

"I'll come see you after the dinner," I promise as we finish packing our stuff up to head out.

NOW

My eyes open, and I blink at the bright morning light streaming in through the cracks of the blinds. I stretch, grateful to have slept in for as long as I did. My body needed this. I reach for my phone and see a text from Goldie, inviting me to have coffee with her on the porch when I wake up.

I smile sleepily and send her a text. I love her and having coffee with her. After getting thirteen hours of glorious sleep last night, I might love her coffee even more on this cool autumn morning of my one and only day off.

After I get dressed and brush my teeth, I step onto the porch, slipping on a cardigan as Goldie carries two cups across the path from her house to my cottage.

"Good morning," I call to her with a smile.

"It's afternoon now, but same to you." She hands me a cup. "Peace offering?"

"Oh, that's right, I haven't seen you since you bamboozled me," I murmur.

"Bamboozled. Now there's a fun word," she teases, bringing her mug to her mouth and taking a sip.

I sip my coffee and stare at her over the rim with one eyebrow raised.

"Oh, honey, you know I love you both." Her eyes soften. "I just want you to be happy."

"I am happy."

"This is your first day off in how long?" She gives me a side-eye.

Shrugging, I stretch my feet out and stare at the birds flying around the feeder in the yard.

"That's not living, honey."

"I'm doing what I love," I protest.

"I just worry about you. I want you to get plenty of rest. Do some things for you." She sets her mug down and rocks in her chair next to me.

"Did you get your car fixed?" I tip my head toward her.

She murmurs, "Oh yes, it runs perfectly now."

"Imagine that," I say dryly. "Mine is in the shop now. I have a loaner from Sam."

She turns in her chair to face me, giddy with relief. "I'm so glad you brought it up. How did that go?"

Well, it appears the gossip train in Freedom Valley is alive and well if she already knows about SJ towing me.

I shake my head. "It was awful. He acted like nothing happened."

"Give it time," she soothes.

"He's had twelve years, Goldie."

"How do you feel seeing him after all this time?"

I blow out a breath. "Sadness, betrayal, anguish, attraction, and bitterness. A tornado of emotions. I don't like it." I huff.

"He's always been a good boy. Now, he's a good man." She's always had a soft spot for SJ.

"I wouldn't know," I say in defiance. "I don't know him anymore."

"It's time to change that," she says as she takes a sip of coffee and rocks gently in her rocking chair across from me.

"I told him I was seeing Thad," I tell her.

A few dinner dates with Thad doesn't mean we're exclusive. I don't even know why I told SJ that. It just came out.

"I forgot about Brad. He's not very memorable." She stares blankly out into the garden, not having anything to add to that statement. Her mouth is in a firm line.

"Thad," I correct her and giggle. That's one thing about Goldie—she'll always tell me what she's thinking, unfiltered.

I know Thad and I aren't going anywhere. As much as he and my parents are trying to will it to happen, it'll never happen. I just don't have the energy to deal with him yet. And to be honest, he puts no energy into me, so I haven't been in a hurry to shut it down. Shutting it down will make even more of a mess. Being with Thad is like how my parents are together. For status, not for love. I grew up in a loveless house. No thanks. I'm back in Freedom Valley for Goldie, who is my real family. My parents and I have tried to reconnect since I've been back in Freedom Valley. I hate having conflict with them, but everything feels like a battle, and lately, it's been getting worse. They're trying to mold me into a version of themselves, and it's just not me. I'm happy living here in Goldie's cottage and not in a big house, spending every weekend at the country club like they do. It's just not the life for me.

After a brief and calm silence of us listening to the birds and sipping coffee, she clears her throat and says softly, "Sometimes two people who are meant for each other will face some of the greatest challenges to be together."

My thoughts are interrupted when I look up to see Thad pulling up in his Corvette.

Goldie tenses up. "Look what the cat dragged in," she mutters.

"Shh." I laugh then mutter, "Speak of the devil."

Thad steps out of his car with the top down on far too chilly of a chilly day. He walks up wearing a polo shirt and slacks for golfing. Thad is very rigid with his workout routine and is very fit. He runs, lifts weights, and golfs multiple times a week. He won't miss a workout for anything. Even at the hospital, he'll do his workout somewhere when he's on his break. He's a driven and focused guy, I'll give him that. He'll make some lady happy; it just won't be me.

He's wearing Ray-Ban sunglasses and looks like he has a fresh haircut. He always looks impeccable. Sometimes I just want to mess up his hair. It's weird that he's always so perfect. Like a real-life Ken doll. I rarely feel as put together as he is, and it seems to frustrate him. It's almost like he wants me to be his match, only that's never going to happen.

On a few occasions, he's asked me to dress nicer when we've attended events together or asked me to wear more makeup. I brushed it off, but it annoyed me. Sauntering up the walk, he stops, puts his hands on his hips, and scolds me, "Babe. Don't you know how to answer your phone?"

I cringe. The endearment scrapes against my brain like an unsharpened ten blade. Did he seriously just call me *babe?*

This is how he talks to me. No pleasantries, no concern about how I needed help. Yet this guy is hinting at getting serious when it's clear he doesn't care about me. It's so weird.

"Nice to see you too, Thad," I mutter, trying hard not to roll my eyes.

"Where's your phone?"

I look down and realize I don't even have it. "It's in the house." I shrug.

"What if the hospital tried to call?" he persists.

"It's my day off, Thad," I plead. I know what he's going to ask me. Or rather demand of me.

He ignores me and continues, "I need you to cover my shift. I have tee time with your father at the club." He takes off his sunglasses and cleans them with his shirt.

"You want the job, right? The board will be meeting soon.

You need to make a good impression and be a team player."

My heart drops, thinking of my plans to enjoy a nice fall day with the windows open and maybe take a hike later. It's not happening now.

I'm beginning to loathe Thad. He uses me and makes me jump through hoops for this job. And because he knows I want it so badly, I'm trapped and frustrated that I can't say no. Otherwise, my job will be in jeopardy. I shake my head, seething inside.

"I'll make it up to you." He leans down to kiss me, but I quickly turn my head so he gets my cheek instead. He saunters back to his car without looking back. He speeds off too fast out of the driveway, spitting gravel and dust everywhere.

He never once acknowledged Goldie or waited for a response, just ordered me to take his shift and left.

I look over at Goldie. Her mouth is set in a line, and she says flatly, "That man has the intelligence of a carrot."

THEN

It's late when my window slides open and someone grunts as they land on the floor of my room. I flip on my light, and it's Callie in a rumpled dress, her hair wild and her face streaked with tears.

"What happened?" I rush to her, looking her over to see if she's hurt.

"It was bad. They were drinking and really angry." She sniffs, wiping her tears with the back of her hand.

"It's okay, come here." I close the window and pull her toward my bed, tucking her in and comforting her.

"On the way home from dinner, my dad was screaming at me

that I better not throw my life away and that I'm their future doctor and they're counting on me," she says, shaking.

I hold her close because she's shivering. "Callie, you're only seventeen. You don't have to take care of anyone, and that's not right," I whisper, pulling her closer.

"They talk to me like I'm their cash cow, and they can't wait to cash in on their prize."

My heart clenches, and I close my eyes. I wish she could just stay with me and my dad. I want to protect her so badly from her parents.

"I'm tired of walking on eggshells every day and trying to be perfect for them," she says with a sob.

I nod my head as she continues, "I can't do this anymore. I wish I could just live here with you and Sam."

I look at the door. "I'm surprised he didn't hear you and come in here."

"I think he saw me climbing up the trellis," she admits sheepishly. "There are a lot of bikes parked out front, and they're still hanging out down in the shop."

"I'm sure I'll hear all about it tomorrow." My dad will probably just give me crap about it, but the truth is that my dad loves Callie. My dad doesn't have a lot of rules, but as long as we're safe, he's chill.

"You think he'll be mad at me?" she whispers.

"No, Callie. He doesn't like how your parents treat you, either."

NOW

SJ: Callie, please meet me for coffee. Let's talk.

Callie: How did you get this number?

SJ: The shop.

Callie: I'm not ready to talk to you.

SJ: Get ready.

Callie: We're done.

SJ: We'll never be done.

With a grin on my face and a speck of something warm in my chest, I slide my phone back into my pocket and head into the bakery. Fighting with Callie is better than a lifetime of silence without her.

Coach Murphy sees me across the lobby and lifts his hand in a wave as he chats with the other patrons. He's got a cup of coffee and a plate with a pastry in front of him.

"Coach." I nod and get in line to put my order in. As I scan the menu, a familiar voice calls from the back, "Hey, SJ!" I look over and see Evan's sister, Allie, in an apron with her Baked Inn Love logo on it, carrying a tray of scones to the bakery case. And they smell amazing. I'm kicking myself for not coming in here to try it out before now.

"Hey, Allie, how are you?" She's older now too, and not the little kid sister that I remember. It's crazy to me that she's a mom. Evan, Allie, and I have so many memories together. Allie tagged along on a lot of our adventures out at the inn growing up.

"Doing great! What can I get you?" she asks cheerfully, stepping over to the register.

"Black coffee and one of those scones?" I point at the pumpkin scones that smell amazing.

"For here or to go?"

"Here." I nod to Coach, sitting at a table.

"The boys enjoyed the game the other night."

"Thanks, it's great to be back. I met the future Eagles," I say as I tap my card on the machine.

"They told me all about it. It's good to have you home. I just came back last year myself. I was out in California for a while."

"The place looks great," I say, looking around. It smells great in here. I make a mental note to come back.

"Thanks, it's a dream come true to finally have my own bakery," she says as she slides my coffee over to me. "Let me get your scone. They're still warm."

"Thanks." I look around. A large round table in the back full of older ladies looks away quickly as I glance over. One of them giggles, and another says something, and they all sneak a glance over at me. This makes the rest of the table erupt in laughter, and a few sneak glances back at me.

I smile politely and look away. I recognize a few of them from around town.

"Here you go," she says as she slides a plate over to me. "Ignore them," she whispers. "They're playing matchmaker. Word on the street is that you're the most eligible bachelor in Freedom Valley," she informs me.

"Um, I'll pass on that," I say with a shake of my head and smile as I head to Coach's table.

"Thanks, SJ," she calls as she helps the next customer.

"How are you doing, son?" Coach leans his forearms on the thick dark wooden table. He still looks the same, just an older version of the coach I remember as a kid. He's worn a Freedom Valley Eagles hat and hoodie as a standard uniform for as long as I've known him.

"Doing good. How about yourself?" I slide in across from him.

"Just wanted to touch base and see how you're doing." He takes a sip of his coffee, and his eyes go from me to the table in the corner, watching me.

"Friends of yours?" he asks with amusement.

"Friends of the owner." I shrug. "I don't know them."

He nods. "Ahh, okay."

I go back to his previous question. "I was hoping you'd have news for me about the coaching position."

His face fell for a second, and I didn't miss it. "The board was supposed to vote and make you the assistant coach until I officially retire. They haven't done it yet. The word is, they were waiting on funding for the position. We haven't been doing so great in the past years, and they say they don't have the funds yet. That's what they're telling me anyway."

I take a sip of my coffee and set it back down. "Can we be real, Coach?"

"Always." He leans in.

"Do you actually think this is going to happen?" Sitting back, I fold my arms across my chest and stare at him.

"They'd be idiots not to hire you. Hell, you're doing it as a volunteer right now. If that doesn't count for something, then I don't know what does."

"It's not about the money. I already have a job. I *want* the position. But I'm starting to wonder if people on the board are hosing up the process on purpose."

"What do you mean?" he asks, scratching his jaw.

"Hamilton McGraw." I sigh.

The thorn in my side, Callie's father. The man who simultaneously destroys anything in his proximity. Doesn't matter what it is—jobs, businesses, families. He doesn't care as long as he gets what he wants. And I suspect he wants to make sure I never become a football coach.

Coach scoffs. "I won't let that happen."

"He plays dirty. I wouldn't put it past him to get other board members on board with whatever he wants."

"Then we fight back," he counters.

"And how are we going to do that?"

"We win games."

I nod and grin. "We can do that."

"I'm glad you're back, Reid. You're going to be a fine head coach," he says proudly.

It feels good to hear this from him. In high school, football was the only way I felt like I belonged. Now, I want to coach because I want to make sure that any kid who feels like I did in high school doesn't. I want to be a mentor to these kids and make sure that town bullies like Hamilton McGraw don't fuck up the next generation like they did to me. And Hamilton McGraw better understand that he's not running things anymore. I am.

CHAPTER 7

Callie

THEN

"Can I come over and work on my science project after school?"
I ask as I take a bite of my sandwich.

"Yeah, we can get pizza," he says as he slides his cake across
the table to me.

"Why do you always get the cake when you don't even like
cake?" I grin and take a bite.

"I don't like the cake, but you do."

"You get an extra piece just for me?"

"Yep."

"Why?" I ask, my heart melting.

"You're my otter, Callie," he says.

"Thanks," I whisper, trying not to get sappy. He always does little things like this, like saving a piece of cake for me. My own parents have been out of town on vacation for a week now with friends and haven't even bothered to call and check in on me. Yet SJ knows where I am and what I need. He pays attention to the little things. I doubt my parents know little details about my life, like what desserts I like. My parents are rarely sober and rarely aware of anything but their social status and trips. Unless it benefits or affects them in some way. It feels good to know that someone in the world cares about me.

I'm in the back corner of Sam's shop putting together my science project with headphones on and my music playing when someone taps me on the back. It's Sam. "Hey, kiddo, pizza's here." He points with his thumb as he picks up a few tools from the worktable and slides them onto a hook where they belong on the wall.

"Thanks, Sam." I turn off my music and head to the back. I walk into the break room of Sam's Auto Body shop and hear the loud roar of laughter. Two of my favorite bikers, Bear and Smoke, are sitting around the table with SJ making plates of pizza.

"Hey, Callie, you want one?" Axel calls from in front of the fridge. He's holding up a can of soda.

"Yes, please," I say as I slide between Bear and SJ. Bear looks over at me and says, "What are you building out there?"

"It's my science fair project. I'm competing in Concord in a few weeks. If I win, it's for a partial scholarship." I hold the box open so he can take another slice.

"Listen to you, smartypants. Your mom and dad must be so proud," Bear says as he takes a bite of pizza.

I laugh, and SJ snorts.

"What?" Bear says with his deep, protective voice. To others, he could be scary. He's got serious dark eyes, a beard, and wild, long hair. But to me, he's my Bear. He looks out for me and makes sure I get home. He's become like another dad like Sam to me. People can say what they want about the Eastern Bones, but they've never been anything but kind to me.

SJ just shakes his head. "Callie's parents are always gone. That's why she's over here all the time."

Sam looks at both of us and crosses his arms. "Where are they now?"

"They haven't checked in," I mumble. "I'm not really sure." I think they went on a cruise with some friends. But I don't want to tell them that. It's embarrassing.

"Who is looking after you?" Sam shuffles his feet.

"I can look after myself," I reply, taking a bite of pizza.

I look up and four sets of angry and concerned eyes are on me. "What?" I mumble, my mouth full.

"No," Sam finally bites out. "You can stay here when they're gone. We have the third bedroom. He points at SJ. "You clean that room and put fresh sheets on for her. And both of you, no funny business," he says pointing at us.

"Okay," SJ mumbles, sneaking a look at me.

Warmth fills me, and I look at Sam and say, "Thank you. For the pizza, too."

"You can stay here until they come back," he clips. I can tell he's really mad.

It's a foreign feeling to have someone care about my comfort and safety, yet, it feels…nice. I'm not sure what to do with this feeling, but it does make me feel warm and loved.

"Thanks." It's been lonely at home by myself. But I didn't want to tell them that. It's just been easier to stay here after school and only go home when it's time to sleep.

He nods and reaches into the fridge, pulls out a beer, and snaps the lid off, shaking his head.

I sit and eat quietly and watch as these big bikers have created a family-like environment that is more of a safe space than my own family. They've accepted me as one of them. I look over at SJ, and he smiles at me, his warm brown eyes reassuring me.

It's not lost on me that these bikers are all members of the local motorcycle club, and they sometimes make questionable choices. I don't pay attention to club business, and they've been nice around me. My parents have ranted about them and made it known that they don't approve of SJ or Sam. They think they're all trash and have told me as much any time it comes up. And *here they are looking out for me, feeding me, and keeping me safe. My parents would freak if they knew I was here with them as much as I am. This house may be unconventional with Sam and SJ living above the shop and surrounded by a motorcycle club, but they're a family. SJ is safe and loved here. At my house, I am not loved or safe. I'm alone most of the time. My house is volatile, and I'd rather be lonely than have the nights where my parents fight with drunk rage and keep me up.*

NOW

Let's try this again, I think as I put my phone in do not disturb mode and get ready for my hike. If Thad or the hospital calls, they won't reach me. I'm not on call because I'm not a permanent employee. If they want me on call, they need to give me a full-time contract. Today is mine. I won't be taking a shift. I'm unavailable. I'm taking Goldie's advice and doing something fun for me.

One of my favorite trails on the outskirts of town is perfect today. The weather feels warm, and a hike to clear my mind and figure out everything that's going on sounds like just what I need. It's quiet out here, and all the tourists who come to look at the foliage are out on the main highway while I have my spot to myself. I even brought a book with me and might even read.

This is where I used to come with SJ. It's where we fell in

love on countless hikes and picnics. I haven't been out here since I've been back, but it's time. This isn't just a place of memories with him anymore. It's mine now, I've decided, and I'm going to make new memories here. That's what I tell myself anyway.

The wildflowers are dying down, and the trees are all popping with stunning, vibrant colors that are almost too pretty. I'm so glad I'm back here, and this alone was worth moving back. Our lookout is just a few miles out of town but not known by too many people, and it is one of my favorite places. The autumn sun beams down on me, warming my face.

I've always loved all things about autumn. I'll admit that in my college apartment, I sometimes left fall decor out year-round. It reminded me of my home in Freedom Valley. We have the best fall season here. The weather, all the pumpkin-flavored treats, festivals, spooky decor, I love it all. This is all part of why I came back here to settle in and start a new life. I missed it here.

I tighten the laces on my boots and take off on a path you'd have to know to look for that's rough and not defined. Fall is showing off right now, and the foliage is beautiful. I couldn't have picked a better day to come out here. This is my place of peace, just coming out here and staring at all the stunning colors—especially this time of year—makes me so happy. About a mile into my hike, I stumble across a new clearing where someone has built a gorgeous cabin. It has a perfect rustic wooden deck off it with outdoor seating to die for and a huge stone firepit. I hang back so as not to trespass or bother the people living here. Longing fills me because this was my favorite spot, and I dreamed of building my dream home here once upon a time with SJ. And it looks like someone has beat me to it and built my dream home down to every detail. A firepit with four white Adirondack chairs around it. A chimney with smoke curling out of it. The smoky smell makes me close my eyes and inhale the crisp autumn breeze. I hear a crunch of leaves and look over to see a shirtless SJ standing in jeans, holding an axe.

"Jesus, SJ, what are you doing out here?" I yell, surprised to see him. He scared the hell out of me. His skin is still tanned from the summer sun, and holy crap, he has even more tattoos snaking across his chest. Beads of sweat cross his face. Wood chunks are in a pile next to him, and he has a big stump with a piece of wood lying on it that he's chopping.

He looks equally surprised to see me. Relaxing the axe over his shoulder, he tilts his head and grins. "I could ask you the same. Miss me?"

"No," I scoff. "I'm on a hike. And where are your clothes?" I look away but not because I want to. It's because I can't stop staring at his massive chest and gorgeous pecs. Why does he have to be so good looking? It's not fair to waste good looks on such a jerk.

"Inside." He nods toward the cabin I was just drooling

over.

My mouth hangs open. "*You* live here? *Here?* No way."

This was our place, and he comes back here and builds our dream cabin? I see he's been busy in the past year since he's been back. I suddenly realize that I don't know anything about him. Nothing. My head is spinning. My chest feels heavy. He built this without me.

He doesn't say anything, but his mouth turns up and goes back to cutting the wood. He positions the wood on the stump and steps back and picks up the axe and smashes it down onto the stump, splintering the piece.

He doesn't say a word to me, but he glances at me curiously between chopping.

His body is tanned, chiseled, filled out, and lean. That kind of body doesn't come from the gym. It comes from chopping wood, lifting heavy things at the shop, and probably building that stupid cabin that was supposed to be mine. Grown-up SJ is not the cute high school boy anymore. He's all manly man muscle. There's a darker, unnerving energy about him now. He's not the cute affable kid I once knew. This man has secrets. He has small lines fanning out at his eyes. A crease marring his brow from overthinking and brooding. He's taller, more solid, a canvas of tattoo art and a dark happy trail leading down into those jeans. I don't move and watch him repeatedly cut more wood. He stops to wipe the sweat from his forehead. "Want to take a picture?" He smirks.

"Dickhead," I clip, narrowing my eyes.

"You're the one watching *me*." He chuckles with a grin as he looks me over from head to toe, slowly. My body warms at his perusal.

"You're the creepy one in the woods with serial killer energy," I push back.

At that, he laughs and leans against the axe. "I've missed you."

"You had twelve years to find me," I retort.

"I found you now."

"Too late."

His face falls. "Don't say that, Callie."

"You left me," I bite out.

He sighs and wipes his brow with the back of his hand. "We were just kids doing the best that we could. You had your issues with your parents, and I had mine, too."

My face falls when he says that. "Have you heard from either of them?" I ask about his mom and sister.

He shakes his head. "No. You?"

I shake my head. Family secrets are what destroyed us, and now here we are, and it feels like we've come full circle.

He shakes his head and leans down to reposition another piece of wood to chop. I know he's acting like it's not a big deal, but he's been through a lot. I heard he had joined the military, but I tried to shut him out and wouldn't let anyone bring him up again after he left and didn't contact me.

Goldie tried to talk to me about him, but I always shut her down. I didn't want to know. There's so much about SJ that I don't know. So much he took from me. I never imagined we'd be strangers like this. I didn't want to hear about him through Goldie. I wanted him to care enough to reach out to me himself.

"Change your mind on that coffee yet?" he asks. His husky voice incinerates my panties.

I narrow my eyes. "No."

"Come on, we used to be best friends."

I bark out a laugh. "Best friends?"

He nods, his whiskey eyes on me.

"A best friend doesn't just *leave* without a word. Not one word. Friends don't even do that, let alone best friends."

"That's not true," he says softly. "Did you know that I wrote you letters every day for a year? I sent them to your house, and Goldie even tried to give you some."

I didn't know that. My hand flies to my mouth. I never got any letters from my parents. I vaguely remember that with Goldie when she mentioned SJ. That was a horrible time for me with my parents, and I never felt more alone in my life. I left not long after so that explains why I never got any of his letters. I'm sure they just threw them away.

"It's too late for us." I shake my head. We can't fix this.

"Nope," he says. "This is our spot." He waves his hand. "Why would you come back here if you didn't miss me?"

"I'm surprised you remember that," I say quietly. "You forgot about me so easily, I figured you forgot everything else about us. And it isn't our spot anymore. I guess it's just yours now. Enjoy your spot."

He throws the axe into the log and stalks over to me like a puma, sleek and dark, his torso dewy with perspiration, his long legs eating up the distance between us, stopping in front of me. The look on his face is determined.

"Not a day has gone by that I haven't thought about you. Not a single day."

As he says this, he gets closer until I can see his eyes, and they're locked on me. I close my eyes. I can't look at him. My SJ. He's not mine anymore. His face is so close to mine, his mouth inches from my lips.

I open my eyes and see hope in his, and I can't take it anymore. I reach up and pull him to me, and my mouth crashes into his.

And he pulls me in, his mouth taking over and his hands cradling my face, not letting go and kissing me like he was meant to do. And it feels...right. God, it feels right. And wrong. He built this home and a life here without me. This was our spot. And now I don't know what any of this means.

"You weren't just my best friend, SJ. You were my everything." I pull back, choking out a sob.

I turn to walk back to the path, wiping my eyes as I go. "Now you're my nothing."

"Callie," he clips in a hoarse voice.

"What?" I call back without turning around. I can't look at him. I brace myself because I know whatever he says has the power to destroy me. He holds all the power, always has. And he's dangerous with it.

"I was your first kiss. I plan on being your last." He goes back to chopping wood and the back view of him is even hotter than the front. Jesus.

THEN

Tonight's our first home game of the season, and I can't let Coach Murphy or the team down. They're counting on me. My nerves are shot, and I feel like I'm going to be sick. Pre-game nerves always rattle me, but then during the game and after, I always feel better. Then the adrenaline letdown and exhaustion set in, and I'm so hungry I could eat a horse and then sleep for days after every game. So much pressure to perform and do well. How the town approves or accepts me depends on how well I play and whether we win. I've seen people shake their heads at me in disappointment after we've lost. It's as if I'm the direct result of our losing, and it's solely my fault. And the way they clap me on the back and tell me good job after a win is the high I chase every time. To belong. I don't know why it matters to me so much, but I want to belong here. I don't want people to look down on me.

At lunch, I was relieved when Callie passed me a few PB & J sandwiches she had packed for me from home. She knows they are the only things that calm my stomach before a game and that I need to eat. I smile at her, grateful for the sandwiches. She reaches over to hug me, and it feels like everything will be all right. "Knock 'em dead tonight, SJ."

The team is ready in the locker room. Coach talks to us and amps us up, and then we run out. The stadium lights are bright across the stadium. It's darker now, and the crowd is cheering. I smile as I look because I know Callie is out there cheering for me and wearing my number.

Someone grips and squeezes my arm too tightly. I jerk back and look up, and it's Callie's dad, Hamilton McGraw. He looks over at me and sways slightly back and forth, his eyes glassy and unable to focus on my face. His breath and body sweat reeks of alcohol. "Better win, son," he slurs, spitting as he speaks. My first thought is Callie and where she is and if she's seeing her dad drunk like this at the game. I know she'd be so embarrassed.

I put my head down and scooted down the bench closer to my team to escape him. I don't want to be seen with him. My eyes dart up to the stands to check on Callie and make sure she's okay. I see her sitting with a few friends, and she's unbothered *and unaware of her drunk Dad showing up at the game and starting stuff with me. I look over, and Callie's mom Cheryl is watching me with her lips pursed. It looks like she didn't miss seeing me looking up at Callie. And the way her eyes are glassy, she looks lit too. She's holding a tumbler that probably contains alcohol. I wonder who drove here. It's amazing how much I used to care about whether these people liked me. But I know they never will. To them, I'm just the son of a biker who isn't good enough for their daughter. I'll never be accepted by them. The truth of it is that they'll never be good enough for Callie. They may not accept me, but it hurts more to see them treat her the way they do. She deserves better.*

I look up into the stands, and my dad is watching me. No doubt he caught the exchange with Callie's dad. I watch his eyes narrow on Hamilton. His body language is rigid and tight. He sees me watching him and lifts his chin and his hand in a wave. My dad is a good guy and runs a good business here in Freedom Valley. I could never understand why he isn't good enough. Why am I not good enough? I have good grades. Not as good as Callie's, but they're good enough for college. And I play varsity football. I do all the right things. I can't help who my dad is, but he's a good person. My dad, the colorful biker as they want to see him, is here at the game without any alcohol in his system. He's here with his friends to cheer me on. Why does it matter that they rode here on bikes? Hamilton and Cheryl McGraw are the ones people should be worried about.

NOW

I wake up cold and sweaty from a nightmare. I sit up and scrub my hand over my face and take deep breaths and reach for my water. I've barely slept since I saw Callie again that first night at the game, and when I do sleep, the nightmares have come back, and this time, they're all of me leaving her.

When I first came home, building my cabin was fueled by insomnia. But I'm done hiding how I feel about Callie. I'd rather risk facing everything head-on. And my deepest pain is the way I hurt her by leaving. My biggest fear is that she'll never forgive me. I knew I wasn't good enough for her. I knew she was better off without me. But now? I'm not sure of anything anymore other than I still love her. Somehow my feelings for her are even stronger now.

I watch the sunrise over the ridgeline as I wait for my coffee to brew. When it's done, I take my cup out to the porch and watch the sun rise with my feet propped up. Callie and I used to always come here and sit on a blanket up on top of this cliff and watch the sun set. She used to say it was the only place she felt safe and peaceful. I wanted her to have this. I wanted this for us. I always hoped maybe she'd come back, and we could work things out and build a life together. But now I'm messing it all up. I can't get it right for anything.

When my dad told me this land was up for sale about six

years ago, I knew I had to have it even though I was still stationed in Texas. I bought the land but didn't start building on it until a year ago. Building the cabin has been the best thing for me. Callie was right; this place is peaceful. When she surprised me out here the other day, it made me feel like I had a sliver of a chance at winning her back. Kissing Callie was...everything I imagined it would be. I know that we're meant to be. I just need her to see that this is it for us. We're ready for this. I think she does, but she's just still so upset with me, and I get it. I was a shit. I'll do anything to fix things. As I look back on the past several years, every decision I made was a driving force toward getting her back. I bought the land, finished college, got out of the military, and got myself healthy again. I want to be a better man for her.

Having Callie back here feels like a switch has flipped in me. It's funny how someone you think you know everything about can live an entirely different life for the past twelve years, and I have no idea what that has been like for her. I want to know everything I missed. It feels like we've both lived an entire lifetime since eighteen. And I don't really want to tell her any of it. Most of it wasn't good. The Army was tough. It healed me in some ways, but it broke me, too. I've seen a lot of things and done a lot of things. I don't regret any of it, but I regret what happened with Callie. I want to explain everything to her and make her understand.

That night, when I went to tow her and found her asleep in her car, she looked so fragile and exhausted. Not like the strong and fearless Callie that I used to know. Then when she got mad and screamed at me, I knew she was still in there, the Callie I know. I deserve every bit of it. I'm sure she's been through it with her parents. And that's the part I can't forgive myself for. Leaving her here with them. I didn't think I had a choice back then, but I do now. Eighteen-year-old me and thirty-year-old me are two very different men. And a few people in this town need to realize that.

I pull up to the inn on my bike, and Caleb and Kase run up excitedly. "Coach Reid, can we see your bike?" They jump up and down.

Pulling off my helmet, I say, "Who wants to go first?"

"Me, me!" little blond Caleb shrieked, raising his arms.

"Alright." Lifting him, I put him on the bike, and his arms barely reach as he leans over to touch the handlebars. I hold his little leg up so it doesn't touch the hot exhaust pipe.

"Future riders on our hands," Evan calls from behind me. "But don't tell their mothers." He chuckles.

"When are you going to get a bike?" I call over to him. "You can ride with me."

"I wish I had time." He shrugs. "Does this mean you are going to be an official member of your dad's club?"

"Nah, I like riding, but I've just never gotten into the club. Too busy with other things. But I support my dad in whatever he does." I shrug.

I switch Caleb out for Kase to have a turn. "I'll let Dad know we have future Eastern Bones members."

Evan snorts and leans down to pick up Caleb and spin him around. "Things good?"

"Can't complain. You?" I ask Evan as I take in the updates to the inn property. This place has always felt like home to me. A real home.

"Better now that you finally made it out. Beth has been on me to have you over."

"You guys ready for the fall festival?" I set Kase down.

"Not even close. We still have a million things to do." He scrubs a hand over his face. "But I could use your help with the tractor. We need it for the festival and can't get it to start. Pete and I have worked on it all week. We can't get it going."

"Happy to take a look," I say as we walk out to the barn. The boys and Bossy and Chip, the black and white dogs, trail us.

I turn around and take in the inn and the property. It's changed so much since I've been back. It looks like business hasn't slowed as guests mill around, and Pete, the handyman, is across the yard working on a project. I lift a hand to wave. He's been here since Evan and I were kids.

"What do you think?" Evan asks proudly, standing next to me.

"You've done it, man. You're carrying on your family legacy. Richard would be so proud."

Evan's dad, Richard, passed away a few years back. Goldie let me know in a letter, and I was devastated for Evan. I can't imagine losing my dad. I know coming back and taking over the inn after he passed has been rough on Evan. Then, when he came back, Hamilton McGraw tried to take the inn from him by manipulating the bank. He ended up getting fired for that. But that probably only freed up more time to manipulate through other ways around town. Like he's doing now.

"Thanks." He smiles sadly, then says to lighten the mood, "We did have some fun out here, didn't we?"

I look at the ancient beat-up tractor that's more like a pile of rust at this point than tractor. "Is this the same tractor we accidentally put in your pond?"

"Yeah." Evan smiles wryly. "My dad was so pissed."

"Yeah, my dad was too. He had to come fish it out and get it running again for Richard." I laugh at the memory that is funny now but wasn't at the time. We got in so much trouble for that, but it was just kid stuff. The inn was a safe place for all of us kids, including Callie. *Callie.* I wonder if she's been out here to the inn and if she'll be at the fall festival. We always used to go together. I wonder if I could get her to go with me this year. To spend time with *her*, get to know the new version of her, and show her how much *I've* changed. I'm a different man, who just so happens to love her exactly the same. That's been the only constant in my life, it seems. The sun rises in the east, sets in the west, and I love Callie McGraw.

I open Evan's toolbox and find what I need, and after about an hour and a half and one trip to the auto parts store, the tractor is up and running. As good as it's going to get for the pile of rust that it is.

Evan stacks straw bales in the corner of the barn and turns to me. "I hope you planned on staying for dinner because everyone will be disappointed if you aren't," Evan says as he hands me a bottle of water.

"Sure, thanks." I take a swig and set the bottle back down.

"Want to play football with us, Coach?" Caleb asks, holding a football up that's comically huge in his tiny hands.

"We'd better get to practicing if you're going to be future Eagles." I hold up my hands to catch the ball.

"Yeah!" both boys cheered.

After we tossed the ball for a while, they got bored and wandered off to play on their playset. Evan leans in from his Adirondack chair next to mine and says, "How are you really doing?" His forehead crinkles with worry, and I know he's wondering how my mental health is doing. He's one of the few people I allow into my bubble, and he has been there for me.

"I'm okay," I say firmly. And I mean it. I really am.

"Don't bullshit me," he hedges, a small smile on his face letting me know we're keeping this light and he's just checking in on me.

Nodding, I sigh. "The truth is, I finally feel like I have the fire back in me. It's a good feeling."

"And Callie's the match?" Evan smirks.

"Very funny." I snort. But Evan is exactly right.

"Everything good with football?"

"Still waiting to hear something. It's frustrating. When I started volunteer coaching, Coach Murphy told me that I would be a shoo-in for this position, but to be honest, I'm not sure it's going to happen. With my past reputation and history here, I just don't know. A lot of people in this town don't respect me or seem to think I'm capable of stepping in Coach Murphy's shoes."

"You've done more than you're giving yourself credit for. More people than you realize are rooting for you to get that job," Evan hedges. "And you're a great guy. Everyone who matters knows that. And if they don't, that's their problem, not yours."

"Thanks. I'm tired of Hamilton McGraw thinking he's running this town, and it's got to stop."

"I agree." He nods. "That's why we have to fight back. This is our town now. We're going to make sure that it stops, and this town is protected."

"You can count on that. I'm not backing down." I promise.

"I'm so proud of you. Glad you're back."

"Proud of you, too. You've got a beautiful family and inn here. You deserve this. You've been a good friend, and I won't forget how you were there for me when I came back."

"You deserve this, too, you know." Evan looks over at me. "And you'd have done the same thing for me."

"The only person I want this with doesn't want anything to do with me."

"You sure about that?"

"I'm not sure about anything anymore," I quip.

CHAPTER 9

Callie

THEN

It's been over thirty minutes, and I know he's not coming. My dad was supposed to give me a ride to Concord for my science fair today. I reminded him, texted him, and even had his secretary at the bank put it on his calendar. I figured he'd be home in time to take me. I checked my watch again. I pulled my phone out of my backpack and called him. It rings and finally I get his voicemail. I hung up and called my mom. She answers and sounds like I caught her mid-laugh. "Hello. . ." She's loud and I can tell she's probably at the club with her friends and likely already several glasses in.

"*Mom, do you know where Dad is? He's supposed to give me a ride.*"

"*Oh, sweetheart, you know he has a work thing. He can't make it.*" *I suspect there's no work thing. He's probably drinking at the same club, too.*

I pinch the bridge of my nose, trying not to cry. "I have to go, Mom." I hang up, and tears fill my eyes. They forgot about me. Again. And this was important to me. I've been working on this project for months. It's all I've talked about. I can't rely on them for anything. Time and time again, they leave me to figure out everything on my own, yet they still put all this pressure on me to do well in school.

I take a deep breath and call SJ.

"*Hey, what's up, Cal?" SJ answers.*

"*He forgot about me." I sniff, trying not to cry. "And I can't get it loaded by myself without breaking it.*"

There's silence, and I hear shuffling, then he says, "I'll be there in ten minutes. I'll bring Dad to help load it. Don't worry, I'll get you there on time."

"*Thanks, I really appreciate it. Bye," I say as I hang up the phone. I worked on this project at Sam's shop for a month, and then it took two of us to get it to my parents' house so that I could be ready for the science fair.*

I sit with my knees to my chest and try not to cry. It's fine. I'll get there, I'll have a smile on my face, and it'll all work out. This doesn't matter, I say to myself.

I hear them before I see them. SJ pulls up in his dad's older model green truck, and Sam and Bear are on their bikes and pull in and park in our circular driveway behind the truck.

SJ jogs up to my front door as I open it. "I'm so happy to see you," I say with relief, giving him a hug and kissing him.

"It's okay. Road trip, it'll be fun," he says as he reaches for my backpack and carries it to the front seat of the truck. "I should have just planned on taking you anyway." He's right, but my parents would have had a fit if they knew SJ had taken me, so that was why I had asked my parents months ago. Now, it doesn't matter, I decided. I won't be asking them for anything, and I'll be taking care of myself from now on, just like I usually do.

"Hey, girlie," Bear calls, and Sam squeezes my shoulder as they enter my front door and pick up my science project, a paper mâché replica of the human body with all the organs and bones labeled and painted. It's super fragile, and they bring it to the truck and slide it in the back seat, careful not to let it bend.

I look at SJ, and he snorts. Apparently, we both find it funny to see these two bikers arguing over how to keep my science project safe by trying to buckle it in. It looks like they just carried a human body out to the back of the truck. And then seeing them at my parents' big ostentatious house is funny too. My parents would have a coronary seeing them here. They should have thought about that before they forgot about me and how much this day means to me. Jerks.

"You should be all set, Callie," Sam calls. "Drive careful,

son," he calls over his shoulder to SJ.

"Thank you," I call as they swing their legs over their bikes, straightening their leather vests and sliding on their helmets. Both give a wave as they take off from the driveway. Tears prick my eyes as I wave back, and I think about how Sam and the club show up for me, and I'm not even Sam's kid. And that makes me feel wanted and safe when I'm with them.

"Ready?" SJ calls from the driver's seat of the truck.

"Ready." I slide into the seat beside him.

"I can't believe I won!" I say excitedly as we drive back to Freedom Valley.

"I can. You deserve it. You worked so hard."

"I couldn't have done it without your help and your dad letting me work on it at the shop," I say gratefully.

He looks over at me. "Can I ask you something? Why did you want the scholarship money so bad? Isn't your dad going to help you with school?"

I shrug. "I can't rely on them or trust them. I'm also not sure that they have as much money as they'd like for people to believe," I say quietly. I don't want to tell him, but most of my parents' fights of late have been over money and lack thereof it. I don't want to take anything from them or owe them down the road.

"We don't need them anyway," he says.

"Do we have time to stop for burgers and milkshakes? I'm starving," I ask, trying to change the subject. I don't want to think about my parents anymore today. It's been a great day, and I don't want to ruin it.

"Only if we get onion rings," he agrees as he pulls into the diner.

NOW

I'm gazing out at the atrium, daydreaming with my coffee cup in my hands that's long gone cold. I'm tired but trying to take a break from the hustle of the ER. I asked Thad to meet me here for coffee to talk, but he didn't show up. It's typical of him. He's probably still taking a nap in the on-call room. He's not even working an eight-hour shift today. I roll my eyes. Thad is the laziest doctor we have. I don't know what I was ever thinking by ever associating myself with him. I just went along with what my parents wanted. Autopilot like I have been doing for the past twelve years. Going through the motions of college, med school, residency. Like I've disassociated myself with my life to the point that other people were making decisions for me. I start to think about what I want, what makes me happy, and I know that the life my parents have and want for me has never been it.

My coffee cup is snatched from my hands, and I scoff as I watch it land in the trash not far from where I'm sitting.

"What the. . .?" I look up and then back down to a fresh warm coffee cup from Baked Inn Love that slides between my hands. SJ's big hands wrap around mine and the cup. I look up into his eyes that peek out from under his dark blue Eagles ball cap.

He's wearing a dark gray Henley tight over his chest and with muscles in all the right places. He must have shaved, but he already has that five-o'clock shadow again that hits me right in the lady parts when he grins, and his single dimple pops. He slides into the chair across from me and leans in toward me on his elbows. And that's when my eyes land on his lips. The same lips that I kissed the other day at the lookout. I think about those lips and imagine them on mine again. I shake myself out of these thoughts and remember that we're not friends anymore, much less kissing buddies. Nope.

"What are you thinking about?" His mouth turns up, taking a sip of his own coffee and looking at me with satisfaction because he knows exactly what I was thinking about.

"What are you doing here?" I ask dryly, irritated that he knew I was looking at his lips and probably guessed what I was thinking about. I hate that he has this effect on me.

"You wouldn't meet me for coffee. So I brought coffee to you," he says as his whiskey eyes drink me in from across the table.

"Do you need to take a picture?" I mock him like he did to me the other day.

"I don't need a picture to remember you. I remember everything," he says evenly.

I gaze back at the atrium, trying not to look at him.

"What's on your mind? You look lost in thought," he asks as he looks out over the atrium.

I clear my throat and shake myself back to reality, but having him here right across from me casually drinking coffee is something I dreamed about for over a decade. I've thought about this moment and what we would say. This all feels so surreal. I finally have my chance to tell him everything and ask anything, but I don't even know where to start.

I stare at him and finally say, "I was thinking about how messed up it is that you can go from planning your future with someone to becoming complete strangers."

He leans closer. "We'll never be strangers," he says firmly, his lips forming a line.

"We're strangers now."

"Let's change that." His dimple pops again.

"It's too late."

"And I told you it's never too late," he says as he takes a drink of his coffee and his throat muscles flex. Damn. How is it even possible that his throat muscles are sexy, too?

"One thing I've learned is that no matter how much love

you have for someone, it doesn't mean they'll love you back the same. Every person in my life has shown me that. Except Goldie." I stare back at him and tilt my head in a challenge.

"That's not true." His face softens and he sits back, crossing his arms.

"It is true. Too much has happened. We're not the same people anymore."

"I know we're not the same. I want to know you and everything that I missed."

"Why are you doing this, SJ?" I sigh in frustration, turning the cup in my hand around, grateful to have something to focus on instead of his face.

"I need you, Callie. I'm making myself crystal clear right now so there is no mistaking what and who I want. It's you. A lifetime with you. There has never been a time when it wasn't you. If I have to show up every damn day at the hospital with a good cup of coffee just to get you to glower at me, then that's what I'll do. Because I'll take what I can get from you. I'm not going anywhere," he says with his eyes focused on me.

I squirm in my seat under his warm gaze.

Crap. He means this.

CHAPTER 10

NOW

"You have customers," Ty calls over to me, nodding to the front of the shop. I made the mistake of offering to work a day shift, and the shop has been very busy.

"Huh? Why are they *my* customers?" I mutter, glaring at Ty because I know he's messing with me.

I look out to the front of the garage bays, and two ladies are waving at me excitedly.

"What do they need?" I asked Ty.

"They're back for the fifth time."

"Is something wrong?" I ask, confused, running a hand

through my hair and then pulling my hat lower.

Ty smirks. "Your dad told them they could have their fluids topped off for free between oil changes. They're here for wiper fluid. Again." He laughs, clearly enjoying this.

"Wiper fluid? Why?" I mutter as I reach over for the fluid cart to top them off.

"This is what you get for being Freedom Valley's most eligible bachelor, Coach." He laughs. "They keep coming back in hopes that they'll see you, and today is their lucky day. Don't disappoint them."

"This is why I work nights," I grump.

"How are things going with Callie?" he asks as he raises a car on the lift.

"Not that good. Nothing's working," I grumble.

"Go for a ride on your bike."

"I don't want to go for a ride, and how would that help?"

"With her. Go pick her up tonight. When Mellie's mad at me, I take her out for a ride. It's hard for her to stay mad at me with her arms around me taking in a nice ride at sunset." He shrugs. "Also, maybe if people see you with her, they'll stop considering you the next contestant on the *Bachelor*."

That's not a bad idea, I muse. "Alright, I can do that." I would love to get Callie on the back of my bike. And less attention from people in town would be great, too. Now the hard part is going to be getting her to agree to it.

I sigh as I put on a friendly smile and head over to take

care of our customers. I make a mental note to steer clear of day shifts.

CHAPTER 11

Callie

THEN

"Then you put the cap on, just like this," Sam says patiently, as he looks over at me. "You do the next one."

"Okay," I say, determined as I push the cart to the next vehicle lined up in the bay.

"You're doing a good job," he encourages as he cleans up the tools he has laid out on a workbench.

"What are you guys doing?" SJ calls as he steps into the shop, his football bag slung over his shoulder, sweaty from practice.

"Your dad's teaching me how to change the oil and top off the fluids." I motion to the last car we've just finished.

"Cool," he teases with a grin. "You can finally help out around here."

"I would love to help out," I say as I lean in to repeat the process from the last car.

"It's good for you to know this stuff in case anything happens to your vehicle when you're off at college," Sam says. "Now how many quarts of oil go in the car?" he quizzes me.

I look at the car and guess from memory. "A four cylinder, so four quarts?"

"Five on this one," Sam says. "Close."

"Thanks for showing me all of this," I say, grateful for him taking the time to teach me all of this. My own dad doesn't do things like this, so it's been fun to learn something that I'll need to know someday. Although I'll have SJ with me, and he always helps me with things like this, I want to know how to do it myself.

"It's no problem." He grunts. Sam is a man of few words, but underneath that hardness, he's a kind soul.

"I heard you're playing at McGuiness tonight with a few others?"

"Yeah, we're going to do a few sets. You and SJ should come down."

"I'll try," I say. "My parents probably won't let me, though."

Sam doesn't say anything, but he looks like he wants to.

He finally turns and says, "Alright, you did good. Go hang out with SJ until you have to go home."

"Thanks, Sam," I say as I put my arm around him and pull him in for a hug. His body stiffens, then relaxes. He pats me lightly, and I release him, dashing up the stairs.

SJ calls down, "Dad, I ordered subs. Callie and I are going to pick them up. Be back soon."

"Let's go," he says, pulling me close and kissing me as we dart across the parking lot to his truck, hand in hand.

NOW

As I scroll through my phone, I sip my straw and lean against the bar with my elbows. It's Friday night, and I'm at the McGuiness Tavern. I haven't been out much since I've been back, but I'm trying to step out of my comfort zone. And if I'm being honest, I might run into SJ. My stomach fills with butterflies at the thought of seeing him again.

"It's about time you came back," a familiar voice says next to me.

"Sam!" I cry out as I launch myself into his arms to hug him.

"It's been a while. Look at you all grown up, Dr. McGraw." He smiles proudly at me.

"Thank you." I smile. "It's so good to see you."

"I hear you've been giving my boy hell." He grins.

I roll my eyes. "Well, he deserves it."

"That's probably true," he agrees.

"I see we've got your car in the shop. You didn't remember all the oil change lessons we had?" He pretends to scold me. His hair has a little bit of gray speckled in it now as does his beard, but Sam is still just a slightly older version of SJ. I didn't see it as a kid, but now that I'm older, I realize Sam is good-looking. SJ comes by his good looks honestly.

"Of course, I remember." I grin. "I'm too busy saving lives. I leave the professional oil changes up to the best," I tease.

"We'll get you taken care of," he promises as he pats me on the back.

"You're playing tonight?" I ask, now noticing his guitar case beside him.

"Yeah, are you sticking around?"

"For a little while." I smile.

"Good to see you," he calls over his shoulder as he heads to the stage where a few other band members have begun setting up.

Looking at Sam now and picturing him at my age with a fifteen-year-old is hard to wrap my head around. Sam was a super young dad and picturing him as a thirty-three-year-old with an eighteen-year-old kid is just wild to me now. I've always looked up to Sam, and he's always been kind to me. Even after SJ left, he looked after me before I moved in with Goldie and left for college. It had been painful being around Sam when SJ dumped me. At the time, I was hopeful that SJ would come back or call or something. He never did, so it hurt like hell when I left for school. It still does when I let myself think about it. I felt pathetic pining after someone who didn't care about me.

"Callie? Are you Callie?" a younger blonde with glasses calls over to me from a few tables over.

"Yes." I smile and look over at her nervously. I'm suddenly feeling shy and wondering if I should have stayed home. *No, I need this. I need to make friends and get out,* I remind myself.

"I'm Beth, Evan's fiancé." She smiles. "You already know Allie. And this is Mellie and Paige." She introduces me to the other ladies with her, who smile at me curiously and give friendly waves. "Want to join us?"

My heart warms, shyness gone. This is Beth, who is Evan's fiancé. She looks young and sweet and welcoming. This is definitely making me glad I came out tonight.

"Sure." I smile and slide off my stool. "Hey, Allie," I call to the familiar face and wave to the others.

"It's good to see you again, Callie," she says, leaning in to hug me.

"Good to see you too," I say, sliding onto the seat next to them at their high-top table. "Having a girls' night?"

"Yes, Evan is playing." Beth swoons as she waves to Evan on the stage. Evan waves back and then strums his guitar. "We're having drinks and catching up." She waggles her eyebrows at Evan, who is warming up with his guitar.

"Stop ogling my brother. It's gross," Allie teases Beth.

"I can't help it. He makes pretty babies." She shrugs with a grin.

"Speaking of babies. Who has Benny and Eden tonight?" Paige asks.

"Margie. She loves Grandma time. She has all the kids tonight and she loves it," Mellie says.

Allie looks over at me and says, "How are things with you and SJ? I've heard rumors about you two getting back together." She grins. "Hoping they're true."

"What have you heard?" I ask, curious about what the rumor mill is spreading these days.

"Just that the chemistry is off the charts with you two," Allie says. "No offense, but everyone is rooting for you two to get back together."

"I don't know if we can get back together. There's too much to fix." I shake my head.

"He's a mechanic. I'm sure he can fix anything," Allie teases.

Thankfully, the music starts, and I realized I've missed hearing Sam play. He used to practice his guitar all the time at the shop, and while it drove SJ nuts sometimes, I always found it soothing to listen to him while I was doing homework or we were hanging out while SJ worked on a car. He can play almost any cover song. In a way, it's the sound of my childhood, and it's comforting to hear him play again. It also takes me back to memories with SJ. And that isn't where

I want to go tonight.

"I'd love to have you come by Turn the Paige bookstore and see it," Paige says sweetly. "We just opened, and I'd love to show it off."

This is what I've missed. Friends. Having a community to call home again. I knew I needed to come back to Freedom Valley. "I'd love to come by. I used to read a lot, but I haven't been able to read for fun for a long time. I'm excited to get back to it again." I sip my drink. "And how cool is it that we finally have a bookstore here in town?"

Next to me, Paige's eyes widen, and she says, "Is that him?" Nudging me.

All our heads turn to look, and SJ stands in the doorway with his back turned to us, talking to someone. He laughs at something the person is saying to him, then looks around until his eyes land on me. Even from this distance, I can tell that look is aimed at me, blazing with unrestrained heat. The way he used to look at me. His face is impassive, cool, and calm, but his eyes smolder. A flicker of surprise at seeing me is evident on his face. He looks good. Too good.

"*That's* your man, Callie?" Paige breathes. "Add to cart."

"Um…" I mumble. I'm at a loss for words just looking at him. He is easily the best-looking man I've ever seen. And not just because I used to be madly in love with him. He just naturally looks like a blue-collar hottie in his flannel shirt. And I just happen to know that he's the best kisser and lover.

Or used to be anyway. God only knows what he's like now as a man. And then I think about who he's been with over the past twelve years, and my eyes narrow. I don't want to think about him with anyone else.

Allie nods. "Yes, Callie needs to add to cart."

"No." In my mind, I'm shaking my head no, but instead, the words come out as I'm nodding.

"Why not?" Beth asks. "He is one good-looking man. Like a mini-Sam." She looks up at Sam and back to him. "If those are his genes, that's what he'll look like in about twenty. And it's not bad, Callie."

I snort. "It's a long story. But he's not my man."

"Go ahead," Mellie encourages. "We have all night."

"Also, let's exchange numbers so we can add you to our friend group chat." Allie pulls out her phone and slides it over to me to add my number.

I add it and then sip my drink. My eyes still catch his as he makes his way around the tavern, catching up with people. "We were high school sweethearts and supposed to go off to college together. He ended up leaving without saying a word, and he joined the Army. He never said goodbye or anything," I explain.

I look up to see their faces staring at me and their jaws dropping. "What?"

"Oh, this is going in a book," Beth says with satisfaction.

Allie laughs. "Beth writes romance novels, and my

husband is her literary agent."

"Wow, that's really cool, and go for it," I say as I sneak another look at SJ.

She laughs. "Of course, but is this not the making of an epic second-chance romance book or what?"

"I don't think this one will have a happy ending like in books," I say as our server delivers fresh drinks to our table.

"Why'd he leave?" Paige asks dreamily, putting her face on her palm and leaning forward, eating this all up.

I shrug. "I don't know. That was always the biggest mystery," I say. "It doesn't matter anymore. We're done."

Allie scoffs. "It does matter. You and SJ were the ideal couple that everyone idolized. We were all shocked when he left."

I glance over nervously at the bar, and he's watching me. He has a bottle in his hand and tips it up to me and winks. Freaking winks. I give him a side-eye and turn to face the girls practically swooning over that wink.

"Okay, see? That's what he does. But why should I give him a second chance to break my heart again?" I ask.

"A lot can change with time. People grow and change. SJ could be an even better man now. He was only a kid twelve years ago making dumb decisions," she says thoughtfully as she swirls her straw in her glass.

"Go talk to him," Mellie nudges me.

"No," I say nervously.

"SJ! Come over here!" Allie calls.

I want to die in this spot. I want to vaporize and go away at this very moment.

SJ gets up from where he's leaning against the bar, walks over to our table, and stands beside me. Too close. He smells so good, and I'm trying to keep calm with him standing right there, close enough to touch him. "Ladies," he says, acknowledging everyone, then turns to me and murmurs, "Callie."

"Crap. You're even hotter up close," Paige breathes.

"Um. Thanks?" he says nervously as he takes a sip of his drink and looks down at me for help.

I look away. I'm not helping him. He's on his own.

"Have a seat," Beth orders with a smile. "Let's talk about you getting back together with Callie."

"Sure, a topic I can get behind," he says as he sits down and casually drapes his arm around my shoulders. I turn and glare at him. But secretly, I like it. The girls exchange a wide-eyed look of satisfaction.

Mellie is fanning herself. "They're so cute," she mouths to Paige.

I shake my head and try to hide my grin, busying myself with my drink.

"How's your cabin coming along?" Beth asks. "Evan says the floors look great and are all finished."

My heart warms hearing about the cabin. I wonder what

it looks like inside.

He nods. "It's almost finished. You should come out sometime and bring the babies."

I squirm at the thought of SJ holding Beth and Evan's babies. I bet my ovaries would catch on fire if I saw that. Just picturing it makes it feel hotter in here. Imagining SJ as a father does things to me. Makes me feel like I could go feral seeing him having a family with someone else.

"When are you two going to start dating again?" Allie asks, and I shoot her a look, letting her know she's dead. Her book club is dead, and her bakery is dead. Wait, maybe not the bakery. I like baked goods too much. And I can't live without her coffee now.

He turns his eyes to me, giving me his full attention. His voice is low and sincere, and his eyes are full of regret and something undefinable as he says, "When she knows I'm not the same man I was and finally forgives me." The words are meant to answer Allie's question, yet he is looking at me as he replies. This was meant just for me.

He's warm, and he feels good sitting next to me. I'm going down fast like the *Titanic*. This ship is sinking. It was safer being mad at him. Forgiving him is the unsafe part.

All their eyes land on me for my response, and I squirm but can't hide my grin. "You're all dead to me," I whisper.

SJ leans over, kisses the side of my head in comfort, and pulls me toward him into a hug. "All in good fun, Cal."

Letting me know they're all just joking.

"What's everyone's plans tonight?" he asks casually, his arm still around my back, holding me as if this is completely normal. I look around, and a lot of people are watching us curiously. And when I look, they look away quickly.

"Just you know...catching up with everyone. Getting to know Callie," Beth says.

Allie looks at her watch and says, "I'll be right back. I have a set to do with the band. We're singing the cover of 'I Remember Everything' by Zach Bryan." She stands and heads up to the side of the stage to warm up.

"Still never learned guitar like your dad?" I ask him.

I want to get to know SJ and find out who he is now. Holding on to the anger from him is festering inside me, and it's harming me more than anything. I'm grasping at straws here to change the subject and learn more about him.

He shakes his head. "Music gene skipped me, I guess."

"What do you like to do, SJ?" I ask, my drink making me bolder with him.

His eyes brighten, and his face softens at me finally not being mad at him. "I like being with you."

"What are you doing here?" I ask, twirling the straw in my drink.

"It's a free country. I can come out for a beer with our friends, can't I, Doc?" He pulls me in and kisses my cheek again. "I've been waiting to call you 'Doc' for years."

I roll my eyes again and look away to hide my mouth turning up. I look over, and Beth, Mellie, and Paige are still eating this up. Beth looks like she wants to take notes.

"Beth says we're going in a romance book," I say dryly.

"Keep watching, it's about to get good," he says again with a wink.

My heart feels full in my chest. What is he talking about? *What does that even mean?* He's persistent, I'll give him that.

"Dance with me?" SJ asks, looking at me, and his gaze softens. He looks at me differently than anyone has ever looked at me, like I'm the only person who holds his attention and interest. Like I matter. He reaches over and tucks a strand of hair behind my ear, and his thumb glides over my cheek as he does it.

"Will you go away if I do?" I interject. I'm trying to hold him at arm's length and failing hard. He's making me accept him back in, and I feel like I'm on the edge of a cliff, and damn if I don't just want to jump all in again with him.

"No." He smirks and continues looking at me adoringly.

"Let's go," I say grudgingly.

He takes my hand in his, guiding me to the dance floor, never letting my hand go, his other hand lands on my waist, which feels so intimate and close. Butterflies are back in my tummy, and they're out of control. His fingers clasp between mine, something he used to do back in high school.

"I love this song," he whispers in my ear.

I'm feeling nervous and awkward, not sure where to touch him. Sensing my nervousness, he loops my arms around his neck, his hands pulling me tight, his hands wrap around my waist.

His flannel smells like fall, rosemary, cedar, musk, and black pepper smell. Unfamiliar yet still somehow familiar at the same time.

Being in his arms makes it hard to stay mad at him. I feel everything when I'm around him. Every touch feels amplified, and I've never wanted someone more than SJ.

"Are you ever going to forgive me?" He pulls me closer, kissing my cheek again, this time even closer to my mouth. Third time if anyone is counting. And I'm counting.

"I want to...but I don't know how. I don't know what we look like now that we have so much history," I answer honestly.

"I'm not interested in the way we were, Callie. I want to be your forever," he says, his eyes drinking mine in. "Let me in."

My heart softens. I want that too, more than I realized. I just don't know if I can trust again. "How about I try? Just... that's all I have right now. I can try. But no promises? We're different now," I admit.

"Whatever it takes. I want us to work." He continues. "If that's what you can do, I'll take it," he says, looking relieved.

"For now, let's just dance," I say as I lay my head on his shoulder, and we dance to the song, Allie's velvet strong voice belting out with Sam's.

"I love you, Callie. Never stopped."

My heart clenches hearing this. I want to believe him. But I thought he fell out of love with me and that I wasn't enough for him, and that's why he left.

I close my eyes. I don't say anything back because I still have doubts.

After our dance the night before, SJ escorted me back to our table, kissing the pulse points of my wrist softly and leaving me a stupefied mess without saying another word. Thanks to that encounter, I spent the night tossing and turning, barely getting any sleep. And now here I am, finishing up my shift at the hospital and then headed to my dreaded dinner.

I agreed to meet my parents for dinner at their country club, and Thad is unfortunately going as well. Tonight is the last time I'll be interacting with him outside of work. I'm setting him straight. We are never going to be a couple. The sooner he knows this, the better. And no, I tell myself, it has nothing to do with SJ being back. I'm taking back my life and no longer coasting while going through the motions and doing what other people expect of me.

My parents have taken me to dinner at their country club a few times since I've been back. All painful interactions where my mother spends the evening berating me on my clothing choices and telling me that my hair needs a treatment, and I could stand to "trim up a little." I put up with these dinners because they're my parents and I'm trying and hoping they'll somehow become normal. I feel obligated to go to them, but I dread them and from here on out, I'll be attending less of these, too. I just don't have the time and energy for this anymore.

Tonight's the night. I'm going to let Thad know that we are done at the end of the dinner. I'll be speaking to my parents too about this, probably later. If they continue to socialize with him, then they can do so without me.

I get to the parking lot and am opening my car to get in when he strolls out from the hospital door and says, "Let's ride together."

I stare at him and sigh. "Hi, Thad." I can think of a million things I'd rather be doing tonight. And being with him in a car or at a dinner is not one of them.

"What are you wearing?" His eyes scan down my pants and the nicest shirt I own. Nice enough for the country club, but I honestly didn't put effort into it.

"Are you trying to embarrass everyone?" he huffs and then laughs like he's trying to make a joke and not an insult.

That stings me because that's something my parents say to me. I'm always embarrassing them with my clothes, hair, whatever they can pick at, and I see Thad has picked this up now, too. He didn't start this way. He paid me compliments at first but slowly over time it's like I'm his Playdough and he's trying to mold me into whatever version he'd like to see instead of who I really am. Another reason we'd never work out.

I roll my eyes and glare at him. "I thought we could just drive separate, and I'd meet you there."

"I need you to drive. I need to do a few things on the way."

This is going to be inconvenient when I let him know we're not a couple at the end of the night. "Okay, I have to stop for gas." I slide into the driver's seat.

"Why don't you already have gas?" he chides as he pulls his phone out and focuses on it, ignoring me.

We pull in to get gas. I'm numb, and I want to be done with Thad. I probably won't get hired at the hospital, considering Thad's on the board and decides whether I get hired or not. *Not a conflict of interest at all,* I think to myself. Hopefully, my reputation so far will hold up, but I can't count on that. I have a feeling Thad won't take the rejection well. I've seen him flip out on people at the hospital for dumb little things. I imagine this won't go over well.

I'm distracted as I get out to pump the gas. I'm startled when a warm hand covers mine on the nozzle. "I got this," a deep, familiar voice says softly.

I look up, and it's SJ, and he smells familiar and good. Like motor oil, spicy soap, and clean. I breathe him in for a quick second and say, "What are you doing?"

"Pumping your gas, what does it look like?" He shrugs his wide shoulders and puts a hand on my lower back. He's wearing a red and black flannel, with a black leather jacket. Even back in high school he was always looking out for me, taking care of me. And I miss it. I miss it to my core. I felt good and safe with him. This familiar feeling feels… comforting. I haven't had this in so long.

"I've got it," I say, too full of defeat.

"And what's he doing?" He nods to Thad who has his head down in the front seat.

Thad leans out the window. "Hurry up, we have a reservation," he clips.

I close my eyes, dying of embarrassment when I notice SJ's jaw stiffens, and he looks like he wants to kill Thad.

His eyes are on me, and they don't move. This is what we used to do. We'd have full-on conversations with our eyes, and we're doing it now. I want to look away, but I can't. Neither of us moves. Over a decade of emotions washes through us like a tidal wave. We both feel it. The current has changed between us.

The gas pump pops, startling me, and I nervously reach over, and SJ already has it and is screwing on the cap. He turns and leans in to me. "You deserve more than that. That's not even the bare minimum. I'll be waiting." He turns and saunters back over to his bike in the next stall and swings his leg over it. He slides on a helmet and looks over at me pointedly. He's saying, "Your move, Callie." He does it with just a look. And it makes my breath hitch.

I take a deep breath. My move. I know what I want.

We never made it to dinner. We got to the country club and my mom texted that she didn't feel well. Probably drunk already. And then on the way back to his car, Thad got called back into the hospital, so that worked out nicely in my opinion.

When I pull in to drop him off, I say to him, "Thad, we're not going to work out. You and me? We're not going to be a couple. I just wanted you to know. I want us to be friends and work colleagues."

He turns and says, "We can talk about this some other time when you're thinking clearly."

"I am thinking clearly," I snap. "I'm pretty sure I've never been clearer with you."

I'm livid. I'm so tired of not being seen and heard and being dismissed like a child. Fire burns in my chest, and I want to scream.

He says nothing and gets out and walks away still on his phone.

I drive home, relieved to be done with him, and wonder where SJ is tonight. The thought of him out with someone else makes me stir-crazy. I think about texting him, but instead, I text my new friends.

Me: Anyone have any advice on how to trust someone again after they've betrayed you?

Paige: the best way to get over a man is to get under him.

Allie: lol! That is NOT the saying, Paige. But yes to getting under SJ.

Beth: He's in the cart. Complete your purchase.

Mellie: Take that cart for a spin, girl!

Me: You all are not helping. Lol

CHAPTER 12

THEN

"How did you get your parents to agree to this?" I ask Callie nervously as she opens the door, and I follow her into her house.

"They didn't say no exactly," Callie replies nervously, her hand tightening in mine.

My eyes widen. "But did they say yes?"

"They said I could bring a friend to dinner," Callie adds.

"Callie," I groan. "This is going to be bad."

"After last night's win, they'll be happy to see you. My dad even said you're the best football player on the team," she says proudly, pulling the door closed behind us, which is like a jail *door swinging shut. Being inside Callie's house is like a prison cell.*

"Callie, is your friend here?" her mother calls from the kitchen.

"Yes, he's here," she calls back.

"He?" her mother calls back in a confused tone. I shoot Callie a look. She shakes her head as if telling me not to worry about it.

Callie's mom comes into the hallway and winces just a little when she sees me. "Samuel," she calls. "It's nice to see you." I cringe at her calling me Samuel. My mother used to call me that, but no one has called me that since. I've always been SJ for Sam Junior. Never Sam, that's my dad, and I'm most definitely not Samuel. She's been reminded before and does it to try to get under my skin, and it's working.

I force a smile. "It's good to see you, Mrs. McGraw. And thank you for having me. It's just SJ. Not Samuel," I remind her, politely.

"Oh, right," she says in a flat, friendly tone that gives me a small sliver of hope that this dinner might go well. I won't hold my breath, but maybe this time will be different.

"Dinner's about ready. I'll get your father." Her heels click on the tile as she leaves.

I side-eye Callie, and she mouths, "I'm sorry," and gives me a tight smile.

"Hell of a game you played, son. You really made us proud," Hamilton says as we sit down to eat. It smells good, but honestly, I'd rather go eat dirt than sit at their table with them. I'm doing this for Callie. His words give me more hope that maybe this will be a good dinner, after all.

"Thank you, sir. How are things at the bank?" I ask politely, sitting up straighter. Eating in their formal dining room makes me nervous. Their overcomplicated meals make me feel even more out of place. I glance over at Hamilton staring at me, and his mouth turns up a little, and my suspicions are confirmed.

He chuckles. "Aren't you just the little man? Things are good." Hamilton smirks. He always loves to talk about himself. I figure if I can get him to talk more about himself, he'll interrogate me less. I wince at him calling me a little man. Always belittling or being passive-aggressive toward me any chance he gets.

"Samuel, where will you be attending college in the fall?" Cheryl asks as she takes a sip of her wine and looks pointedly at me. I also noted that's her third glass she's poured since we sat down. She hasn't been eating. Hamilton is on his second bourbon.

Thankfully, Callie interjects and says sternly, "Mom, it's SJ. And he's gotten into the same schools as me. We're just waiting to decide where we both want to go," she says as she reaches over and squeezes my hand. We've already decided, but we're not telling her parents yet about our plans. Her mom's eyes land on our hands and snap to Hamilton's face. He looks over at me and says, "Will you still play football?"

I wipe my mouth with my napkin and say, "I'm not sure yet, still weighing my options."

"Are you going into medicine like Callie?"

"No, that's not for me, sir. I'm thinking possibly business." I smile politely.

Callie takes another bite of her prime rib, still eyeing me. We're walking on eggshells. And it's getting crunchy.

"Well, you'd better figure it out soon," Hamilton chides, then changes the subject. "Your father must be so proud."

"Where's your mother, Samuel, honey?" Cheryl interrupts, and I don't miss the slur in her voice.

"Mom!" Callie snaps.

Hamilton and Cheryl just stare at me and wait, ignoring Callie calling them out for being rude.

"My mother left when I was five. It's just me and my dad now," I remind them flatly. Here we go. I'm not even hungry anymore. I set my fork down, anticipating it all falling apart from here. It's time to start planning my exit.

"Oh, you poor boy," she coos. I look over and don't miss Hamilton rolling his eyes. Dick.

"Do you think you'll go into the biker business like your dad?" Hamilton asks in a condescending tone.

"I don't know, maybe. I like working on cars. But I also want *to go to school." I shrug. I look over to Callie, and she nods. I'm being honest. That's the thing I can't respect about Hamilton and Cheryl. They're so fake.*

This is why I hate being around them. It's a game for them, and we're pawns to play with every chance they get. We say the wrong thing, and it all goes south. It's always a game to get it over with and get out before that happens. It usually ends badly.

"Well, I just hope you don't get mixed up in that biker gang stuff," Cheryl says as she watches me, waiting for a reaction.

"You know, I think I'd better get back to the shop. I have to help my dad with a few things. This was delicious, Cheryl, thank you." I stand and set my napkin down.

"I'll walk you out," Callie says quietly, shooting her mom and dad an angry look.

Hamilton and Cheryl say nothing as we leave. They're probably disappointed that I left before all hell could break loose this time.

"I'm so sorry," Callie whispers.

"That was awful." But just as awful as it usually goes whenever I have an interaction with them.

Just a few more months and we'll be gone," she whispers. But I'm starting to wonder if we'll ever be free from them.

Callie

NOW

I hurried out to my loaner Prius when I realized it's not where I parked it, and I frantically search the parking lot, and my eyes land on him. He's leaning up against his motorcycle with his legs crossed with a helmet in his hands, staring back at me with a sexy smirk. Dimple engaged.

I drink him in, standing there in his dark jeans, boots, and a black hoodie. He looks so good that it's painful, and his mouth turns up at me like he knows what I'm thinking. Dammit, I hate it when he does that.

"What are you doing here?" I call, pretending to be chill.

Except there's no chill in me right now. Not a bit. My heart pounds nervously in my chest.

"Your car's done. I left it in your driveway. Come on. We're going for a ride."

"I can't ride with you." I shake my head. *But I want to. I want to really bad.*

"Get on, Callie. Now," he says firmly. And something in his tone makes my toes curl. Bossy SJ is sexy. *Fine.* I reluctantly walk over and take the helmet he's holding out and slide it on.

He puts his helmet on, swings his leg over the bike, and effortlessly pulls me onto the back of the bike. He reaches up and starts the bike, then reaches back and pulls my arms around his waist. He's warm and solid. He feels so good.

I hear him in the speakers of the helmet. "We're just riding, Callie. No talking. We need this," he says as he looks back at me. I nod in exhaustion and lay my cheek on his back. His body relaxes with relief at my agreement, and tension pours off him.

Feeling him, being near him is calming to me, despite all the pain between us. It's crazy to me how someone can hurt you so badly, yet you still love them so much. It's not fair.

He takes off, and we stop in front of my house. He gently takes my backpack off and drops it on my porch. He waves to Mrs. Winters as he jogs back to the bike, and I wave at her as well. She looks like she's about to break her arm, waving back at us excitedly. She looks so happy. I grin at her, shaking my head, knowing she will grill me about this later.

The sun is about to set, and I'll admit that it's perfect weather for fall riding here in Freedom Valley. He takes the road toward the lookout, like I knew he would. He doesn't stop, though. He takes highways with the most fantastic autumn foliage views appearing golden with the sun setting. On the highways of our high school rides, we'd take in his truck with music playing and not a care in the world. Now, I feel like we have the weight of the world on our shoulders. We used to take a lot of drives where we didn't talk, just listened to music and were together, just like now.

I lean in and breathe him in. Fuel, motor oil, and soap. He feels like home. Old home. The kind of time travel back to your childhood home in a time where you felt safe and secure. And in my childhood, he was that place for me. Him and Sam. And then Goldie.

And for this ride, I'll soak it up. He didn't talk to me, just like he promised. Sometimes he'd point at a bird or animal, and I'd squeeze him a little so he knew I saw it too.

Healing energy swirls through both of us as we ride. My arms wrapped around him, feeling him, and being with him is what my soul needed tonight. I didn't realize how much I needed this. How much *we* needed this. He was right.

He turns and heads back to town and pulls up to the side of my cottage behind my car. We get off, and he takes my hand as he walks me to the door and leans in, kissing me softly, taking his time. And when he does, a tear falls down my cheek. He takes his thumb and swipes it away. "Why are you crying?"

"I don't know. It's been a long time since I've let myself cry over us. And you come back here, and all these emotions are trying to pour out of me. It's like a part of me stopped living and having emotions when you left. I bottled it up and kept quiet."

"When you're quiet, you're crying the loudest," he says softly. "No more bottling. I'm here. Let's work it out."

"I haven't even let myself cry or have any emotions, SJ. I've buried everything with work and school," I admit.

"You promised you'd try," he says, pulling me in and kissing the side of my head. His hand wraps around my waist, pulling me closer to him. "Also, there's no more school, and the hospital doesn't own you. You don't have to work that many extra hours. You deserve to be happy. Let me make you happy," he says, his eyes searching mine, trying to read how I'm feeling just like I'm doing to him.

"You were my otter," I say quietly. "I have to try."

I can't just throw away what we had, but I honestly have no idea what I'm doing here. I feel like this is all happening so fast, and it feels exhilarating and nerve-racking. I don't want to mess it up and make him want to leave me again.

"I'm still your otter," he says, taking my hands and

searching my eyes.

"What does this mean for us?"

"I want you, and I want us. A fresh start."

I stare at him; his confidence hasn't wavered. He really wants me. His pursuing of me after all this time is confusing and stirs up so much in me.

He pulls me in for a soft and tentative kiss, making me lean into him and kiss him back until his tongue licks along my bottom lip, asking for entrance. I open my mouth, and that's the permission he needs, and he tastes me, exploring me heavy and fiery. Our passion feels out of control.

He tastes so good, and his arms come around me and pull me up and into his arms.

When he finally pulls back, I'm breathless. He stands with his hands in his pockets while I get the door unlocked. Satisfied that I'm safe, he pulls me in for another kiss and off my feet, making me see stars when he finally sets me back down.

He turns to leave and calls out into the darkness, "Good night, Goldie!"

She coughs and says nervously, "Oh...good night." Pretending she hasn't been eavesdropping from around the corner on her porch.

I laugh and head over to her as he rides off. I slide my chair next to hers and put my feet up on the railing, reaching for one of her porch blankets to wrap over me with the chill of the fall night setting in.

Goldie says quietly, "That boy has always been yours, honey."

I sigh and lean back. *Mine.*

"Don't let that carrot get in the way of you finding your way back to your soulmate."

CHAPTER 14

THEN

"Do you think we could find my mom?" I ask her as we both sit at the table in the library looking at the computers along the wall.

"Yeah, I bet we could. Are you sure that's what you want?" she asks, tilting her head.

"I just wonder what happened to her. What was better than me and my dad. What made her feel like she had to leave and take my sister and not me, too," I ask wistfully.

"Let's do it." She snaps my textbook closed, then shoves back and settles at the computer.

"*What's her full name?*" *Callie pulls up Google on the computer.*

"*Michelle Pamela Reid was her name. They divorced, though, so I don't know what it is now.*"

Callie types it in and waits. "*Okay, there are three people with that name close by.*" *Her fingers fly over the keys, and she says,* "*Bingo.*"

"*Whoa, that was fast. Just like that? Why didn't I do it sooner?*" *I wonder.*

Callie reaches over and tears a sheet of paper out of her notebook and grabs my pen and writes down information, looking up at the computer and back down.

"*Want to take a road trip?*" *She looks at me.*

"*What do we do when we see her? Should we talk to her?*" *I swallow nervously, wondering if my dad will feel bad if he knew I was doing this.*

"*No, we don't have to. We can just see what she looks like. Maybe we'll see your sister. She'd be what, about twelve now?*"

"*How far away is she?*"

"*About an hour, I think.*"

"*Okay.*" *I nod.* "*Let's do it.*"

"*Are you sure this is it?*" *I stare up at a big house. It's not as nice as Callie's, but it's big.* "*It looks expensive.*"

After grabbing snacks and drinks from the gas station, we

park across the street. Callie joked that we're on a stakeout, and everyone knows you need snacks when you're on a stakeout.

My snacks lay in my lap untouched. I'm too nervous. My mom lives here. An hour from me and she never bothered to check on me. See if I was okay. It hurts me that she just didn't want to be my mom.

We waited until just before it got dark, and Callie was squirming and said she had to pee.

"Okay," I say as I snap my seat belt on and get ready to start the truck, disappointed we came all this way and didn't see her.

"Wait." She puts her hand on my arm, and her eyes go wide. The front door to the house is open, and a dark-haired petite woman steps out with a teenage girl following her and both of us freeze and take in what we're seeing.

"No way, that's really them," she whispers.

"SJ, look at me," she demands, snapping me out of my thoughts. "Do you want to know why she left? Tell me now. We can do this if you want," she says urgently, looking over at her and back at me.

I swallow nervously and nod. "Yeah." We've come all this way. I need to know.

"Okay, let's go." She's unbuckling, and I'm frozen, staring at my hands still on the wheel. "Come on," she coaxes. "I'm going with you."

She hurries across the street and up the driveway as the woman has her hand in her purse searching for her keys. "Um,

Mom," the girl says, tapping her mom's shoulder.

"Kit, where are my keys?" she mumbles and looks up. She sees Callie first and recoils like she's seen a ghost. Then her eyes snap to me, and her eyes soften as she freezes. Her hand goes to her mouth.

"Samuel," she breathes. "Are you Samuel?" she says, getting emotional, her voice catching.

I nod, my hands in my pockets, not moving. I look over, and Callie isn't moving either. Her jaw is dropped, and that's when I notice Kit. She is the spitting image of Callie. It's like looking back in time to the seventh grade when I met Callie. What.The. Hell. There are a few differences, but it's striking. They have the same hair color, a very light pale blonde and bright blue eyes. No mistaking it.

"Did he send you?" she asks Callie. "Why are you here?" she asks, looking back and forth between us.

Callie and I say nothing. We're still staring in shock.

"Who are they, Mom?" Kit asks, turning to her mom, looking justifiably confused. Even her voice sounds like Callie's.

"Is that…?" Callie shakes her head. "No…"

"Look, I promised I wouldn't ask for more money. Did he send you? Because I haven't asked for anything. I kept my promise."

"What are you talking about?" I finally ask.

"Hamilton," she says with a sigh. "I told him I didn't want anything after he signed away his rights."

I turn and look at Callie wide eyed, and she's looking at me with her jaw dropped. She looks like she's about to throw up.

I hold up my hands. "Can we talk to you? Just give us ten minutes, please."

Ten minutes is the bare minimum of what she owes me. I look at Callie and back to her. Callie looks like she needs a paper bag to breathe in, and the way she just dropped this bombshell of information so casually is not appreciated. Not only has she hurt me, but now she's hurting Callie. She needs to explain herself.

She looks like she wants to say no but puts her head down and then looks up and nods. "Okay, ten minutes. Kit, go over to Karrie's. I'll come get you in a few minutes."

"Mom," she says at us and back at her mom like she doesn't want to go.

"Go," she says firmly. "Now."

We follow her inside, and she sighs when she shuts the door. "I expected that you'd find me someday. But I didn't think you'd be with her," she says, looking confused back and forth between us.

"Can you explain everything from the beginning?" I ask patiently, trying not to let my voice shake. "I just need to know."

She swallows and looks down. "I'm not proud of it, but I had an affair with Hamilton when I worked at the bank. Sam found out, and we fought. At first, he tried to accept Kit as his own, but...it got too hard for me. I was embarrassed by what I'd done. I never should have left you. I've regretted it every single day. I *am so sorry. Every day that went by, I felt even more guilty like I had no right to come back and that I didn't deserve you."*

"Kit is my half sister?" Callie asks, shocked.

"You didn't know?" she asks, looking horrified.

We didn't say anything, but Callie slips her hand in mine. I can feel her shaking next to me.

"No, we didn't know. Callie's my girlfriend. We've been best friends since the seventh grade." I squeeze her hand reassuringly.

She looks back and forth between us like she's trying to understand. "Hamilton gave me money to start over and signed over his rights to Kit. He said that he'd tell everyone that I tried to trap him, and if I stayed in Freedom Valley, he said he'd ruin me. And then he'd ruin Sam."

"Why'd you leave me?" I finally choke out.

"I couldn't take you from your dad," she says. She puts her head down, and a sob comes out of her as she covers her mouth.

"He begged me not to go and then lost it when I tried to take you with me. He didn't deserve that, and neither did you. You didn't deserve to lose your dad for what I did. I thought you two would be better off without me. At least that's what I told myself when I left." She wipes her eyes with the back of her hand.

I'm trying to process this, and I just can't. I'm shocked. Callie squeezes my hand. She looks equally shocked. I want to tell her that is not how I remember it. I remember that day she left me. And she didn't even look at me, much less try to take me with her.

"Look, I know I don't deserve to know anything. But are you happy? You are so handsome. You look just like your dad." She smiles at me sadly through her tears. She looks like she wants to reach out and touch me and hesitates, pulling back.

I start to choke up. Callie looks at me, and I stare at her. She nods and continues for me, knowing that I need her to answer for me. I'm on the verge of losing it and crying.

"He's happy. He's had a good life with Sam. He's the kindest and strongest person I know. He's a talented football player. I'm sorry that you missed out on getting to know SJ. Because there's nobody better than your son."

"I'm so sorry," she breathes through tears. Her face looks full of regret.

We stare at each other for a while. I don't know what to do, but I don't want to regret it if I don't, so I pull her in for a hug, and we stay like that for a long time. I thought I'd feel something. Like a connection to her as my mom. But there's nothing. I feel like I'm comforting a stranger. She sobs into my chest. I pull back, put my head down, and take Callie's hand. We leave and walk hand in hand out to the truck. I need to get out of here. She pushes me over into the passenger seat and buckles me in. I'm numb and feel like I'm in shock of what just happened. I put my face in my hands and sob, my shoulders shaking uncontrollably.

"It's okay, SJ. It's okay, I'm here. Let's just get out of here

and then we can talk about it." She buckles and pulls out and heads toward home.

We don't say a word the whole ride home, and when we pull up to our lookout spot, she looks over at me and says, "Well, at least we're not related. That would be super awkward at this point."

We both look at each other disgusted. "Gross." And both of us break into a fit of laughter.

"We share a sister," I say as I look at her, feeling dumbfounded.

"We share a sister," she repeats, equally stunned.

"Gross," we mutter at the same time.

"What are you feeling about all of this?" she asks.

"I feel worse, honestly. I thought maybe she'd want me; she'd want to spend more than ten minutes with me, and I don't know...want to be my mom?" I say, my chest feels heavy with sadness.

I shake my head with disbelief. "And I never thought you'd be dragged into this. I can't believe my dad kept this from us all these years."

"I think your dad's just doing his best. He's the only reasonable parent we have out of all of ours," she says with a deep sigh.

"Just when I thought your dad couldn't be any worse," I say, shaking my head again, still trying to unpack everything that just happened.

"Well, this explains why my parents never liked you, and now you know it never had anything to do with you. It was all about them and their choices." She cringes. "Very strange choices. Imagine my dad mixing up with a biker's old lady. How is he still alive? Your dad really is a saint."

I nod. "It's crazy."

"Why don't you talk to Sam first and see what he says?" she suggests. "I can't talk to my parents. Who knows what will happen if my dad knows we know? He ran your mom off with his own child. No telling what he'd do to us to keep this information from getting out. Imagine what people at the country club would say? He hooked up with a biker's old lady, got her pregnant, and sent her away? No telling how he'd react. Honestly, let's just get the hell out of here. Screw them. They're all a bunch of selfish pricks."

I stare out at the lookout, still processing everything. I can't even believe this.

"I'm surprised Sam and the club haven't crucified my dad," she continues.

I nod. "Yeah, let me talk to him. He'll be straight with me."

This is not how I pictured that reunion with my mother would go. Things just got even more complicated.

CHAPTER 15

NOW

It's late, and I'm finishing up a few cars that Ty couldn't get to today. After a long practice with the guys, it feels good to zone out and work. I have music playing loud, and I'm in the zone, focused on changing out a fuel filter, when the music suddenly turns off.

I look over my shoulder to find Hamilton McGraw standing in the shop across the room, wearing a less-than-pleased look. He hasn't aged well. His skin is red and splotchy and lined with wrinkles. His hair is thinning, and he's almost bald on the top. He's probably around sixty but looks a lot older than his age, likely due to his drinking.

I stare at him and the audacity and disrespect that he has to come into my dad's shop. It's time for him to meet the grown-up me. And grown-up me sure doesn't take shit from someone like Hamilton McGraw, the weakest man I know.

Hamilton crosses the room. "I think it's time you and I had a little talk, son. You didn't hold up your end of the bargain," he says.

I turn around and continue wrapping up what I'm doing and say calmly, "I've never made an agreement with you, and I sure as fuck never will."

"You were supposed to stay away," he snaps pensively.

"Funny, I don't remember ever agreeing to that," I say calmly as I snap the hood back down and walk around to stand in front of Hamilton. His eyes widen as I come almost toe-to-toe with him and cross my arms. He's only five-eight to my six-two height now. And I'm enjoying this. He was a bully to me when I was a kid, but now, he isn't going to push me around. I stare at him and enjoy watching him squirm under my gaze.

"Stay away from my daughter," he bites out. He looks angry, but what I see on his face is that he knows he's already lost.

"Which daughter?" I hedge, looking bored.

"Don't play games with me, boy," he quips, growing angry.

"Boy?" I toe his feet with my boots until he backs into a

stool and almost falls. I stand in front of him, arms crossed, leveling him with a glare. "I'm not a boy anymore, Ham. I'm a grown man."

His eyes darken. He's losing without the reaction from me that he wanted, so he's grasping at straws now. "Did you know that I sit on the board that decides Coach Murphy's replacement?" he asks, trying to be coy, but it's not working. He knows he's out of his league here.

I make no reaction, thankful for the years of military training. He'll get no reaction from me, nothing. And after he waits and realizes I'm not biting, he continues, obviously nervous, "So it would be in your best interest to do as I say."

"And just what are you trying to say, Ham?"

"I will ruin you," he threatens, spitting when he talks. He's never liked it when people called him that.

"I'm not worried." I shrug, walking over to begin work on the next car. "You don't have the power that you think you do. Get out." I dismiss him, annoyed that he's here in the first place. He wants me to yell so he can tell people I lost it on him and get sympathy. Instead, I make him irrelevant by staying in control.

"It would be a shame if your dad lost his shop," he says, kicking an empty container of oil across to hit me in the boot.

I look down at it and back at him and chuckle. "It's really cute that you actually think that's possible." I reach over to grab a wrench.

"Oh, I know it's possible. I've brought many businesses down here that didn't fall in line," he says smugly.

"Oh, like you tried to do with the Golden Gable Inn?" I remind him of his failure. "How's it going at the bank? Oh wait, they fired you after that stunt you pulled with the inn." Evan filled me in on everything. "This town is tired of you. It's time for you to go. It's your turn to leave town."

"You don't know who you're messing with," he threatens again, loudly. This makes me laugh. The loudest person in the room is always the weakest. Meanwhile, I've remained calm and collected.

"You think messing with my dad is a good idea?" I smirk, shaking my head.

"Nobody cares about the little scooter booter trash your dad is affiliated with," Hamilton huffs.

I don't have to respond because I can already see them lined up behind Hamilton's back.

"Get the fuck out of my shop," my dad thunders from behind him, and Hamilton turns to see my dad, Bear, Axel, and Smoke standing there glaring at him, arms crossed, looking like menacing bikers.

Hamilton stills and glares at me and turns to go. I don't miss the look of fear flashing in his eyes. Just as I thought. Hamilton is a weak man.

"Oh, and Ham?" I call. He stills but doesn't turn. "You took twelve years from me. You won't be taking any more. I'm coming for what's mine."

He slams the heavy metal door behind him.

"Poking the bear, I see," my dad calls with a smirk.

"I'm not worried. He told me years ago he'd destroy you if I didn't leave. I believed him."

Anger flashes in my dad's eyes, and he shakes his head. "You know that wouldn't have happened."

"I know that now, but I didn't then."

I'm not a kid anymore. And neither is Callie.

And judging by the conversations my dad is having with his club in the back right now, I have a feeling that Hamilton won't be messing with people much longer. He's about to feel the fire from everyone in this town he's tried to cross.

CHAPTER 16

Callie

NOW

The speaker crackles in the stadium. "It's Friday night here in Freedom Valley, and Coach Murphy and Coach Reid and the Eagles are ready to take on the falcons. Tonight, we have Coach Reid here for a quick interview. Coach Reid, when will you be officially taking over for Coach Murphy now that he's announced his upcoming retirement?"

"I'm not sure about that," SJ says calmly, "but tonight, we're here to play football. I'm grateful to be out here on this field helping the next generation of Freedom Valley claim state." He nods as he ducks back out to the field, taking his place next to Coach Murphy.

I feel lighter being here at the game this time, and a sense of hope and possibility fills me being here in the stadium and not at odds with him. *He could be yours again.* The feeling in my heart reminds me.

"Well, you heard it, folks. The Eagles are here to win. Let's go Freedom Valley Eagles!" the announcer calls.

"It was much easier to talk you into a game with me this time," Goldie muses. "I didn't even have to break my car."

I eye her suspiciously. "You didn't actually break your car, did you?"

"No"—she shrugs with a wry grin—"but I know a good mechanic if I need one."

Luckily, I don't need a mechanic anymore. "My car is fixed, and strangely, the tires even look brand new." I need to remember to ask SJ about that. I got my car back in perfect shape and detailed. Spotless. I need to leave Sam's shop a five-star review.

"Oh look, here come our snacks," Goldie says excitedly, shifting next to me on the bleacher.

One of her past students hands her our food. "Here, Mrs. Winters. I got extra mustard like you like."

"You're a sweet boy, Ethan," she calls to him and turns to me.

"How do you get them to always go get you food?" I shake my head and laugh.

"Here, honey, eat up. We need our strength to cheer," she says, ignoring my question and handing me a hot dog.

"We are not cheering," I dryly remark.

Like a magnet, my eyes travel down and land naturally on SJ. As if he can feel the heat of my gaze, he looks back up at me and smiles, making that dimple pop, then looks back at his clipboard.

Goldie nudges me. "What was that?"

"Nothing." I shrug innocently and take a bite of my food, grateful for the distraction.

"Where's that carrot tonight?" she asks curiously, looking at me out of the corner of her eye with disdain.

"No clue, not my carrot." I don't even like carrots.

"That boy sure is handsome," she says, ignoring my response. I look over at where she's looking, and sure enough, she's focused on SJ. He's wearing dark jeans, his Coach Reid polo shirt, and his Eagles hat. He *is* handsome.

"What's keeping you from going all in with him?" she asks, breaking my thoughts.

I swallow and look away for a moment. "I'm scared but optimistic about SJ. It feels good but still scary."

She tilts her head and looks at me curiously. "He doesn't look like he's scared, honey. He keeps looking at you like he's ready to play this game." And by game, she's not referring to football. I'm the game. And I didn't like how the game ended the first time.

"Maybe he was meant to be just a high school boyfriend, but not my forever person."

"Oh, he's still your forever person. Just look at him. Stop letting fear ruin you from being with your soulmate."

I look down, and he's looking up at me with his arms crossed and a mile-wide smile. The man I was supposed to build a life with. Together. He's back, and he wants a second chance.

CHAPTER 17

THEN

I hear the window again and look over. 2:36. "Callie, what's wrong?" I sit up and stare as she kicks off her shoes and slides under the covers next to me.

"Same crap. I feel safer here," she says as she burrows in next to me.

Still groggy, I sit up, feeling angry with her parents. I'm considering going to get my dad and having him step in. But his stepping in might mean it could get worse for Callie. He and the club don't always handle things above board. And if they did do something, it could tear Callie and me apart.

"You gotta be careful climbing up that trellis. What if you fall?"

"I thought you put the ladder there for me?" she murmurs.

"What ladder?" I ask, confused. "I didn't put a ladder out there."

"I think your dad did it, then," she murmurs as she drifts off to sleep.

Warmth fills me that my dad looks out for both of us. I will never take for granted having him for a parent when I think about what kind of parents Callie has had to live with.

I reach for her hand and drift off to sleep with her.

NOW

"Saw Callie on the back of your bike," Bear says as he scoots his stool over toward me at the shop.

I look over at Bear. He's in his mid-thirties, not much older than me, yet my dad is only fifteen years older than me, so Bear has always been like a brother to me. My dad raised me like a son, but he's been almost like an older brother to me at times, too. We've all grown up together.

"It's like going back in time, seeing you two together again." Bear swirls a toothpick in his mouth.

"Yeah, well, time screwed us both over." I wipe my hands on a rag and sit on a stool.

"You two used to be inseparable."

"A lot can change," I reply. "I'm trying to fix it."

"Does she know why you left? Hell, I'm not sure you even understand why you left."

It feels weird to say out loud why I left, and it feels dumb when I think about it now. "I walked away from Callie because if I didn't, she wouldn't be the doctor that she is today with me dragging her down."

Bear groans. "You weren't dragging her down."

"When her parents repeatedly told us both that I wasn't good enough? Hell, this whole town made me feel not good enough. I was only good enough when I was winning football games. When football was over, I was useless here. I left for her."

"You have always been good enough," Bear says.

"I joined the Army to be better for her and to make her proud. There's no better man than a soldier. I went to hell every day to be a better man for her."

Bear sighs. "You *are* a good man."

"Still not good enough, apparently. This town won't give me a job."

"You're both adults now. Can't nobody tell you shit," Bear says.

"You better worry about your own love life." I grin and set my water back down, changing the subject.

"What love life?" He grunts. "Why, you know any single ladies?"

I laugh. "They seem to line up to get their fluids topped off repeatedly. Stick around and find one."

"That's a strange metaphor for getting laid," he mumbles, looking at me weirdly.

"It's not a metaphor. They literally want their fluids topped off five times a month."

"Oh, like literal fluids? Not..."

"Bear," I groan. "No. Gross."

He laughs. "Just giving you shit. I need one willing to date a biker."

"Well, that's on you. I'm not a matchmaker. Go down to Baked Inn Love, and that's where they all hang out."

"SJ!" my dad yells down from his office.

I swing around and look up, and he's got his phone to his chin, holding up my phone, which is lit up with an incoming call. He puts his phone aside and says, "Your phone's blowing up. You better come check these messages." He looks concerned.

I take the stairs to the office and reach for the phone I'd left up there charging. I scroll through the messages, and my heart drops. No, no, no. I drop my head and scrub my hand over my face.

I stare down and hang my head. Pressure builds in my chest, feeling tight and unable to breathe.

"You good?" Dad asks, standing next to me, his hand on my shoulder.

"No. My Army buddy Sparks died. That was his mom messaging and calling me. I need to get out to Oregon." I cover my mouth with my hand, almost wishing I didn't have to say those words out loud.

"I'm sorry." He squeezes my shoulder, concerned. "Take as much time as you need."

"I'll keep you updated." I head down to grab my keys and coat.

"I heard that," Bear says. "I'm sorry. You need me to help with anything?"

"Can you keep an eye on Rook and the cabin while I'm gone? I'll be out of town for a few days."

Bear nods. "Will do."

I head out and make the drive home. I don't even remember how I got there. I was on autopilot and feel numb. He was killed in a car accident. We did all that time together and went through hell on back-to-back deployments, only for him to make it back home and have it all end before he could even live his life. I shake my head and punch the steering wheel. "Dammit!" I scream. I should have called him more. Hot, angry tears streak my cheeks.

I walk out to my porch that overlooks the mountains. My heart is so heavy with sadness. Sadness I've fought hard to overcome. I'll never understand some things and why they happen. Sometimes we're not meant to understand them. I miss my friend, and I won't ever have the chance to have a beer or go on a hike with him. He'll never come to see my new cabin we talked about together. We had plans for him to visit as soon as I finished it. Now that'll never happen, and I can't wrap my head around this.

I pack a bag quickly, book my flight, then sit and think about everything that has happened over the past decade. I send out a quick text to Coach to let him know I'll be out this week.

Jesus, I can't bury any more of my friends. I hate this.

CHAPTER 18

Callie

THEN

Sitting with SJ at our lookout spot is my favorite place. We lie back on a flannel blanket and watch the clouds slowly pass as I try to make out their shapes.

"What are you thinking about?" I trace his jaw with my finger, leaning in to kiss him.

"I'm going to marry you someday," he says matter-of-factly.

I laugh. "We can't get married."

"Why not?" he asks as he turns to me.

"Well, first of all, we're seventeen." I laugh.

"Well, I'm obviously not marrying you at seventeen. That

would be weird." He shrugs. "But someday."

"You're my best friend." I smile and lean in to kiss him. "I never want that to change."

"That's how it starts. You find your best friend, then you fall in love." He kisses me softly.

"Done."

"I can't give you a fancy life like your parents have," he says with a sad smile.

"I don't want fancy. I want simple. Our lookout spot and you. I'm good. That's all I need."

He reaches over for my hand and kisses me.

NOW

I lean over the back seat to grab the pizza and beer I picked up from Freedom Pie and hear a familiar voice. "Hey darlin', let me help you."

"Bear!" I shriek and pull him in for a hug. "How are you?" I murmur into his worn leather vest. "I've missed you."

"Missed you too." He chuckles. "What are you doing here?"

"Pizza and beer as a thank you for fixing my car. Where's SJ?" I ask, looking around.

"Sam's inside, but SJ is gone."

My heart drops. I freeze, and my body runs cold. My hands tremble as I almost drop the pizza boxes. My breath catches, and my body feels numb. "What do you mean, gone?" I've heard this before.

"Come on, I'll fill you in," he says as he takes the pizza and carries it inside the shop. My heart drops, and I'm hoping he's just gone for a day or something. Just when I was trying to give him a chance, he's gone again.

Sam stands and smiles at me as I walk in with Bear and hug him. "Did you eat yet, Sam? I brought pizza and beer."

"Nope, but that smells good." Sam heads to the sink to wash his hands.

"Where's SJ?" I ask as I set out a few paper plates from the cabinet.

"He had to go out to Oregon," Sam says. "A buddy of his passed away unexpectedly."

"Oh no," I say, sadness filling me for SJ. Relief fills me that he's not gone for good again. But hearing about his friend and how he must be feeling right now fills me with remorse, and I'm heartbroken for him. I wish I could have been there for him and helped him. He must have been so upset when he found out.

Bear clears his throat. "But he asked us to ask you if you'd look after his house for him while he's gone. Do you think you could help him out with Rook?"

"Why would he want me to do that?" I ask as I set my pizza down and reach for a beer.

Bear shrugs innocently. "He was upset, and that's what he

asked when he left."

I don't miss the side-eye that Sam gives Bear. Bear says nothing and continues to eat, staring straight down at his plate like it's the most fascinating thing in the room.

"I guess I could." My heart races at the thought of being in that cabin in our spot. Being in his space. He wanted me there. My heart also breaks for him losing a friend.

Bear reaches into his pocket. He slides a key on a keychain over to me. "You know where his place is?" he asks innocently.

"Yeah, I know where it is." I tilt my head. "Do you know when he'll be back?" I look between them both. They're up to something.

"He said a few days," Sam adds as he grabs another piece of pizza.

"Okay, I guess I can do that."

"Good, I'll let him know," Bear says.

"How have you been, Sam? It was good to hear you play the other night."

"Been alright. Shop and the club keep me busy," he says. Now that I'm older, I see Sam differently. He's a good person. I wonder if he has a girlfriend or is seeing anyone. I saw him bring a few women around when SJ and I were in school, but he never seemed to be serious with any of them.

"I see you put the ladder away," I tease.

"I figure you're old enough to know how to use the front

door now. You were then, too," he adds with a snort.

I bumped into him with my shoulder. "Missed you, Sam."

He doesn't say anything, but I don't miss how his mouth turns up slightly.

"Wait, who is Rook?" I ask, finally.

"His cat," Sam says with a laugh. "SJ took in a stray that kept coming around."

"Okay. Anything else I should know before I head out there?" I ask. "Are you sure you're both not up to something?"

"I'm not up to anything." Sam shakes his head.

"No, that should be it," Bear adds, not answering the question.

I sigh. "Okay."

I missed this. It feels good to be back here with them.

I sit parked in SJ's driveway, and it feels so strange to be here. It's so quiet and peaceful. No noise. I lived in the city for so long that coming back has been so calming. I'm still getting used to the idea that SJ is a grown man now and not a kid sneaking out to the lookout with me to make out. And he built an entire grown-up house at our spot. This is so wild.

The gravel crunches under my shoes as I walk up to the house. The front porch has a large stained dark wooden deck with natural rocks landscaped around it. There's a lot of trees surrounding it and the view is spectacular, especially with fall in full swing. I noticed the other day that he'd built it in the perfect spot.

The front is shaped in a craftsman style, and it has a metal roof with a large chimney. It feels like coming home. Only this is his home and not mine. *He made it without me*, I remind myself. He built a whole life without me.

A pang of sadness fills me. It feels like he continued without me. I take a deep breath and brush these thoughts aside. I'll admit, I'm dying to see the inside of the house. The house we were supposed to have built together. The house we dreamed up on countless picnics here. One time, we used rocks to lay out where we'd put our living room and kitchen, and he'd even made up a garage where he said he'd work on his truck. I look around and don't see a garage, but I see a big open space next to the house where a garage could go. Maybe he has plans for that. I wonder what else SJ has planned for his future. He's been making it clear that he wants me, but I've heard that from him before.

Something brushes up against my ankle, and I look down to see the ugliest gray cat I've ever laid eyes on. He only has one eye; he's missing part of an ear, he's covered in scars, has bald patches where he's missing fur, and he looks downright terrifying. Like a *Pet Cemetery* cat off a horror movie. But his tail is up, and he's purring like he's friendly.

"Well, hello there, you must be Rook." I coo as I lean down and scratch him between his ears. He leans into the scratches and purrs even deeper.

"You're a friendly little guy," I say, relieved that he isn't as rough as he looks. "Are you hungry?" He responds by purring and sitting patiently by the door where his water bowl sits.

I pull the key from my pocket and open the front door to find a large and cozy living space. It's sparsely decorated and still smells like new construction. The kitchen has a backsplash that's partially finished, and I see the glossy tiles stacked next to the counter in a box. It's still a work in progress and as I look around, I can feel that SJ has poured love into this place. He's made a beautiful home here.

I open the pantry to find cans of wet cat food. I grab a can and head back out to the porch, where Rook waits patiently, watching me through the glass door. I set the can down, and he chows down on it. I refill his water dish and set it back down for him, giving him another pet and scratch.

He happily eats and watches me, and I realize he has no teeth, either. What a peculiar cat. It makes him even cuter. "You've been through some stuff, haven't you buddy?"

It makes me think of SJ and I wonder what he's been through, too. Maybe this cat was meant to find SJ and they need each other.

Stepping back into the house, I'm surprised to find it's even bigger than it looks from the outside. It has two bedrooms downstairs and two upstairs. The bathroom on the lower level is huge and has a deep oval bathtub that overlooks the mountains with a huge circle picture window. "Oh yes. This will be happening," I murmur as I run my hand over the edge of the gorgeous bathtub. I mean, he wanted a house sitter, right? It's only fair he lets me use his bathtub. He's not here and won't know. I grin.

Everything is tidy and has a place. Very military-like. This is not the high school SJ who always had a messy room full of smelly football gear and clothes piled up with motor oil and gasoline smells from the shop.

I look at my phone and wonder if I should text him. I find it odd he didn't text me, but his buddy died, and I'm sure he has a lot going on. I'm glad he wanted me to help him. I wouldn't say no. We have our history, but I'd do anything for him. Anything but give him my heart completely again, I reason.

I text him just to let him know I'm thinking of him.

Me: I'm sorry to hear about your friend. I'm here if you need anything.

I don't wait for a response, and I lock everything up and head back to town for the rescheduled dinner with my parents. Not looking forward to it, but I need to get it over with. My dad said he wanted to talk to me about something important tonight, and I'm curious about what he wants. I also need to let them know that Thad and I won't be seeing each other again outside of the hospital. Since I dropped him off the other night and talked to him, I haven't heard from him thankfully. Hopefully, he's moved on. I park in front of the cottage, and Goldie is out watering her mums and waves to me.

"Hey, Goldie." I wave as I cross the driveway.

"How have you been, Callie?"

"Been good. I'll be gone for a few days. I'm going to look after SJ's cat while he's gone."

"Oh? Where's he gone?"

"Out west, a friend of his passed away."

"That's sad. Glad you can help him out," she says with a side-eye to me.

"Just helping out a friend, Goldie. Nothing more," I call out.

"Sure," she says, but her face says she doesn't believe it for a second.

I shake my head and head in to pack a bag of scrubs and pj's. I shower and get ready for my dinner, putting on a dress and heels. It does feel good to get dressed up for me and not be in scrubs for once. I get to the club and park and head in, wishing I'd grabbed a cardigan before I left on this chilly fall night. I think about how they always want to have dinner at their club and never a casual dinner at home. No, this is all for show. They want to show me off and parade me around their friends.

A hand wraps around my arm and grips it too tight. I'm

startled when I look over and see it's Thad. "There you are, late as usual, I see." He smiles.

I cringe and snatch my arm back. "Ow, Thad." I glare at him. "What are you doing here?" He didn't listen to a word I said the other night. And now he thinks he can invade my personal space and put his hands on me? Absolutely not.

He ignores me and waves to my parents, plastering another fake smile on. "Your parents invited me."

My parents wave enthusiastically from across the restaurant, and I head to their table with Thad on my heels. He pulls my chair out for me, and I slide in, ignoring him. I'm seething that he's even here. I thought I was having dinner with just my parents. I truly believed that I'd never have to be around this man outside of our work environment ever again. And now I'm here, trapped at this table with three vultures picking at me and negating my appearance.

Growing up and not being a priority to my parents made me who I am. Someone who unfortunately became a people pleaser and lets others choose and walk all over me. And I'm not doing that anymore. This stops now.

"Glad you both could make it, busy doctors and busy schedules," my mom croons.

"How are things at the hospital?" my dad asks.

"It's been—" I start to speak, and Thad interrupts me and begins to talk over me, giving me a dirty look as if I interrupted him and not the other way around. I stare at him in disbelief and then at my parents, who clearly saw what just happened and still lean in on every word Thad says as if he's the most fascinating human on the planet.

"I've been so busy and exhausted. Your daughter has it easy down in the ER," Thad says, landing another blow.

And the hits just keep on coming, I think to myself.

I side-eye him and mutter, "Really? The ER has been very busy. I've been busting my butt nonstop during my sixteen-hour shifts, including the one you were supposed to work that you dumped on me while you were busy golfing with my dad. Did I ever get a thank you? Nope."

Ignoring what I just said, and looking like she's disassociated and in another world, my mother says, "Callie, you look so tired, darling. Have you had a facial lately? And your hair? We need to get you into the salon as soon as possible." She tsks as she looks at me from head to toe, inspecting me—and clearly not pleased with what she sees. I put effort in this time, and still, it's not good enough.

Great, this dinner is going to be one of those. I reach for my wine and take a generous sip, bringing my lips together and trying to bite my tongue.

Thad reaches over and tries to cover my hand. I pull it away and glare at him. He reaches again and grips it hard, glaring back, like he's trying to remind me that he thinks he's in charge. Unbelievable. I yank it back and glare at him and no one at the table says anything or seems to notice.

"Stop it," I hiss quietly.

"When are you too going to make it official?" My mom throws out there, looking over at Thad hopeful.

"Mom," I hiss, sending her a look. I grit my teeth and shake my head. I feel like I'm not even seen at this table, and all three of them are in their own little world.

Thad smiles a big smile that doesn't reach his eyes. "Callie and I just have to work some things out," he says as his eyes roam over my body. I cringe.

He's delusional, and I glare at him. "There's nothing to work out," I say, gritting my teeth. "We're done."

"Then someday we'll have two Dr. Douchets." My mom smiles broadly, taking a gulp of her wine. She reaches over to pour more, not even paying attention to what I'm saying.

I snort. "That will never happen," I reply. Oh, hell no. This needs to stop. I'm shutting this down.

Thad ignores me and continues, "Callie won't need to worry about working when we're married. She can spend time at the club with you, Cheryl, and do charity work." Thad waves at the server obnoxiously and points for another drink, not even bothering to use his big-boy words or manners. The server looks like she wants to roll her eyes, and I shake my head, grimacing at him. Her mouth turns up a little at my reaction. He's such an ass. He's oblivious to how he treats everyone around him. He reminds me of my dad.

"We will never be a couple," I say to him. He's already on

his second drink, and we just got here. "Did you drive here?"

"Shut up," he whispers, then smiles big at my dad. "Hamilton, are we still on for our tee time this Saturday?"

"You bet," he says, reaching for his bourbon.

"I'm not working your shift if you're scheduled," I murmur, shaking my head.

The rest of the dinner was boring and droned on with my dad and Thad talking nonstop about the club and golfing. My mom fills us in with all the club gossip and upcoming events that I couldn't care less about. I smiled and nodded politely when it was needed. I counted down the minutes.

"Callie, you can help me with the upcoming gala for the club," she says, setting down her wineglass. I noticed she didn't ask me; just informed me that I could help her.

"No, thank you. I'm busy with work." I would rather put a fork in my eye than help her with anything. I have no time for that, nor would I ever want to.

"You need to put yourself out there more with respectable people in town. It would be good for your career, you know," she says pointedly.

"I'm sure the board will be meeting soon about your position," my dad muses. "You want to make sure you're impressing the right people." I look over at Thad, and he smirks as he takes a sip of the fresh drink his server just set down. I also noticed that he didn't say thank you again, either.

"Also, I need you to make a little investment in something, Callie. But we can talk about it later," he waves his hand, his eyes already glassy. I wonder how much he had to drink before he came to dinner.

I have no money for any of his investments or whatever he's short on cash for. I'm already exhausted trying to come up with a way to tell him no without him losing it and throwing a fit like he usually does until he gets what he wants. And his idea of an investment really means that I just give him money, and there's no repayment or investment. He likes to remind me that he helped me in college and that's why I need to help him with his investments. The reality is that they never helped me with college.

"I'll help you with anything you need, Hamilton," Thad hedges.

"That would be great, Thad. I'm so glad I'm going to get to call you son one day." My dad drains his glass.

I choke on my iced tea when he says this. "You're all idiots. How can you all be so dumb? I have repeatedly told you that we're done. And you sit here with them and do this?" I glare at Thad.

I don't know if it's having SJ back that is giving me confidence or that I've just simply outgrown this and come to realize that I don't have to take this anymore. I can stop being the nice person who gives chances. I don't owe my parents anything. They're never going to change.

I've learned with Goldie that the family you create is more important than the family you come from. This one doesn't deserve me.

I would rather be having a burger right now with Goldie. I'd rather be anywhere but here. This will be the last dinner that I attend with any of them.

"Callie," my mother hisses, admonishing my outburst.

"I'm leaving," I say as I stand, disgusted as I toss my napkin down. As I head out, I hear my mom complain about me, "That girl…" Then I hear Thad say something about a little disagreement. *No, Thad, you are the disagreement.*

I get to the car and check my phone for texts. Nothing from SJ. My heart sinks in disappointment. I'm worried about him and hope he's doing okay.

I look in the rearview mirror and whisper, "I need out of here." Coming to dinner with my parents and having Thad ambush it just solidified for me that I want to try with SJ. I owe it to my past self to see if we can fix us. I know what I need to do.

I ignore the calls and angry text messages from Thad that come rolling in blowing up my phone. I hit the block button. Tonight, I'm going to my happy place, the lookout. Thad would never know to look for me there and it feels good to be done with him. But for tonight? This is my night. I'm not letting anyone ruin it. I'm done letting people walk all over me.

CHAPTER 19

THEN

*"Callie, Mrs. Clark needs your help at the baked goods table,"
Cheryl McGraw declares as she walks up to our table. Callie
and I are working at the ticket booth for the Eagles football
fundraiser, and her mom looks back and forth between Callie
and me as she makes it her mission to separate us, as usual.*

*Callie looks at me wistfully. "Okay." She stands and heads
toward the back of the gym. This leaves me alone with Cheryl,
and it's awkward. I don't like to be alone with her, but I can't
leave my table that I'm responsible for.*

"Samuel, dear, how are you doing? Did you decide on a

college?" Her voice is not sincere and dripping with fakeness. Now that Callie's not here, I wish she'd just go away and leave me alone.

Resisting rolling my eyes, I calmly correct her, "It's SJ, Mrs. McGraw. No one calls me Samuel," I add politely.

"Well, that's...that's fine," she says, pursing her lips. "I suppose we need to talk about a few things, anyway." She drums her long, bright red fingernails on the table.

And here we go.

I shift in my chair uncomfortably. I wish I was at the baked goods table with Callie. I look back, thinking about leaving to go back there.

Cheryl jumps right into it as if she can tell what I'm thinking about doing. "I think you and Callie are probably getting a little too serious, don't you think? Callie has her whole future ahead of her to think about. You wouldn't want to get in the way of that, would you?" she purses her lips.

"And SJ has his whole future ahead of him, too," I hear and look up to see Mrs. Winters, her arms crossed glaring at Cheryl.

"Goldie, I'm having a private conversation with Samuel," she admonishes in a condescending voice. My breath hitches at her trying to bully Mrs. Winters. My fist clenches under the table angrily.

"No, you're being a bully, Cheryl," Mrs. Winters says, not backing down.

I stand. "I'm going to check in with Coach Murphy if you're here to watch the cash box and table," I say and walk quickly toward the locker room, relieved to be away from Cheryl.

I look back before I turn the corner, and Mrs. Winters looks angry. She's always advocated and been a friend to everyone. Some people in town treat people like they're on a hierarchy scale. Not Mrs. Winters. She's always made everyone feel safe and the library a place where everyone belonged.

Both women are staring each other down when I walked away and I'm not getting in the middle of that. But I will admit it felt good for Mrs. Winters to have my back. Not very many people do.

Callie finds me later and says, "Did you hear that our cash box was short? My mom is throwing a fit. She says sixty dollars is missing."

I look at her and shake my head. "There's no way that money is missing, Callie."

"I know. She's ridiculous." She bites her lip.

"What?"

"She's telling people you took it." She shakes her head angrily. "I hate her. She's awful."

With a sigh, I look at her and say firmly, "The money is there. Ask her to recount it."

"I did," she says. "I have to go. They're waiting for me." Her head is down, and I hate that she looks so miserable as she walks in the rain to their car.

The next day, I'm in my room and hear yelling from down below in the shop. I run down the stairs to see what's going on. My dad and Cheryl McGraw are in a standoff, and she's yelling at him. Customers are watching from the waiting area. He's standing still, his arms crossed, and he looks pissed. He's wearing his navy coveralls, and they're covered in grease. He's been rebuilding an engine all day, and I know he doesn't have time for this.

"He stole that money! This is a fundraiser, for God's sake!" she yells.

"My son didn't steal anything," Sam says calmly, standing still.

"Then where's the money? My daughter certainly didn't take it." She huffs.

Sam doesn't move and stares at her until she realizes she's not getting the reaction from him that she thought she would. This seems to make her even madder. "I'm not surprised. No one should have left that boy in charge of any money. He can't be trusted."

"What has SJ ever done to show that he can't be trusted?" Sam asks, remaining eerily calm. Too calm.

"Well, the apple doesn't fall far from the tree." She smirks, waving her hand around the shop. "What did you expect raising him in a biker gang?" she spits out, looking disgusted at my dad.

"Get out of my shop," he says calmly.

"Give me the money he stole!" she demands.

Sam reaches into his back pocket and slides out his wallet. Pulling out the cash, he throws it at her feet. "Get out," he repeats.

"Dad..." I stammer. He doesn't look at me, but he stares straight at Cheryl.

Cheryl scoffs and bends down to snatch up the cash and stalks back to her Cadilac SUV, mumbling something I can't hear. She opens the door and turns, and her eyes narrow. "Stay away from my daughter." She gets in and slams the door.

My dad closes his eyes and looks pissed. "Son."

"Dad, I didn't take the money."

"I know you didn't. But you have to be careful. There are people in this town that will accuse us of things like this. You have to watch your back."

"I'm sorry, Dad. I'll pay you back."

He just looks at me and shakes his head. "It's okay." He turns and goes back to the car he's working on, and I hate this. I hate that he has to be involved in this and pay for it.

Callie shows up that night with the sixty dollars in her hand, her eyes red as if she's been crying. "I'm so sorry," she whispers.

"What are you sorry for? We didn't do anything wrong." I'm still mad about Cheryl coming here, but I know it's not Callie's *fault.*

"She found the missing money tucked underneath the cash drawer in the box. She didn't know that Mrs. Winters had told us to put the twenties and larger bills under the drawer and keep tens, fives, and ones separate in the drawer."

I hung my head, relieved. "She came to the shop and embarrassed my dad in front of customers, accusing me and dad of being thieves and in a biker gang."

"I'm so sorry. She's horrible." Callie has tears streaming down her face now.

"Why isn't she here apologizing to my dad?" I ask, frustrated, throwing up my hands.

She shakes her head. "She'll never do that. She did give me the money to give back to Sam."

"It's not about the money, Callie. It was so embarrassing for my dad. He didn't say anything and went back to work, but it shouldn't have happened. Who is going to go tell all the customers that we aren't thieves after all? She badmouthed us. The damage is done."

"I'm so sorry. I love you."

"I know," I rest my forehead on hers. "I love you, otter. It's not your fault."

But will it ever be enough for us? We come from different worlds. Her family and most of this town will never accept me, especially not now. People will still gossip about what happened, but they probably won't find out that it was all a mistake and Cheryl was wrong. They'll just think I'm a thief. I don't know what this means for Callie and me moving forward. I can't lose my best friend. I hate this. But I'm so tired of having to fight to be with her and be accepted in this town. People like the McGraws make it miserable for people like my dad and me. I'm so sick of it.

NOW

It's been a long and hard past couple of days. When Mrs. Sparks called me out to Oregon, I didn't realize what she was about to ask of me. And I would never tell her no. The funeral was just as sad as I expected it would be. I'm exhausted mentally and emotionally saying goodbye to one of my best buddies. I swing my truck into my driveway and find Callie's car parked there.

Seeing Callie's car in the driveway is like a sign from heaven. Relief and elation zap through my body, knowing she's here. She's in the home that I dreamed of building for both of us. I have no idea how or why, but if there was ever a day when I needed a break, today is that day. I've dreamed of the days Callie would be here for me and I'd be there for her when we need each other the most.

"Harley, it appears we have company," I told my new friend.

Harley sits up in the seat and looks out the window. I've

never seen a sadder dog in my life. The funeral was as hard and sad as could be expected. But seeing Sparks' yellow lab service dog lying next to his flag-draped casket, refusing to leave his side, even after he'd passed, gutted me. His mom asked if his service dog could come and stay with me. She said it's what he would have wanted. I couldn't tell her no.

I've never considered myself a dog person, and I'm not sure what to do with this one. She's been quiet and hardly moved, even as we flew home. People smiled at her in the airport and looked at her curiously in her service dog vest. She walked with her head down and tail tucked under her and stayed next to my leg. She's barely eaten, and it's heartbreaking to watch. She just lost her person, and that's devastating for those of us who do understand it, let alone the dog that doesn't understand it.

I scratch her head and say, "I know. I miss him, too. This is your new home now. Let's go meet Rook. Don't eat him. He's a good boy."

"Come." She climbs out of the truck and stops next to me, looking up at me with sad eyes, waiting for instructions.

"Go do your business." I nod to the front yard, and she reluctantly trots off, looking back to make sure I'm waiting for her.

All the lights are off, and it's late. After Harley is all set, I unlock the door and set my bag down in the kitchen. "Harley, stay," I whisper.

I walk quietly and open the door to my room and see that she's asleep. *She's in my bed.* I'm not sure why, but again, no complaints. It's like the universe stopped fucking up our lives and put us right where we belong. Finally.

Callie stirs. She sits up and leans to turn on the lamp and rubs her eyes. "SJ?" she says sleepily.

I lean against the doorframe and say, "I see you're back to sneaking into my bed, just like old times."

She sits up straighter and looks confused. "Bear told me you asked me to house sit for Rook. He didn't say when you'd be home, and you didn't answer my text."

I grin. I'll thank Bear later. And I'll figure out why I never saw that text. I had the worst signal in the mountains of Oregon. I feel like the past few days were the worst and all blended.

She stands and looks around for something.

"I also see you're wearing my shirt again." I lean on the doorframe and smile at her. Damn she looks good in my shirt and in my bed.

"What are you talking about, SJ?" She mumbles in frustration as she finds jeans and pulls them on.

"I saw you at that first game wearing my shirt, Otter." I slide my hand into hers, and the electricity surges between us.

She stands and grabs a bag and walks toward the door, but I pull her into me, stopping her.

"Where do you think you're going?" I say softly. "It's late."

"Home," she says with determination, but her eyes meet mine, and they're vulnerable. Like she's asking me to tell her to stay but doesn't want to say it out loud. I hate the look on her face that doesn't trust me. I put that there, and I'd give anything to take it back.

"I've been waiting for twelve years to have you back in my life and my bed. I'm not letting you go," I murmur into her ear, kissing her softly on her collarbone.

Her eyes soften, and she stills. "SJ..." She glances out in the hall and stills when she sees Harley sitting there patiently waiting. "Oh. Who is that?"

"This is Harley." Emotion catches in my throat when I say it, and watching her with Harley fills me with unexpected emotions. It feels like all my worlds colliding with my military past, Freedom Valley past, and future.

She leans down to pet her and examines her vest. "Is she your service dog?"

"She was my buddy's, but he died. She's with me now. But I think she's broken. I don't know how to fix her."

Harley nudges Callie, sniffs her, and leans into her, tail wagging.

"What do you mean, broken?" Callie asks, examining her and looking her over.

"She's sad. I haven't seen her wag her tail or do any dog stuff until just now with you."

"Of course, that makes sense. She's sad. Her best friend is gone," she says softly. "Losing a best friend is a big deal." She looks up at me and then back at Harley.

Her look hits me right in the gut. I close my eyes. It feels like a freight train hitting me. I flew out there, helped with everything, and I've held everything in. Until now. I couldn't be vulnerable in front of his family. They needed me to be strong and help them. But with Callie, I could always be vulnerable. It also reminds me of what she must have felt when I left, and I hate it. But I'm here now. And we can live and honor Sparks and Harley. I want that with her.

I turn and rest my arms on the sink and look out over the trees silhouetted by the moon, hanging my head. "Yeah, it's a big deal," I say, emotion catching in my throat.

I take deep breaths and concentrate on the trees, and exhaustion sets in. I need my person. I need Callie.

Her arms circle me from behind, and she holds me. And the tears come. I can't make them stop now. My shoulders tremble as my body shakes with my sobs.

She rubs my back and holds me for a while and finally I take a deep breath and my voice croaks, "It's okay." I pull her to me and wrap her in a big hug. I didn't realize how much I needed this. Needed her. Tears release. I missed her. Like a piece of my soul was gone until her arms held me just now, reminding me where the other piece was all along.

"I'll stay with you," she says softly.

"Okay," I say hoarsely, relieved to have her here.

She pushes me gently onto the bed. She pulls my shirt off, and I pull her to me, kissing her slowly. I don't know what I did to deserve her here, but I'll take it.

"Just one night," she whispers. "I can't break again."

"I won't break you," I promise as I reach for her face and kiss her softly, hoping she feels how sorry I am.

If one night is all I can have, I'll take it. I've missed her so much. I'd take anything if it meant it was with her.

Because I love her, and she loves me. Somehow, I'll show her we're meant to be together. But tonight, I'm going to show her. One orgasm at a time.

CHAPTER 20

Callie

NOW

I open my eyes and smell coffee. The sunlight streams down the hall from the big picture windows, and I turn over and find SJ sitting beside me in bed. He reaches over and pulls me close, tucking me under his chin. My body feels boneless after sex with SJ last night. I wanted to comfort him, but we ended up comforting each other. *Twice.* I smile to myself. And it was amazing. SJ is like a fine wine that ages even better with time.

"How did you sleep?" I mumble.

"I don't sleep much," he says as he kisses my cheek. "But

I did sleep better last night than I have in months."

"How come?" I ask as I stretch and kiss his neck.

"Multiple orgasms," he teases, kissing me.

I sit up and lean into him. "What's been going on, SJ? Why don't you sleep?" I say softly, full of concern for him.

He closes his eyes and swallows and looks away. "I have PTSD. When I came back, I was broken too. Just like Harley, I guess. Evan helped get me sorted out with the VA. I'm okay now," he assures me.

"I'm sorry you were struggling." I stroke his shoulder blade, running my hand over his tattoos. "It's okay not to be okay. You can be real with me, always."

"I know." He nods and looks lost in thought for a moment. Then he says, "When I first came back, every place in this town reminded me of you. I couldn't go anywhere without remembering us, and it brought up all the memories. When I found out you were back, I had hope. It made me work harder on myself to be the best that I could be. For you." He kisses me softly, pulling our hands up and kissing the back of mine.

"What are we doing, SJ?" I whisper.

I feel it; he feels it. But I need to hear it. Being with him again feels like everything is as it should be, but I need to know that I'm not one-sided here, and he feels it, too.

"You're mine," he says, looking over at me. "And you know it."

"I know," I whisper. "I love you." Loving SJ was never the question. I have always loved him. Trusting him, on the other hand, is a little more difficult. Loving him was never hard.

"I love you, Otter," he murmurs into my ear and kisses me.

I'm not sure what the future of us looks like, but I don't want to tell him that right now. We had a good night, and he needed me. I needed him. I'm not sure what we are now, but friends are a good start. I've missed my best friend. Maybe this is a start...

Shirtless SJ looks indescribably hot standing at the stove, making us eggs while barefoot and in jeans. I'm lying on the floor next to Harley, giving her pets and love, and she whines and makes me keep petting her every time I try to get up to sit at the counter.

"I think she put me under a spell. Hypnotized me or something," I say into her fur as she nuzzles into me.

"I'm not sure what to do with her," he says as he sets down two plates.

"She can be your service dog, right?"

"Yeah, I guess. I'm not even sure what exactly she needs and can do. I've never thought about having a service dog before. I feel like she's on another level, and I don't want to mess her up."

"I think she'll be really good for you." I say, "And I bet the kids on the team will love her."

"Yeah, but I'm not even sure she likes me. She seems to like you, though." He puts eggs on plates and watching SJ cook for me is hot.

"Of course, she likes you. Why don't we call Axel's sister, Ophelia? She just started a dog rescue and training facility out by the inn. She'll know what to do." Axel and his sister, Ophelia, practically grew up being raised by the club. After their parents died, the club stepped in and took care of them, and they were always around. Axel owns the tattoo shop in town called 603 Tattoos and still helps Sam on occasion at the shop. I've heard Ophelia is working with dogs.

"That's not a bad idea," he says as he sets down our plates.

"She could always retire from the service dog part and just be your emotional support dog." Harley barks at me. "What?" I pet her again. "She's definitely happy here and seems relaxed."

He leans back and watches us with a smile on his face.

I wrap my arms around him and pull him close to me. "Thank you."

"You're welcome." He kisses me and hands me a fork. "Let's eat."

I sneak glances at him, convincing myself that he's real and not just a dream from the past.

"What?" he asks.

"Just making sure you're real."

He laughs softly and smiles at me. "I'm real."

"I feel like we still have so much to work through."

He nods. "We do. We have twelve years to catch up on. I want to know everything about you, Callie." I love the way he says my name.

"That's a lot to catch up on in not a lot of time." I look at my watch. "We only have an hour. I have to be at the hospital soon."

He looks up at me and says without missing a beat, "We have forever."

He believes in us. And seeing everything he's built here; he believed in us before there was an us again. And spending time with him here doing these day-to-day things like playing with Harley and eating breakfast gives me hope that maybe we will have forever.

After breakfast and another quick round with SJ, I make it to the hospital and kick myself for not grabbing a coffee along the way. I smile with relief when I look over and see my favorite nurse and friend Ramie carrying two coffees. She hands me one.

"You're a lifesaver," I say, grateful for the caffeine.

"Wow, look at you, you are glowing," she smirks. "Would this have anything to do with hot coach daddy Reid?" She flutters her eyelashes. "Wait, did you get laid," she whispers.

"Eeew, don't call him that. It makes me think of his dad." I shake my head. "And maybe."

Ramie looks relieved. "I'm so glad you're not with Dr. Dick. I can't stand that guy."

I shudder at the thought of him. He's probably still angry with me for the other night. Not that I even remotely care. I'm still high on happy from being with SJ. He's not going to ruin it. "Is he in yet?"

"No, but he's scheduled," she says as she opens the med cart and lays out medication.

I filled her in on the other night and how rude he was to me and how he isn't listening when I tell him that we're done.

She stares at me. "Cut him off right now by the way he talks to you alone. Just no. He's not even a friend. He's a colleague at this point, nothing more. Ridiculous," she says as she shakes her head.

He's a creep. I know it, and hearing her validate that helps. He and my parents just ran right over me the other night. I will never put myself in a position like that again.

"I'm glad you're seeing it. I've wanted to punch him in the balls repeatedly for as long as I've worked with him," Ramie confirms, sipping her coffee and flipping through med orders on the computer.

"Don't do that, you'll lose your job." I sip my coffee.

"Honestly, I'm not sure I'll be able to keep mine."

"I wouldn't be so sure of that," she says. "Word on the street is that the board hasn't been happy with Dr. Dick for some time, and you, my friend, are a great physician. We're lucky to have you here. He can go kick rocks."

"Thank you, I appreciate that." I'm relieved to hear good feedback. "Let's do this," I say as I pull my hair back and grab my coffee and head to the pit, ready for our shift. And if they ask me to stay longer? The answer is hell no. I'm unavailable. I've got SJ back. I'm busy. And I plan on being *very* busy with him. We have twelve years to make up for lost time.

By noon, I've already done sutures on two patients, helped a handful of people with the flu, and sent a broken arm off to surgery. The nurses here are all a godsend, and we all work well together. We have a great team, and if I'm not able to get hired here full time at this hospital, I'll miss everyone. Except Thad. There are a few other local hospitals that I can apply at, but I really wanted to be back here in Freedom Valley with Goldie and now SJ. I realize I'm smiling when I'm thinking of him.

I'm putting in a few orders at my desk when I hear one of our nurses raise her voice, and a patient says even louder, "What, are you dumb? I *said* I want a male doctor."

I stand and walk toward the patient's room in case things

get out of control.

"Dr. McGraw is our doctor on call, and she's great—"

"I said *male* doctor. If it's that blond Barbie out there, then no." The male voice interrupts.

"We're a smaller hospital, and she is the doctor we have on call," she repeats calmly to the angry patient.

It's not the first time this has happened. It has happened a few times now, and we usually just try to get these types of patients fixed up and out of here quickly to avoid any further issues. When I did my residency in Boston, this didn't happen. If a patient came in like that, they'd have been tossed out. No one played around in the busy big Boston hospital emergency rooms. Hell, the other patients would have tossed this angry patient out. But here in the town of Freedom Valley, this hospital tolerates more than it should have of entitled patients.

I stand and walk over to where the irate patient is standing and pacing in front of Carly, one of our newer and nicest nurses. He's obviously distraught and angry.

"Everything okay?" I ask politely from the door.

"No, it's not. I told this nurse that I want a *real* doctor," the man practically spits as he says this.

"Is there a particular reason you would specifically like a male physician?" I ask politely, trying to be kind and understand where he's coming from. I always like to give the benefit of the doubt, but my gut is saying this guy is just being a jerk.

"Listen, if I wanted tits and ass, I'd have it. When I need medical attention, I want a real doctor," he leers as he paces and glares at Carly and me.

I take a deep breath and respond as calmly as I can to this moron.

"Alright, here's what we're going to do. You have two options. You can stay here and treat our staff with respect and receive the very best care. *Or* you can leave and find another hospital to take care of you. I'm the doctor on call today. And I can assure you that I *am* a real doctor. I spent over two and a half decades in school, and I'm qualified to assist you if you choose the first option. Which will it be?" I remain calm and firm as I give him these options, but I have a feeling about which way this is going to go, and I'm not looking forward to dealing with the fallout.

"No. I told you, I want a real doctor," he says stubbornly and crosses his arms, glaring at me in disgust.

"What's going on here?" someone says behind me, and Thad steps into the room. "I'm Dr. Douchet. How can I help you?" He smiles as he moves in to stand next to the angry man, assessing the cut on his arm wrapped up haphazardly in a bandage.

The patient looks relieved. "Thank God, this stupid Barbie here was trying to make me leave," he says accusingly, pointing his finger at me.

"Oh, now we can't have that. I can help you out. What's the problem?" he asks, ignoring all the things that are wrong with this situation. Carly looks at me wide eyed in disbelief, and I shake my head and toss my gloves in the trash as we head out of the room, her on my heels.

"What in the actual hell?" she whisper-breathes like a dragon.

"Stay calm, Carly. I'll handle it," I say as we head back to the pit. I sit down to finish my orders, but I'm shaking and too angry to focus. I know if I freak out and get upset, Carly will, too. I'll deal with Thad. I spent over ten years living in New York and Boston. I can handle myself just fine here in small town Freedom Valley.

A couple of minutes later, Thad steps out and whistles obnoxiously at me to get my attention as he heads toward the pit where I'm sitting. I ignore him because I'm not a dog. I roll my eyes and continue to do my work. He stops by my desk and says, "Callie, I need you to get this gentleman..."

"Can I have a word with you, Dr. Douchet?" I snap as I stand and walk toward an empty room. I turn, and he doesn't follow me, so I hold the door and wait for him, glaring at him.

"Callie, I don't have time for this," he chides as he sighs and enters the room. "What do you want?"

"First of all, my name is Dr. McGraw. Second, that patient was abusing me and my nurse, and you stepped in and allowed it. Not appropriate. And third, we're done. DONE.

You and me? We're not together. We're not even friends. We are colleagues and you will treat me with respect. Do you understand, Dr. Douchet?" I stare at him and don't waver. He scoffs and steps back, shaking his head glaring at me.

He rolls his eyes and checks his watch. "Callie don't be stupid," he says with indifference.

I stare straight at him, wondering how someone can be so ignorant. "There is nothing further to be gained from this conversation. Do not speak to me again unless it is in a professional capacity. And I will be speaking to human resources about this incident."

Carly and Ramie stand outside the door, watching this all go down. "Taking my break," I call out to them as I turn and head down the hall.

I make it to the stairwell and collapse to the floor, putting my face in my hands and breathing hard and angry.

The door opens, and I look up, bracing myself for Thad. It's Ramie. She's carrying two wrapped sandwiches and a few bags of chips. She hands me a sandwich as she slides to the floor next to me. Relief fills me that it's her.

"That was *epic*," she says reaching over to give me a high five. "I mean, you should have seen his face. He was *pissed*. He barked orders at us and then demanded to know where you went."

"What did you tell him?" I ask, unwrapping my sandwich.

"We told him you were on the seventh floor taking your

break."

I turn to her. "We don't have a seventh floor."

"I know," she says. "It was funny to watch him take off to find you, though. That should keep him busy for a while."

I snort. "Thanks."

"Here," she tosses me a bag of chips.

I sigh. "Is it too much to ask to be respected?" I ask as I take a bite of my sandwich.

"From people like him? Yes. We've got your back."

"Thanks," I whisper with relief. "This is good." I didn't realize how hungry I was.

Thad isn't going to let this go.

I did my best to avoid Thad for the rest of my shift. There was an extra shift to take, and I didn't take it much to the scheduler's dismay. I grabbed my stuff and headed out when Thad shows up and grabs my arm as I walk out of the locker room.

"Get over here," he bites out, trying to drag me by my arm off to the side. "We're going to talk about that little stunt you pulled earlier."

I shake my arm loose. "Don't ever touch me," I snap and glare at him. I turn and head to my car, walking quickly trying to get away from him. Fear chases through my veins, something I didn't think I'd have toward Thad. Mostly I've just always thought he was a moron, but now I'm concerned for my safety and the staff at the hospital. Adrenaline pulses, and I quickly walk, almost running from him. I'm not taking any chances by leaving myself in his vicinity.

"You are such a dumb bitch!" he yells after me.

I'm almost to the safety of my car, my heart trying its best to climb out of my chest. His fingers dig into the flesh of my upper arm once more, pinching the skin, no doubt about to leave a mark. He tries spinning me back around to face him, but I don't make it easy, struggling and squirming. I'm just about to scream at the top of my lungs, but before I can so much as get my mouth open, a wall is between Thad and me. Warm, hard, and smelling so familiar.

"What the fuck do you think you're doing?" SJ barks at Thad, shoving him so hard he falls on his behind, rearing back in fear.

"This is none of your concern," he says angrily, scrambling to get up. "I'm talking to my girlfriend."

"I'm not your girlfriend. I've made that very clear repeatedly, and you do not touch me," I yell. SJ holds me firmly to his side.

He laughs bitterly. "What, you think you're better off with this guy? The greasy mechanic? Don't you work at the place I take my car?" He sneers at SJ and looks at him like he's beneath him.

SJ ignores him, looking at me. "Are you okay?"

"I just want to go home. He won't leave me alone." I shiver.

"Callie, get over here, now!" Thad snaps his fingers at me and points next to him.

"You don't get it, man," SJ says. "I know you can't be this stupid."

"Oh, what don't I get?" he goads.

"If you touch her again, it'll be the last fucking thing you do," SJ says eerily calmly.

"She's too good for you," Thad spits out.

"Oh, she most definitely is." SJ shrugs. "But *you* were never going to have her."

"You're scooter trash like your dad," he sneers. "Hamilton was right."

SJ swings his leg over his bike and starts it, ignoring him. "Callie."

Without hesitation, I throw my leg over and wrap my arms around him after I slide on the helmet he hands me. I'm ready to get out of here.

"Callie, if you leave with him, we're done," Thad threatens. "Everything is done for you here."

SJ throttles it and takes off.

I feel relief with my arms around him. Safe. I'm safe again with him. Whatever happens from here on out with the job, my family, or anything, I know things have changed with SJ and me. They're going to have to take us both on.

We're at his house, and Harley's at my feet and has been following me everywhere. She's a really sweet dog. I reach down and stroke her between her eyes, something she seems to love and leans into.

"What are you going to do now that you're single?" SJ teases with a gleam in his eye.

I snort. "I was always single. Dr. Delusion needs a psych consult. I'll stay single until I can find someone to match my energy," I say smugly. "I'd rather be single than be in a half-ass relationship."

He stretches and puts his arms behind his head. "Well, just so you know, I'm full ass."

"You weren't always full ass," I mumble. "But I do like your ass."

He sits up a little. "It's different now. You like my ass?" he teases.

"Yeah, I do," I admit. It feels good just being with him and teasing each other like old times.

"Are you worried about things with your parents now? Your dad doesn't take it well when people stand up to him." He puts his arm around me protectively. "You need me to talk to him?"

"Don't worry about me. I grew up with an angry father. I can handle anything." I grew up having to read the room any time I was around them and try to figure out how the day was going to go based on their moods and alcohol intake for the day.

"You shouldn't have to handle that. I want to be here for you, Callie. If he messes with you again, it will be very bad for him. Nobody better ever put their hands on you."

I stare over at him, his face lighting up in the light of the firepit that crackles. He looks more handsome than anyone has a right to look. And he could be mine again.

"My dad made me feel like I had to figure out everything on my own. I've been doing everything on my own for years. It's new to have someone in my corner like this."

"It's not hard, Callie. You're my other half. You're mine, and I will always be here for you. It's our corner now."

I want to believe this. I want to be happy and pick up where we left off, but I'm still hesitant. "When you left, it felt like you didn't care," I say quietly. "It shattered me."

He says hoarsely. "You're wrong. I cared so much that I left so that you could become who you were meant to be." He continues, "I walked away. Because if I didn't, you wouldn't be who you are today, a doctor and living your dream. I know you don't see it, but I was doing it for you."

"You don't know that. We could have done everything together," I whisper.

"It's the past, Cal. We have to leave it there and move forward."

"If it's in the past, then why am I still hurting in the present?"

"I'll do my best to make it feel better from here on out. I don't feel like talking anymore," he says, his eyes darkening.

"What do you feel like doing?" I ask.

"You."

CHAPTER 21

THEN

"Hand me that wrench, son," Dad calls as he reaches his hand out from under the truck he has up on the lift.

I hand it to him and say nervously, "Dad, I have to talk to you about something."

He stops and rolls out from under the truck and sits up. He reaches for a rag and stares over at me as he wipes his hands. "What's up?"

"I don't want you to be mad at me." My stomach turns nervously.

He sits and doesn't say anything as he waits, concern in his *brown eyes that match mine.*

"I went and saw Mom."

He closes his eyes and doesn't say anything.

"Are you mad?"

"No, I'm not mad. She's your mom. You can see her."

"Why didn't you tell me why she left us?" I ask, waiting for him to get upset, but he doesn't seem as bothered as I thought he'd be.

He takes a deep breath. "You know, we were both young when everything happened. I'm sure we both have regrets." He rubs his forearms. "What did she tell you?" he asks, patiently.

"That Kit is Hamilton's. It's freaking weird, Dad. Kit looks just like Callie. How have you known all this time and never said anything? Weren't you mad at them? You're so nice to Callie, and she's the daughter of the man who ruined our family."

He holds up his hand. "Callie's not at fault. Honestly, back then your mom and I were long done when she took up with Hamilton. I always knew Kit wasn't mine. I still tried to make it work for you. But the guilt was too much for her, and we fought a lot, and she ended up leaving, anyway. I think she felt like she didn't deserve to be here. I think Hamilton wanted her gone, too. She was a liability for him around town."

"How have you not lost it on him?" I shake my head, confused.

"Because Hamilton doesn't deserve to matter to me. I have you, the club, and my shop. I'm happy. And your mom wasn't happy with me, so she looked elsewhere. It sucks what she did,

but I can't control any of it. I got to be your dad. And that's what matters to me." He shrugs. "I won."

"Jesus, Dad. You're like a freaking saint."

"I'm no saint. But I did what I did to protect Callie, too. She's become family to us. I knew that if I messed with Hamilton, we'd lose her. I chose to love her more instead of hating him. That is love, son."

He continues, "I knew I'd eventually tell you everything. But you were little when it all happened. And then it just got harder to tell you as time went on. But I knew we'd have this conversation. Does Callie know?"

"Yeah, she was with me. She's pretty freaked out. I think she's worried about what you think about her."

"She doesn't have to worry about nothing." He shakes his head.

"I'm sorry, Dad."

"You don't have to apologize for anything. This had nothing to do with you. Leaving you is something your mom will have to live with. I know she loves you. She messed up, and she probably didn't know how to fix it," he says. "You think you'll stay in touch with your mom?"

"Probably not. She didn't really seem like she wanted to see me." I sigh. "We just had ten minutes."

A dark look passes across my dad's face. "I never kept you from her. She's known where we've been all along."

I hang my head, then I look back at my dad. "I have everything

I need with you. I don't need her," I say as he pulls me in for a hug.

The door opens to the shop, and Callie bursts in. "Hi, guys," she calls cheerfully as she comes over and drops her bag on the floor. She looks over at Sam and then looks away nervously.

I reach out to pull her in and kiss her. "Hey."

"I came to hang out. My parents are gone." She sneaks a glance at my dad and says, "If that's okay."

"It's always okay." Sam rolls back under the truck. "You guys go, I can finish up here."

"You sure?" I look at him.

"Go have fun. You're graduating soon." He shrugs.

I look at Callie, and she grins, swipes up her bag, and we head to the back so I can wash up. "Want to hang out down here while I go shower really quick?"

"Yeah, I have some homework I can work on." She shrugs and opens her bag and settles in at the table.

I grin because I know she hasn't found them yet.

"SJ, when did you put..." She reaches over to kiss me, her eyes shining. "Thanks."

"I figured you might want some study snacks and left them in there during school," I call as I head up the stairs. "Be right back!"

I left a bag of her favorite Swedish fish and a bottle of water in her backpack earlier.

Tonight, we're going to a party that Evan is throwing on

the back property of his family's inn. Senior year is coming to an end and we're all trying to spend as much time together as possible before everyone goes their separate ways for the summer.

I finish getting ready and hear my dad and Callie talking below, and I pause to listen. My dad's voice is deep and serious.

"You aren't responsible for anything your parents do," he says calmly.

"I'm just so sorry, Sam. For my mom and my dad. For them being such bad people."

"Callie," he says, reassuring her. I hear Callie crying softly.

"You always have a safe place here at the shop. I love you, kiddo."

"Thanks," she sniffs. "My parents have never said that."

"What?" he asks, and my chest freezes.

"That they love me."

"Never?" he asks in a surprised voice.

"No."

"Well, I love you, and I know my boy loves you, too."

"You and SJ are my family. Thanks, Sam."

Her own parents treat her like crap. And here my dad is more of a parent than hers, and they treat him like he's the town trash? After the things they've both done to betray us. I shake my head, angry. I'm going to show Callie every day how much she means to me and how much I love her. It kills me that she has to live with them. Not for long.

NOW

The drive out to the Golden Gable Inn is one I've made countless times in high school. Callie wasn't the only one that I left behind when I left. I left behind all our friends, too. And I regret that. In some ways when I left, I needed a clean slate. And I don't know if I can ever forgive myself for that, but looking back, it felt like the right thing to do at the time. I needed to find myself outside of Freedom Valley. To go somewhere where nobody knew me, and I could start over and make something of myself. I somehow always figured that if I became someone and came back, then people would respect that.

I turn into the Golden Gable Inn and pull my truck up and park. Evan and Beth come out onto the wide front porch, both holding a baby. It blows my mind to see him as a dad. I never imagined us older and having families. I knew I'd eventually end up back here, but I didn't ever picture what it would be like.

I get out of the truck and smile. "Hey," I say as I reach out and give him a hug and clap him on the back. Reaching down, I hold one of the baby's feet and admit to myself that they're cute. I never pictured myself having a family, but being back here and seeing Evan with his family makes me imagine Callie and me with a family. And I can see it. I want that badly.

"Hey, Beth." I reach out my hand to shake hers, and

instead, she pulls me in for a hug, and the baby she's holding starts to whimper. I bend down and say, "Hey, there…"

"I hope you can stay for dinner," Beth insists. "Sasha made pot roast, homemade mashed potatoes, and garlic green beans."

"And Allie is bringing pie," Evan adds.

"I'll never say no to any of that." I smile, sliding my hands into my pockets.

"The boys will be happy to see you again. You're like a celebrity in our house, Coach Reid," Evan says proudly.

"Ahh, not officially a coach."

"You will be," he insists.

I step back and say, "Hey, so I brought a friend and wondered if that's okay? She's been sad, and I think it might cheer her up to be around people," I add nervously, glancing toward the truck, wondering if this is okay.

Evan shrugs. "Sure, who is it?" He looks over and scans my truck.

I walk to the truck and open it. "Come on, girl," I murmur as she sits up uneasily and jumps down out of the truck.

"Oh," Beth murmurs in a soft voice, "who is this?"

"This is Harley." Her tail is tucked between her legs, and her head is down as she walks next to me.

"What's going on with her?" Evan asks, concerned, leaning down to pet her.

"She was my buddy's service dog. He passed away and left

her to me. And…well, I think her heart is broken. I'm trying to make her happy again," I say quietly.

"I remember someone else like that once," Evan remarks, and Beth shoots him a warning look.

I chuckle and look down at her. "Maybe so. But I'm trying to take her everywhere I go so maybe we'll find something she likes to help cheer her up."

"Let's introduce her to Bossy and Chip, our inn dogs, and get the boys. I bet we can win her over." Beth reaches down to scratch her ears, and Harley leans in to sniff the baby she's wearing on her front.

"Hey, Harley, this is Benny. Do you like babies?" she croons. Harley seems to perk up a little bit, sniffing the baby. "Want to go get a treat?"

Harley wags her tail a little, but her head and ears are still down as she looks back at me for permission. I nod to her, and she turns and follows Beth.

"We'll help make her happy again," Evan says as we head into the inn.

Relieved, I followed them into the inn. Evan helped me, and I'm hopeful he can help my new dog, too. Sometimes we need our village to help us when we're broken.

"Coach Reid, when do you think Kase and I can play football with you on your big field?" Caleb asks, scooting his chair right up next to mine, looking up at me with adoration.

I tousle his hair. "I have two reserved spots on my team for when you're older." I really hope I'm still coaching and get the opportunity.

"Mom!" Caleb shrieks. "Kase and I will be Eagles when we get big!"

I look under the table to check on Harley and see Sasha hand her a piece of pot roast. I look up at her, and she grins with a guilty look. "What?" she mouths. Well, maybe Harley can be bought with pot roast.

"I missed you, Sasha. Thank you for having us," I say and mean it. I ate here countless times in high school. Evan and I used to clean her out of the kitchen and home. Back then, we brought our teenage boy, football playing appetites, and she'd always send extras home with me. Dad wasn't one to cook much, usually relying on things we could heat up or take out, so these meals here were sacred to me. It's as close to a mom's kitchen as I could ever have imagined.

"Are you coming to the fall festival?" Allie asks as she passes me a piece of warm apple pie with vanilla ice cream on the top. My mouth waters.

"I'll be there," I say as I grab my fork. I take a bite and close my eyes. So good. "Allie, you made this?"

"Yep, so be sure to tell everyone you know to come by Baked Inn Love to get one!" she says as she passes more plates out.

"This is fantastic." I close my eyes. "I'll be by to get one."

"Will a beautiful doctor be joining you at the festival, too?" Margie asks with a warm smile. "We've missed our Callie girl."

Evan and Allie's mom has always been kind to me and treated me like one of the kids and that I belonged.

"I hope so. I plan on asking her," I add. Back in high school, we went to every festival together, and sometimes we were even recruited to help out at them.

"Do you still do the pumpkin guillotine?" I look over at Evan.

"Heck yeah, we do. And it's gotten even more epic," he says. "Pete just..." Quickly looking over at Sasha, he tries to hide a grin and stops. "Nothing, it's great. You'll see." He scoops up the apple pie, puts it in his mouth, and looks away from Sasha's glare, but she smiles and shakes her head.

"Oh, I know all about your sneaky little pumpkin shenanigans," Sasha teases. "You two better be careful."

It feels good to be back here and be around this family that teases each other. A part of it makes me sad that I was gone and shut all of this out for the past twelve years. I should have made more of an effort to get back here to visit or, at the very least, stay in touch.

Evan slides a glass of iced tea to me and looks me in the eye. "You good, man?"

Shaking myself out of it, I say, "Yeah."

"Let's head outside for a walk," he says as I stand and reach for my glass.

I whistle softly for Harley, and she immediately gets up and trots after me.

"Bye, Harley!" Kase calls and waves.

"We'll be back," I call as we head out into the crisp fall night.

We walk a ways up the path, and Evan says, "I'm sorry to hear about your buddy."

I swallow a lump in my throat and nod.

"I think she needs you as much as you need her." He nods to Harley now walking at my side.

"I have no idea what I'm doing with her. I've never had a dog, especially a service dog."

"Your buddy clearly sent Harley to you at a time when you needed her the most. A time when he knew SJ and Harley both needed someone to lean on and get them through," Evan says thoughtfully.

I scrub my hand over my face and nod. "Maybe you're right."

"One day at a time, you'll figure it out. Look at your life now and how everything has worked out. You're a coach. These players need you. Callie's back. Life is good."

"I'm worried I'll mess it up again."

"Honestly, you probably will. We're not perfect. You need to give yourself a break. Wasn't it a Bob Marley quote where he said something like, 'If she's amazing, it won't be easy. If she's worth it, you won't give up.'"

"But I did give up." I hang my head, running my hand over my jaw.

"The truth is, buddy, everyone gets hurt. You just have to find the one worth getting hurt for. Go get your woman."

CHAPTER 22

Callie

THEN

The party is dying down, and I look at the clock and realize that I have to get home before my parents figure out that I'm gone. They're rarely sober enough to parent me. But on the off chance that they do realize I'm not home, I don't want their drunk selves to come looking for me and embarrass me. There's just no telling what they'd do, so it's better not to take any chances.

"SJ, we'd better go," I call to him in the crowd of our friends.

He looks over at me, holding a bow that the guys are shooting at a target affixed to the side of the barn. Music is playing, and there's a cooler of sodas and a small table set up with chips and snacks. Everyone is just hanging out, enjoying our evening with games, laughter, and fun.

"Already?" He looks at his watch and back over to me and nods. He hands the bow to Evan and heads toward me, his eyes fixed on me and full of desire. "SJ." I giggle and reach for him as he wraps his arms around me and leans down to kiss me.

"I don't really want to leave either," I admit.

"I wish you could just stay with me," he says. I squeal as he picks me up and throws me over his shoulder.

"Bye, guys!" he calls as he carries me out to the truck and stops, putting me down to kiss me.

"Just a few more months," I say as we get into the truck, and I slide my seat belt on.

We head down the road, and music is playing softly in the truck.

We don't even see it coming, but all of a sudden, a deer runs across the dark road, and the truck headlights dance off its white chest and antlers.

"Deer!" SJ screams as he instinctively slams on the brakes, throwing his arm across my chest and pushing me back as the truck hits the deer head-on. Headlights are coming at us from the other direction and there's squealing of brakes from the other car as thumps and cracks make their way through the cab of the truck. I scream, and everything goes dark.

"Callie! Callie, wake up. Open your eyes, Callie," SJ pleads with me. I can tell he's crying. I want to tell him that I'm okay. But suddenly, I realize that I'm not okay. I'm hurting, and everything feels like it's in slow motion.

"Dad, I need help!" SJ screams into the phone. "I hit a deer on the highway by the inn. Callie's unconscious."

"Hurry, Dad," SJ sobs.

I hear EMTs and people calling my name. "Don't call my parents," I mumble.

"Callie, Callie!" SJ calls over the noise.

I feel the bumps as I'm loaded into the ambulance, and my arm hurts so bad. Pain shoots through my body.

"Alright, let's get them both looked at." The EMT knocks on the front of the cab, signaling to go, and the doors shut.

"Have you had anything to drink?" the EMT asks, shining a light in my eyes.

I shake my head. "No. My arm..."

"You're okay. We're almost at the hospital," the EMT says as he takes my blood pressure on the arm that's not hurting as bad.

The ambulance doors open, and there are my parents. My mom is yelling at Sam. He's standing off to the side with his arm around SJ, who holds his fist to his mouth with worry.

"This is your fault!" My mom shrieks at SJ, whose eyes are red from crying.

SJ says nothing, and Sam whispers something to him while

glaring at my mom.

"Get out of here," my dad yells at Sam and SJ. "Where's security?" he demands.

The entitlement of my parents is just astounding. We're both hurt, and he somehow blames SJ and doesn't think he even deserves to be at the hospital, too.

Sam and SJ watch me and say nothing and don't move as the stretcher is pushed inside. They quietly follow next to me, making it clear they're not leaving. My dad leans down, and I can smell the booze on him. Great.

Several hours later, I'm able to go home, and my mom drives us. My dad is passed out in the back seat. She says nothing, pretending like this is all perfectly normal.

"What were you thinking, Callie? I just don't understand why you keep throwing your life away for that boy," she snaps. "He's dangerous. He could have killed you."

I say nothing, my pain meds making me sleepy, and I doze off against the cold and comforting window of the car. I just want to sleep. There's nothing that I can say anyway. SJ can do all the right things. My parents can do all the wrong things. None of it makes any sense.

NOW

"Dr. McGraw, a delivery came for you," Ramie calls as I turn the corner. "Look." She motions to a gorgeous bouquet of yellow roses on the desk.

I smile, knowing they're from SJ. He always used to get me yellow roses and knows they're my favorite. I open the card and read his words, scripted in his familiar handwriting that's barely legible.

Callie,
Will you go to the fall festival with me?
I'll buy you a funnel cake.
Love, SJ

I stuff the card in my pocket and reach for my phone to text him, swooning from his message and thoughtful gesture. I feel like we're back in high school. The way he makes me feel is the best.

"Well?" Ramie tilts her head. "From the hot biker coach?"

"I send him a text, my fingers typing quickly. "Yes."

"It's good to see you finally happy." Her voice drifts off as Thad walks up to the pit.

"Callie." Glaring at me, he stops in front of where I'm sitting with his hands on his hips. He stands too close to me as he looks at the flowers and back at me, narrowing his eyes.

"It's Dr. McGraw," I remind him, moving to make space between us.

"Ramie, can you please call radiology for me for room five?" I ignore Thad and continue to work.

"Callie, we need to talk. Now," he demands, still using my first name.

"I'm working and slammed with patients, Dr. Douchet." I look at him. "Unless it's work-related, we have nothing to discuss." And I know it's not work-related.

"I'm the attending here at this hospital, and you will listen to me." He raises his voice sharply, and a few patients look over.

I take a deep breath and stand. He goes into an empty room, expecting me to follow him.

I remain in the hallway. "You can talk to me out here." No way am I going into an empty room with him.

"Why are you throwing away a perfectly good thing we have for that trash," he spits out angrily. "Your parents are so disappointed in you."

I turn, ignoring him, and head back to the pit.

"I'm not done with you!" He stalks after me.

I turn and warn quietly, trying not to make an even bigger scene, "I will call security if you don't leave me alone."

He laughs bitterly. "I'd love to see you try." His eyes shoot to Ramie.

She stares him down and reaches for the phone. He shifts

nervously.

"You're both stupid. I'm not done with you." He shoves past me, purposely shoulder checking me.

"We should call security," Ramie says. "That's two times now he's made unwanted physical contact with you."

"No, don't call." I shake my head.

"If it was me, would you call security?" She tilts her head.

"Yes," I admit. "But I honestly don't think they'll listen. It'll be my word against his." I also don't want to rock the boat in case it comes back to haunt me on whether I get a job. I don't want SJ to get in trouble because he shoved Thad. It's his word against Thad's, and we know how this town treats SJ.

"This isn't right," she says.

I shake my head. I've worked my ass off to get here, and I won't work like this. It's not worth it. I'm shaking, upset from this.

Ramie groans. "I'm going to be pissed if we lose you. Everyone here loves working with you. He should leave. Also, do you know how many stupid mistakes he makes? He's dangerous," she adds quietly.

"I know."

And boy, do I. It's time to talk to human resources. This is beyond me getting a job. It's about patients' lives. I have a responsibility for the patients and employees here to report this.

I park in front of my cottage. I need to check in on Goldie and pick up more clothes. I've been staying with SJ and Harley, and I probably have some explaining to do about where I've been. I feel guilty about not seeing her as much lately, and I've missed her. I don't want Goldie to feel left out because SJ is back.

I knock on her door, and she answers, holding the door for me. "Come in, sweetie." She gives me a hug, happy to see me.

"I wanted to check in on you. How are you?" I notice a bouquet of yellow roses just like mine on her table.

"Beautiful flowers." I smile. "Who are they from?"

"A lovely young gentleman." She smiles widely and wiggles her eyebrows.

"He *is* a lovely gentleman," I agree.

"I'll bet you didn't know that after my Rex died, SJ came and mowed my lawn every week," she says, her eyes watery with tears. "And after he left for the Army, his dad or one of the nice bikers have come ever since to mow for me," she says with admiration on her face. "They never forgot about me."

"I didn't know that, but I'm not surprised." Sam and SJ have always had the biggest hearts. And as much as some people would like to villainize the Eastern Bones motorcycle club, they really do look after our town and the people here.

They do things like this and never ask for anything in return. Sweet on the inside and tough on the outside.

Changing the subject, she says, "I'm assuming you two have been working out your differences?" She feigns innocence.

"Goldie." I snort. "We're doing good," I confirm. "We still have a lot of things to work on and figure out, but we're in a better place."

"I knew it would all work out. I'm proud of you both, honey."

"Thank you."

"Your mom came by here this week," she adds with a frown.

"My mom? Why?" I groan, confused.

"She was checking on you."

"What did you tell her?" Figures she'd poke around instead of just coming to me or calling. She knows I'm always at the hospital and could have come to me.

"That you were busy working." She shrugs and reaches over to cover my hand.

"Thanks. I need to talk to them about Thad."

"She already knows, dear. She wasn't happy. Unfortunately, we didn't end our visit on a good note. She said some choice things about our SJ, and I told her I won't have any of that."

"She's never going to change." I'm thirty years old, and she and my dad still try to control me. My dad tried to get me to give him five thousand dollars last week. He's crazy if he thinks I have that kind of money. And I suspect his money troubles are getting even worse.

She continues, "She asked me why you always come to me and not to her."

"Oh wow. What did you tell her?" I know it's always bothered her that I've been close with Goldie. My own mother has never had any real interest in me or my life. She prefers alcohol. And while alcohol plays a debilitating role in their lives, they are horrible without it. The alcohol just exacerbates the issue. Goldie has been the one to cheer me on and support me with everything I've needed. It's Goldie who drove me to New York for school and came to visit me on holidays. She sent me care packages and checked on me several times a week. Months would go by without any contact with my parents, and that was just our normal. If I needed anything, I knew it wouldn't come from them. No one can say I haven't tried. I have, but being the daughter of two alcoholics who want to control me has been hard. Adding on their manipulation and verbal abuse on top of it all has been exhausting. When Ramie asked me the other day if I would call the police if what had happened to me had happened to her instead got me thinking. If my friend was in my situation and had my parents, what would I say to her? What would I do? And then I ask myself why I don't do that for myself. Why do I settle for this?

"I explained to her that I want nothing from you but your love. And that I'm proud of you no matter what. I'm not sure if she has the capacity to understand that. She must care in some way, but I just don't think she knows how," she says sadly, patting my arm.

School and work have always been my places of escape. Now that I'm back in Freedom Valley and life has slowed down somewhat, I'm having to face everything. It's time to make some hard decisions about my parents and what role I want them to play in my life moving forward. At this point, I'm upset whenever I'm around them, and they don't hear or see me nor do they care about what I want. My dad regularly asks me for money, and I don't have it. My student loans are sucking me dry. And without a full-time contract at the hospital, I have to be very careful, anyway. I can't keep continuing like this with them. I tried to have a relationship with them when I came back, but it was never going to happen. I know that now. Since being back, I've realized that the family you create is more important than the family you come from.

"It's too late," I say. "She's never been there for me. Why would she care all of a sudden?"

"I don't know, honey. But I'm here for you no matter what," she adds.

I smile at her gratefully. "I'm not being treated like that anymore," I say with a determined sigh. "It's been sad but freeing to accept that my mother will never be capable of being the mother that I need her to be."

"It'll be alright, honey," she says with her lips together, nodding.

"Thank you for always being here for me, Goldie. I don't know what I would do without you all these years," I say, pulling her into a hug.

"I love you very much," she says as her eyes tear up.

THEN

The door to the shop opens, and Callie and Bear come in carrying shopping bags. "SJ!" she says, coming toward me and wrapping her arms around me. "Wait till you see what we got!"

"What's all this?" I laugh as I kiss her and wrap my arms around her.

"Bear took me shopping for prom." She happily holds up the bags. "I got my dress and shoes."

"Bear took you shopping?" I ask in disbelief, looking at him in shock.

"I was the driver, kid. Shut it," Bear calls as he walks out of

the back kitchen with a fresh beer.

"Must have been rough if you immediately need a beer," I tease.

"Bear was the absolute best," Callie admits. "He has excellent taste."

I look over, and Bear rolls his eyes, but I don't miss the smile he's trying to hide.

"I'm renting my tux tomorrow." I hesitate. "Callie, are you sure about this? They're never going to let you go with me."

"I don't even care anymore," she says adamantly. "I am going with you to prom."

I sigh and nod. "Okay. And where will they think you'll be?"

"They have a trip planned to the Bahamas the weekend of prom anyway." She shrugs. "I'll be home alone," she says with a smile.

"Okay." I wish it would be okay, but I just feel like things are heating up with her parents. The more interaction we have, the more things escalate with them. It's getting harder and harder for all of us. My dad, her, and me. It's just too much, sometimes.

"Hey," she says, looking into my eyes, "it's going to be fine."

"I hope you know what you're doing, Callie. They're still so pissed at me since the wreck."

"That wasn't your fault. I'm fine," she says, holding up her arm with the bright blue cast on it, covered in black signatures from friends. "It was just an accident."

The truth is, I'm still upset about the accident and Callie breaking her arm. I don't know what I'd do if I lost her. She means everything to me. I've played over and over what happened that night in my head and what I could have done differently, and I feel terrible.

I also don't want to come between her and her family. Sometimes I wonder if her parents are right. I'm in the way, and she has her whole life ahead of her. What if something I do holds her back?

NOW

"Harley, you stink." I sniff in disgust as she gets in my truck.

We drive through town toward the shop, and I pass the dog groomer on Main Street. I park and walk up to peer in the window, looking for shop hours and noticing the closed sign. A huge German shepherd tilts his head and peers up at me from the front window. The groomer has a setup so that the dogs kennel in the front window with an air-conditioning unit set up so that when they're groomed, they're on display for everyone on Main Street to see. Benches sit in front of the window, and I can tell why this has become a busy and popular business here in Freedom Valley. Who doesn't love dogs? Genius move if you ask me.

"Can I help you?" a cautious voice calls out from behind me.

I turn around, and a tall dark blond-haired woman with

piercing blue eyes stares at me expectantly, and then her eyes light up with recognition. "SJ."

"Ophelia? I almost didn't recognize you."

"Good to see you again." She smiles. "I haven't seen you since high school, and I thought you wouldn't remember me."

"I remember you. Axel's sister."

She sets down the bag she's carrying to unlock the door. "You have a beautiful service dog in the front seat of your truck that I've heard about." She grins. "Evan and Beth told me you might need help with a dog you recently acquired."

"That's right. I've heard a lot of good things about you and what you're doing with the dog training and rescue. I didn't realize you worked here, too."

"I own the dog grooming shop and just started a nonprofit dog rescue and training facility near the Golden Gable Inn."

"Busy lady." I nod, impressed.

"I love it. Why don't you bring her in and let me look her over," she says as she opens the door. I hear dogs barking and whimpering from the back of her shop. "I have a full day booked, but I can make time for you."

"Okay," I say, grateful for her help. I turn and open the passenger door, and Harley whimpers, but her tail wags. I look up and realize she is staring at the German shepherd in the window and looks happy to see him. He's on his hind legs watching her and looks happy to see her, too.

"Well, how about that? Maybe you'll make a new friend," I say softly as I scratch her ears. "Let's go say hi."

We step inside, and Ophelia has already donned a black waterproof apron. She walks over and leans down. "Hey, sweet girl."

"She was my buddy's, and he passed away," I say hoarsely.

"I'm really sorry to hear that." She strokes Harley's fur. "I bet you both miss him," she says softly.

"Thanks. It was unexpected, and Harley's been very sad. I didn't even realize a dog could be this sad."

"Of course, they can. Dogs are highly intuitive animals."

I nod and look over to see the German shepherd watching us curiously.

"Do you have any paperwork or records for her?" she asks, looking up at me.

"I do in my truck. Let me grab it."

She has Harley up on the grooming table and nods to me when I return. "I'm going to see how she does with Mr. Pickles."

"Mr. Pickles?" I ask as I set the paperwork down on the counter.

"My dog. I train other dogs with him. He's like my assistant. Mr. Pickles," she calls over to the front window.

The front latch to the dog crate in the front window turns, and he opens the door. He comes bounding in and circles and sits next to Ophelia, then looks up at her like he's waiting for her next command.

"He opens doors?" I ask, surprised.

"Of course, he does. He's a certified good boy. You want to help me with Harley, buddy?" she coos, reaching down to scratch his ears.

She lifts Harley off the table and sets her down and Harley turns into a different dog before my eyes. She looks happy, her ears are perked up, and her tail is feverishly wagging. They sniff each other and begin to play.

"She looks like a really good dog. I'm sorry for the circumstances," she remarks, watching them play.

"Thanks," I say, swallowing a lump in my throat.

"Why don't you leave her here for the morning? She can play with Mr. Pickles, and I'll get her cleaned up. She'll probably feel better with a good bath and blow out, won't you?" she says to Harley, who is currently sniffing Mr. Pickles as he licks her face in return.

"Okay, I appreciate it. I'll just be down at the shop," I tell her. I lean down to pet Harley and say, "See you later, girl." She barely pays attention when I walk out, and I hear Ophelia speaking softly to her.

Callie: Thanks for the flowers. Yes, I'll go to the fall festival with you.

Warmth fills my chest as I get ready for the game. Callie and I are together, I'm coaching, and things are looking up. When I first came home, I didn't know what I wanted. I always knew I'd come back to Freedom Valley. My dad's here and Goldie. But I didn't expect everything to turn out like it has with Callie back too. It's better than I ever could have expected. I didn't expect a second chance with her, but now that I have it, I'm going to fight for her every step of the way. I won't be a self-sacrificing idiot. I won't shut her out.

After I take care of things at the shop, I head out to Second Chance Rescue. I have some time before the game to check on Harley, and Ophelia said that's where I can find her.

I take the familiar path to the inn and stop at the stop sign to turn where the wreck happened all those years ago. I think about that night when I thought I'd lost Callie. The way her parents and the town blamed me. There were rumors going around that I'd been drinking. I hadn't. A bunch of us had been hanging out at the inn, but we didn't have any alcohol at the party that night. It didn't matter because once the rumors spread, there was nothing I could do to convince people of the truth. It was like another nail in my coffin. Evan and his parents vouched for me, but it didn't matter. The damage was done. No one looked at me the same after that. I was just a kid and at their mercy and had to take their shit. But guess who's not a kid anymore? I don't have to take shit from anyone.

I want to coach, but at what cost? To lose Callie again? Lose my position that I've worked for? And I still have stuff to work through with Callie. We still have what feels like a giant elephant in the room of unanswered questions. I'm not sure I can ever make her understand why I left without damaging things even further and losing her trust. When she called me a coward that day in the hospital? She wasn't wrong. I was a coward for leaving. Deep down, I have always hoped that she and her parents would figure things out. I know how it feels to be estranged from my mom, and it's not a good feeling. Sure, Callie's parents are crappy, but they're her family. If she wanted to cut them out of her life, that had to be her choice, not mine.

When I get out of my truck at Ophelia's, I notice that the big barn is dilapidated and barely held together by loose boards patching it in places. This place is in rough shape and needs a lot of work. Ophelia comes out to meet me wearing jeans and a hooded sweatshirt with her rescue logo across the front. Harley and Mr. Pickles trot beside her, tails wagging. Ophelia says something softly, and Harley sits next to her and waits.

I wait and watch. Ophelia gives her another command, and Harley turns and runs back into the barn and returns with something in her mouth and brings it to Ophelia. Ophelia takes her phone from Harley.

She turns to me and then says something softly again to Harley and she bounds over to me and circles me and sits beside me and looks up at me.

"She can bring you things?" I ask in disbelief.

"She's a super smart dog. She's had a lot of cool training. I looked over her paperwork and I called the place that your buddy got her from and found out all her training commands. It's very similar to the methods I use. I think she would like to use that training with you now. You could both really benefit from companionship with each other." She smiles and leans up against the barn. "What do you say?"

"I'm in," I say as I stroke Harley behind her ears. "But are you sure I'm qualified to keep her?"

"Listen, I'm no expert. But sometimes people and animals come into our lives just when we need them. And you and Harley need each other," she says as she tucks her hands into the pocket of her sweatshirt.

I nod, not sure what to say to that. But I do like the idea of making sure Harley is taken care of for Sparks. They both deserve that.

"If it's okay with you, let me work with her a few mornings this week with Mr. Pickles. She's been through some trauma losing her person, and she needs time just like you do to grieve and practice her training to carry it on with you. Then

I'd like to work with you and show you how she can assist you moving forward."

"Okay, that makes sense. She already looks so much happier."

"She's going to be okay. She just needs to adjust to her new environment with you. I also got in touch with my local contact at the VA, and I'm working on getting her registered to you as a service dog here in New Hampshire. They have a great program for veterans and their service dogs here."

"That sounds great," I say, determined. "What will her job be?"

"With your friend, she provided PTSD and anxiety support. But we can talk about how she can be the best companion for you and whatever you need. The VA will be able to work with you on this. She's very special."

I nod, choked up, not saying anything for fear it'll make me tear up. I sniff and say, "That sounds good."

I look around at the property in shambles, piles of scraps everywhere, and it's a mess out here. "How long have you been set up out here?" I ask, motioning to the barn, trying to change the subject.

"Just a few months. I'm busy with my grooming business, but rescue and training are my passion. I like to make sure they all have good training and find good homes."

"Do you have help?" I ask, scrubbing a hand over my face.

"Why, you want to volunteer?" she asks with a hopeful

grin. "I could use a mechanic to look at my new-to-me van."

"My dad and I can take care of that." I nod to her. "Just drop it off at the shop, and we'll get you taken care of, no charge."

"Thank you so much," she says with a hopeful grin.

I need to run it by Coach Murphy, but I could get the team out here sometime for a big cleanup, I muse. "I might have an idea on the property. I'll get back to you on that." I could also get friends to come and help with some small repairs. She's doing good work out here with her dog rescue, and I'd love to see her have help from the community.

"Of course." She shrugs, reaching down to pet Mr. Pickles, who has been watching everything.

"You're so close to the inn." I look around. "Will you be going to the fall festival?"

"No, I don't like going to town things. I keep to myself," she says with a frown.

"Why's that?" I ask, curious.

She hesitates for a moment and says, "My ex-fiancé, Nial, screwed over a lot of people and then ditched town. Some people here believe I'm to blame since he's not here but I still am."

"I'm sorry, that sucks." And hearing this makes me want to find this Nial tool. I'm angry for her. I know what it feels like to be the villain all because someone else creates that version of you for others. I hate that she's experiencing it, too.

"Yeah, well, it is what it is, right?"

"I have my fair share of the feeling of trouble with people in this town not liking me either. I'm dealing with that myself." I nod.

"Any advice?" she asks wearily.

"Yeah, ignore the bullshit and don't run from it." I chuckle.

"Is that what you did?"

"I was gone for twelve years, and I'm back for good now." I sigh and run my fingers through my hair. "I'm trying to coach. But some people don't want to see that happen. But I'm not letting this town mess with my life anymore, and you shouldn't either."

"You're right," she agrees.

"One word of advice?" I offer.

"What's that?"

"Make friends with Beth, Allie, Mellie, and Paige. They are good people, and they will help look out for you around town. I've watched them do a lot for this community, and you can trust them."

"Beth has been trying to get me to hang out. I've just been avoiding everyone. Her friend Paige was one of the people my ex stole money from." She bites her lip and looks away. "I feel like she probably blames me, too."

I shake my head. "Come to the fall festival. I'll be there with Callie. We'll make sure everyone knows you're cool and you didn't have anything to do with what your ex did. I think Callie would appreciate seeing you there, too."

"Okay, I can bring Harley and Mr. Pickles." She looks hopeful.

"Yes, that would be great. Thanks for all that you're doing to help us. I'll be in touch about the volunteering. I need to check with a few people," I add.

"Thanks, SJ." She waves as we head out.

I drive to the stadium and think about how small towns can really screw people over, and seeing it happen to another person who doesn't deserve it makes me even more determined not to let anyone else get hurt. It's time for change in Freedom Valley, which will make some people very uncomfortable. That's not my problem, and I don't give a shit at this point. I'm tired of people like Dr. Dick and Hamilton thinking they can just screw people over and use people for their own manipulation and gain. Hamilton had his own board to make decisions that hurt others. I am going to get my own board together to fight them. It's time to take our town back.

CHAPTER 24

Callie

THEN

"I'll tell you what, SJ Reid, Freedom Valley's star starting player has more heart than any kid I've ever seen on the field. That kid has rose up and played his heart out for Freedom Valley for the past few years. It'll be exciting to see where he goes after this..." the announcer calls over the radio of the local game during an interview. "So much potential," another commentator adds.

Sam strums on his guitar in the corner of the shop. I'm waiting for SJ to finish getting ready so we can head out.

"Sam, can I ask you something?" I ask quietly.

He stops strumming and looks up at me. "What's that?"

"Why aren't you mad at my dad for what he did?" I ask softly.

He takes a deep breath and says, "Because like I told SJ, your dad doesn't matter. The thing is, people are going to do what they're going to do. And you can't control other people. You can just build a life you're happy with and focus on the people who do matter. And not on the people who don't. You matter to me. I keep the peace with your dad for you."

"Thank you for saying that I matter," I say softly.

"He starts to strum a little more. "Of course you matter."

I hear SJ coming down the stairs and I look up to him and tease, "When are you going to learn to play guitar like your dad?"

SJ rolls his eyes but smiles, shaking his head. "When the old man learns how to play football."

Sam shakes his head and laughs. "I know how to play football."

"Riiiiiight, you ready to go?" He looks over at me as he swipes his keys.

"Hey," Sam says looking over at us, "be careful."

"We will. Bye." I hug him as we leave and walk out to the truck into the cold night.

"What were you and my dad talking about?" he asks as he slides behind the wheel and starts it and rubs his hands together to get warm.

"Your mom and my dad," I say meekly.

He looks over at me and raises his eyebrows.

"Has your mom tried to reach out to you since we saw her?"

"Nope," he says resolutely. "She probably won't, either. And I'm okay with that. She made her choice the day she left me here. Seeing her didn't change that and the fact that she's ignored me for twelve years."

My chest feels heavy thinking of five-year-old SJ watching his mom drive away with his little sister and leaving him behind. "I'm so sorry." I can't even imagine how much that had to have hurt him.

He shrugs. "I don't think I'll ever forget the day she left. It's one of the few memories I have of her and my sister. That's part of why I wanted to find her so that maybe that last memory would hurt less."

"I just don't understand it."

"Join the club. She said nothing to me that day. Just picked up my sister and left. I was crying and banging on the front window for her to stop and to come back and she just turned and looked at me and said nothing. Then she drove off. That's the memory I have of my mom, Callie. Even my own mother didn't want me. This puts into perspective why this town doesn't even want me if my own mother didn't," he says with hurt in his eyes.

"Screw her and screw them," I say angrily. "We don't need her or either of my parents. They're all terrible."

SJ reaches for my hand. "I love you, Otter. We have each other. And Mrs. Winters and my dad."

"Love you, too." I scoot closer and lay my head on his shoulder.

NOW

I'm getting ready at the cabin and find a single yellow rose in the kitchen in a jar of water on the counter. SJ comes in and sets his keys and wallet down, and I'm in his arms kissing him, my arms around his neck. When his mouth covers mine, I feel like I'm home. A place that's never felt real until now, with SJ.

"Well, hello to you, too, beautiful," he murmurs, his fingers running through my hair that I have down in curly waves after undoing my braid.

"How was the game? Sorry I couldn't make it, I just now got off from my shift, and I'm so exhausted and need to shower." I have tried to go home a few times, not wanting to overstay my welcome, but SJ has demanded I stay and even uses Harley without shame to encourage me to just stay there from now on. It's been so nice to reconnect with him and get to know him again. I look forward to waking up with him and going to bed holding hands with him.

"It's fine. The team played great. We won. 22-15," he says running his hand up my side and stopping to cup my breast. "Maybe I'll join you in that shower," he murmurs.

"Hey," I ask curiously, "what's with the yellow flower?" I nod to the single flower on the counter.

He pulls me into him. "When that one dies, I know when you and Goldie need fresh ones."

My heart melts into a puddle.

He says nothing but holds me in his arms, looking into my eyes. This is the thoughtful man I love.

"I love you," I whisper.

"I love you more, otter."

"You believed in us when there was no us."

"There's always been an us." He picks me up, and my legs wrap around him as he pulls me into the deepest and sexiest kiss I've ever had in my life. Kissing grown-up SJ is like a dream. I hope I never wake up.

The next morning, we get to the inn and park, and the fall festival is already well underway. The familiar and nostalgic smell of caramel corn and apple cider mixes with the campfire smell from the firepit where people have gathered around to get warm at on this unusually cool fall morning. Holding my hand, we walk to the entrance and take in everything. It's been so long since I've been to anything like this. Being back feels like I'm coming home.

Fall is my favorite time of the year. I have on a long empire waist hunter-green dress with fall colors. I feel pretty in this and have my hair down in long waves. It feels good to be dressed up and spending time with friends.

Pumpkins with elaborate carvings are set up everywhere, and autumn harvest displays are works of art. I missed the fall festival traditions that Freedom Valley has every year. It always brings everyone together, and somehow makes things feel like I'm at home. People are laughing and having a good time. The comfort and familiarity of the inn is a welcome break from all my long hospital shifts. Goldie was right. I needed to make time for this.

We walk in under orange pumpkins strung above us at the entrance back into the field by the barn. Straw bales are set up, and a giant pumpkin and bat display greets visitors. I can see a mixture of old and new traditions and new things to see and do. I see Beth and Evan buzzing around working and setting things up. The inn at the fall festival is the place to be.

A wooden stage is set up off to the side with a pergola of twinkle lights strung over the top. Sam and members of the local band are playing Luke Combs's "Forever After All," and a few couples are dancing and sitting around enjoying the music.

A line of smokers and grills are set up, and the smell of barbecue makes my mouth water. Food trucks and vendor tables are scattered throughout the field, and I can't wait to walk through and see and try everything.

SJ looks at me under the brim of his Eagles hat. "You are the most beautiful woman I've ever seen." He threads his fingers through mine and squeezes my hand.

I smile. "Thanks. Want to go make out?" The way he looks at me makes my heart dip and race.

"Absolutely," he says, his eyes lingering on my mouth as he leans over to plant one on me. He wraps his arms around me protectively. This. This is what I missed. This is the best mixture of the younger version and grown-up SJ. And he's mine again.

SJ looks at a woman walking across the field with Harley and a German shepherd and says, "Do you remember Axel's sister, Ophelia?"

"Yes. But I haven't seen her since we've been back."

"She's helping me with Harley, and she's coming over. I want to make sure everyone meets her and knows that she's cool. She's had a hard time with people in town, so I want to make sure she feels welcome. Want to help me?"

"Of course," I say softly. She was always nice, and I don't like to hear that she's had a rough time. "Let me text the ladies for help."

SJ gives me a smile. He's always been protective of his friends and family, so he's the perfect coach. He's a good role model for his players, and he'll make sure they won't go through what he did growing up here.

Callie: Hey, Ophelia is here, and she's been having a rough time with the town assholes. Have you all met her? I want us to all welcome her into the group if that's okay.

Beth: Yes! We love Opi! Is she here?

Allie: Where is everyone? I'm helping Logan at the baked goods table. But we can meet up by the stage and firepit.

Paige: Preston and I've got Benny and Eden over by the candy drop.

Mellie: Ty and I are supervising candy drop.

Callie: SJ and I are at the firepit.

Beth: Let me get my babies, and I'll head that way.

Paige: We're coming too!

"Okay, everyone is meeting up here," I say, sliding my phone into my pocket.

SJ squeezes my hand and smiles gratefully. "There she is," he says, standing and heading toward her. Harley sees SJ and instantly wags her tail and goes to him. This melts my heart.

She looks unsure of being here and looks around nervously, hanging back.

Hey, Ophelia, do you remember me? I'm Callie." I reach over to pet Harley, whose tail wags when she sees me.

Ophelia nods nervously and looks down. "Yes, good to see you again."

"Hey, Harley." I bend down to pet her. "You look so happy and relaxed." I look up at Ophelia. "How did you do that?"

"I give credit to Mr. Pickles. They're besties now," she says with a grin.

"Mr. Pickles," I coo, reaching over to pet him as he puts his head down and leans into my ear scratches. He has the most soulful, beautiful brown eyes full of expression.

"Come sit with us, let's catch up. The others are coming too, and we'll have a great time," I assure her.

She looks hesitant but comes over and sits next to me by the firepit.

Paige and Beth walk up, and Paige immediately goes to the dogs. "Look at these cuties," she declares, smiling at Ophelia. "Hi, I'm Paige. I don't know if you remember me or not. We went to school together, and I just moved back."

Ophelia smiles back. "Hi," she says shyly. "I remember."

"I heard that Nial was your ex. I wanted you to know that I am so sorry that all that happened," she says quietly to Ophelia to clear the air.

Ophelia looks surprised. "No, I'm so sorry. I didn't know what he was doing until he was gone."

Paige had lost a lot of her money when she first came back to Freedom Valley, and Nial scammed her out of her bookstore. Nobody holds this against Ophelia. She was a victim, too. And nobody knows where Nial went, but I've heard from the ladies that the Eastern Bones took care of him, so things probably aren't looking good for him.

"It's not your fault." Paige waves it off. "But it's good to see you. Do you work with raccoons?" she asks with a serious face.

Ophelia laughs nervously. "Raccoons?"

"Yes." She turns, and her backpack has a big dome on it, and it does indeed have a raccoon in it with his tiny hands pressed against the dome watching everything going on around it.

"Holy cow, you have a *real* pet raccoon?" I lean forward to check him out.

"This is Pancake," she says, taking off the bag so we can see him. Mr. Pickles and Harley sniff the bag curiously.

"That's the coolest thing ever," Ophelia says. "I have no experience training raccoons, but he looks like a nice fella."

"He is." She nods. "He's best friends with my fiancé's dog, Theo. He's around here somewhere with my fiancé, Preston. I hope you can meet him, too."

I look over, and SJ smiles at me as he chats with Ty and Logan. And just like that, we're back with our friends, old and new, and it feels right. We're right where we were supposed to be. We just got here on a different path than I thought we would.

SJ is talking with someone and says something, then turns my way. The way he looks at me makes me feel so wanted. Like I'm the only person he's focused on. The way he walks with confidence and his eyes on me makes me swoon. "Want to dance?" he asks and holds out his hand. And when I look at him, I see it. I can see us here in Freedom Valley growing old here. Attending fall festivals, weddings, and doing daily life together. Forever in love. Here together. I want that more than anything. I realize that I've always wanted that with him.

"Well?" he prompts with a grin, holding out his hand.

"Yes," I say as I take his hand, and he wraps his arms around me and pulls me close.

"This has been a good day," he says, turning me around and holding me close around my waist.

I look over to see Ophelia making friends with Mellie, Beth, and Allie, and I'm glad to be back. Sam was right all those years ago when he told me to focus on the people who mattered and not the people who don't.

SJ's face gets serious. "What were you thinking about when I asked you to dance? You looked lost in your thoughts."

I lay my head on his chest. "I was thinking about us," I murmur.

"What about us?" He kisses my neck.

"Our future," I say as we glance at Sam and Evan playing guitar and singing, looking at us and giving each other a knowing look.

"Oh yeah? And what do you see when you picture our future?" he asks.

"Us. Here. Together." I whisper as his fingers move beneath my chin to turn my face in his direction.

"Me, too," he says. "I always have."

"How long do you plan on loving me?" I laugh as he looks into my eyes.

"Forever."

We were stuffed after two apple ciders, two bags of popcorn, caramel apples, and three hot dogs we roasted around a fire and topped with yummy toppings from a hot dog bar. We sit in chairs and listen to music as I feel like I'm almost in a blissful food coma. Ty and Mellie walk up, looking ready for naps.

Mellie says warmly, "Having fun?"

SJ nods, and I say, "Yes, I love your shirts."

Beth told me that all the inn staff and family wear matching shirts, and it's always been a different color and theme. This year, they're purple with orange pumpkins on them and their names on the back for the inn and sponsors.

"Thanks, this year has been a big success. Even better than last year," she says proudly. She's holding hands with Ty, and they look like the sweetest couple.

"I can't believe how huge your pumpkins are, Mellie. You grew those?" I ask in disbelief. There are four huge pumpkins on display. Their names crack me up: Edgar Allan Pumpkin at 1,134 pounds, Tubby Thomas coming in at 1,078 pounds, Great Scott at 1,356 pounds, and Sassy Squash at 1,689 pounds.

"I did." She laughs. "I didn't think they'd get that big, but they surprised us."

"How did you get them here?" I ask, reveling in their size.

"The tractor and Pete. And lots of cursing. We had five, but one was a casualty." She shrugs.

"Oh no!" I laugh. "Everything looks so great." I glance over when I see a crying kid running to Mellie, holding his elbow that has a little bit of blood on it.

"Kase, honey, what happened?" she asks as she bends down to look.

I lean forward and offer, "Can I help?" I reach behind for my backpack purse and pull out my mini first-aid kit. His eyes widen, and he nods as big tears drop down his little cheeks. Oh, my heart, he's so cute. I look at Mellie, and she nods and smiles gratefully.

"Hey, buddy, do you remember me?" I ask as I examine his elbow and see he's got a gash that won't require any stitches.

"Yes," he whimpers.

"What happened?"

"It hurts," he says. "I fell running."

"I bet it does. That's no fun. Let's get you fixed up as good as new," I say softly.

I clean up his skinned elbow, put some salve on it and bandage it up. "How's that?" I lean in to give him a little hug.

"Thank you," he says as he puts his arm around my neck. He pulls back and whispers, "Are you the real Elsa?"

I throw my head back and laugh and then try to put on a serious face. "Yes, but don't tell anyone, okay? I'm taking a break from Arendale."

His eyes widen and he nods. "I won't tell." Then he leans in and whispers in my ear, "Hans is a butthole. Don't tell my mom I said that," he turns and runs off to play with the other kids.

"What did he say?" Mellie asks curiously.

I just shake my head and laugh, not wanting to tell on him. "He's a great kid."

Mellie says, "Thanks for helping him. Hey, I've been meaning to ask you. We'd love to have you and SJ over to our place for dinner some night. Let me know when you're both free."

"We would love that," I say as I tuck my kit back into my bag and look up to see SJ staring at me with desire burning in his eyes. The kind of burning where he used to look at me like that and I knew where we'd end up shortly. Probably making out in his truck if he has his way. And I like his way.

"We're going to check out a few more things," I say to Ty and Mellie.

"Looking forward to dinner with you, guys. See you around." Ty adds with a wave, his hand on Kase's shoulder.

SJ takes me by the hand. When we get around the corner of the barn and out of view, he presses me up against it and kisses me.

"What's this for?" I whisper as he kisses my neck and pulls me into him, his flannel shirt tickling my neck.

"You're good with kids, doc," he says with a smoldering look that makes me weak in the knees.

"Comes with the territory." I shrug.

"I love the woman you've turned into," he whispers, placing his lips to mine and pulling me into his arms closer.

I never thought of myself as a kid person, but I don't think I would mind having a family of my own. I never really saw myself having kids, but now that I'm here in Freedom Valley, I imagine myself as a mom, and I look over at SJ and imagine what he would be like as a dad. Warmth fills me. I picture us with our little family at the cabin. Eating pancakes in the big kitchen and watching sunsets together at our lookout view. Attending football games, eating dinner at Freedom Pie, and taking our kids to the fall festival to chase down candy and do the corn maze. I want that, but I think I've only wanted that with him. Maybe the reason I never wanted to do that before now or saw myself with a family is because it was never right with anyone else. I didn't have the best family life growing up, but Sam and Goldie showed up for me. They stepped in when they didn't have to and made sure I knew what it felt like to be loved.

"Do you want kids, SJ?" I realize I have no idea what he wants. We never talked about that in high school. High school SJ and grown-up SJ are so different yet...both still feel at home.

He slows and threads his fingers through mine and pulls me closer. "Only with you." His husky voice makes me still.

"With me?" I whisper.

"Wouldn't want them with anyone else, Otter." He tips

my chin up to look at him, his whiskey eyes drinking me in.

I lean in and kiss him softly, then rest my cheek on his cozy and warm flannel.

We walk around and talk to a few people, getting curious looks from people who look down at our hands together and back to us and then to each other with knowing smiles. I don't even care. I want to pinch myself right now. This feels right. I do have a feeling that keeps trying to creep in on whether he'll leave me again, and sometimes I think about it and start to get upset, but it's less and less. *He's here, and he's not going anywhere,* I remind myself. But I didn't think he would leave before. What would stop him from doing it again?

"SJ!" someone calls out, and we turn to see Coach Murphy strolling up to us. He's in his usual Freedom Valley hoodie, jeans, and ball cap. "Callie, good to see you again."

"Good to see you too, Coach Murphy." I hug him.

"Coach Murphy." SJ reaches to shake his hand. "Enjoying the festival?"

He sighs. "SJ, I have an update. Can we talk?" He looks around nervously as if this isn't a conversation he wants to have. It doesn't look good.

"What's up?" SJ asks, pulling him off to the side.

"Listen, the board got back to me. They didn't approve you for the position. I'm sorry," he says, looking disappointed.

"Why?" SJ asks, showing no emotion on his face.

"They don't think you're a good fit."

I bite my lip to keep from saying anything. SJ just nods and shows no emotion. My heart freezes hearing this.

"I thought you said I had this, and they just needed to formally offer it?" SJ shakes his head, confused.

"I thought that. But this is what they decided. You've made such an impact with the team; I honestly don't get it," he says, running a hand over his beard. "For what it's worth, I think you should fight it."

SJ nods and says calmly, "Thanks for letting me know." I can feel emotions rolling off him, though. He may be hiding it with Coach, but I know he's upset.

"Unfortunately, there's more. They...uh, want you to stop volunteering effective immediately. I'm so sorry." Coach Murphy shifts his feet. "But I'm going to tell them you're still volunteering if you'll do it. The team needs you. The board can..." He shakes his head angrily, looking away, not finishing that sentence.

SJ nods and shakes his hand, and we walk away. I'm stunned. I don't even know what to say, my hand gripping his. We get to the truck, and I turn to him. "It was my dad, wasn't it?"

He nods. "Your father threatened me that I wouldn't get the position if I didn't stay away from you. He's on the board."

Hot angry tears well up. "He has no right."

He shakes his head angrily. "It's what he does. We should

be used to it by now."

"I'm not getting used to anything. He needs to stop interfering with us."

"I agree. And that's why I choose you over the job," he says as he plays with my hair, trying to soothe me. I turn to face him. I should be the one consoling him. He just lost his job because of my toxic family.

"We shouldn't have to choose anything."

"I know." He nods.

"But you've worked so hard with these kids, and they need you," I say, getting angrier.

"What do you want to do, Callie?" he says, still eerily calm.

"I'll talk to him…" I pull back. "Wait, you already have a plan, don't you? Why are you so calm about this?"

He softly pulls me to him, kissing me. "I don't have a plan. But I have you. And that's what matters the most. We'll figure the rest out."

"You're not giving up, are you?"

"I'm not giving up on anything, Callie. Don't you get that?"

I look at his familiar whiskey eyes searching mine for confirmation that I understand what he's saying.

"We're in this together, SJ."

"I want to be the first thing you touch in the morning and the last person you see at night when you close your eyes." Then he leans in and kisses me again. "This town can fuck right off if they try to get in the way of that."

My chest aches when I think of all the years we've lost. I'm not losing any more time with him again.

CHAPTER 25

Callie

THEN

"*When were you going to tell us that you and that boy were prom king and queen?*" my mother yells angrily before I can even shut the front door. I look over and take in the wine bottle she's emptying into her wineglass.

"*Hello to you too, Mom,*" I say dryly. It's not even four o'clock. Great. This will be a fun evening. I'm so over her. "*When did you get back?*"

"*Why can't you choose a nice boy with a good family?*" she whines, throwing up her hands and ignoring my question. She's been gone for five days, and I haven't heard from her.

I stare at her, disgusted. "Why can't you just be there for me and actually be a mother?"

She slaps me hard across the face, and I turn and hold my face where she hit me. My skin stings and feels fiery hot. The sting of tears fall from years of neglect and abuse that hurt more than her slap. I guess I had that one coming. The truth hurts.

"I am a good mother." She narrows her red and angry eyes at me. "We give you everything."

"Okay, Mom." I stare at her in disbelief. I'm leaving for college soon anyway. I don't know why she even cares at this point. "He didn't do anything wrong."

"He's not good enough for you!" she yells.

"No, you're holding a grudge against his mother, and he has nothing to do with any of that."

"What are you talking about?" she asks angrily, her eyes darkening.

"His mother. She admitted everything. When were you going to tell me that I have a half sister out in the world?"

The blood seems to drain from her flushed face. She looks pale. "That is not his child," she bites out.

"Okay?" I say in disbelief. "But you could have fooled me since she looks just like me, Mom. We could be twins. It's scary how similar we look."

She turns her head and looks away, taking a big gulp of her wine.

"You are going to throw away your life. I won't have it, and neither will your father," she says, ignoring the bomb I just dropped. I can't tell if she knew or suspected or is just in plain denial.

"Where is he?" I ask. Looking around, I realize I haven't seen him.

"He's on a trip," she says ominously, looking away again.

"What kind of trip?" I push further.

"Does it matter?" she questions.

"Um, because he's my dad, and he's gone?" It's strange that she came back from their trip alone, and he's gone again suddenly.

"Don't worry about it." She turns to walk away with her glass leaving me standing in the kitchen. She stops at the doorway and turns. "Stay away from that woman and her trash kids."

I'm curious, so I look through papers on top of her desk in the kitchen and find a few rehab pamphlets. Wow, I think he actually went to rehab. Maybe there's hope for our family after all. Now if only she could go, too. And if only I could just get out of here and not have to be around them anymore and go live my life with SJ.

NOW

After work, I get to the cabin when I pull in to see SJ's truck already parked. Relieved that he's already home, I look in the mirror to see another truck pull in behind me as I get out. It's Evan, and SJ is in the passenger seat. "Hey, how's it going?" SJ looks like he's passed out in the seat next to him. My heart clenches. "Is he okay?" I ask as I peer in. I've never seen SJ pass out from being drunk before. I only saw him drink a handful of times in high school, and it was usually just a beer here and there at his dad's shop. Seeing SJ in this position worries me because this is not like him at all.

Evan nods grimly. "He will be. He's just really drunk."

"What happened?" I cringe. This isn't like SJ at all. And it brings back memories of seeing my parents drinking constantly. I think that's why he and I never bothered with alcohol much. We saw firsthand with my parents what it feels like to be around a drunk.

"They don't want me to be the coach, Callie," SJ says, obviously drunk.

"Let me get him inside for you, and I'll explain," Evan says, helping SJ out of the truck.

He guides him inside the house, and SJ turns, spinning. "I'm so sorry, baby." SJ slurs his words, his eyes glassy and unfocused as he tries to look me in the eye. "I didn't mean to get this wasted. I just wanted to unwind and take the edge off after a really shhhitty day. God, you're so pretty. How are you mine? What did I ever do to deserve someone as perfect as you? Mine. Mine, mine, mine."

Heat fills me hearing this, but I say nothing but follow

them inside as Evan gets SJ to the couch. We get him settled and step into the kitchen.

Evan turns to face me, running his hand over his beard. "We were at McGuiness having drinks when he just fell apart. He's pretty upset about losing his coaching spot with the kids."

"Is he still not allowed to volunteer?" I ask. "I thought Coach was going to still let him."

"The board is standing their ground and saying no." Evan shakes his head. "That's why he's upset. He loved working with the kids."

"I'm not good enough. I told you," SJ slurs from the couch. "Wasn't back then, and still not now. I can go serve our country and almost die, and I'm still not good enough," he says, sinking farther down on the couch. "I'm dizzy," he mumbles.

"How much did he have to drink?"

"A lot," he says. "He got really upset and just kind of lost it, venting. Honestly, Callie, he needed this. He needed to get all of this off his chest tonight with people who love him in a safe place," he adds.

"Did you find out anything about why the board rejected him?" I ask.

"Your dad," SJ mumbles. "He hates me, always has. That's why he made me leave."

The room is so deadly silent you could hear a pin drop. It's as if my heart has stopped beating, my breath held captive, even the ticking of the clock on the mantel has ceased to make noise. My whole body is still. I haven't even blinked. Evan's gaze falls to my confounded, open-eyed stare, and if I could read his mind, I swear we would be sharing the same thoughts right now. A puzzle piece I've been missing for twelve years has just been found. Sliding into place and completing what was once an incomplete picture. Everything is starting to make sense to me at long last."

"What the hell?" I whisper to Evan. "Made him leave?"

Evans eyes are wide, and he looks at SJ and back at me. "What does he mean by that?" he demands.

"That's what I'd like to know," I whisper.

We're interrupted by SJ's heavy breathing as he's fallen asleep and won't be answering our questions anytime soon. Great.

"I'm sure in the morning when he's sobered up you guys can talk about it," Evan says. "I'd also like to know what he means about your dad making him leave."

"I'll get to the bottom of it," I promise. And I will. Because I'm so mad right now.

"Thanks for bringing him home. I'll keep an eye on him," I promise as I walk Evan out.

"I'll check on him in the morning. It's going to be okay. I'm going to talk to some people and see if we can do something. This isn't over," he says. "I'm sorry, Callie, but your dad has been a piece of shit. Last year, he tried to take my inn from me."

Angry tears prick my eyes, and embarrassment fills me. "I'm so sorry, Evan. I didn't know." Shame fills me for what my father has done to the people I love in our town.

"It's not your fault. But we can't keep letting him run over everyone in our town doing whatever he wants and hurting people. We need to shut him down for good."

"I agree, and I'll do anything to help," I offer grimly.

"I'm glad you're back. He needs you," he says quietly. "See you later."

"Thanks," I say, shutting the door softly behind him.

I take off SJ's shoes and hat and pull a blanket over him as he curls up on the couch. He looks so young like the SJ I remember. Vulnerable. He reaches for me and grabs my hand and whispers as he drifts off, "I love you, Otter."

The next morning, SJ is hungover, and I have a shift to get ready for at the hospital. I wake up to the sun rising out the living room windows. This view is breathtaking. I fell asleep next to SJ after he held my hand and called me Otter. I couldn't leave him.

I take a quick shower and get ready for my shift and smell coffee brewing. At least he's up. I wonder what he meant last night about my dad. What did he do? I'm going to confront him. He can't keep meddling in my life. I gave my parents a chance when I came home, and I tried to have a normal relationship with them. But they have proven once again that they're not capable. I realize that they believe that all the horrible things they've done to us are our fault. They never take accountability for their actions, and they are downright toxic.

I dry my hair and head out to the kitchen to find SJ nursing a mug of coffee, rubbing the bridge of his nose.

"How are you feeling?" I ask.

"Like shit," he says, his voice gravelly.

"Evan is going to help you fight this," I say quietly. "And I'll be talking to my dad."

He holds up his hand. "Don't do it, Callie."

"This town loves you, and these players need you," I remind him. "Also, my dad's a shithead."

That got him to give me a small smile. But he holds me in front of him. "I don't need the coaching position. I can work with my dad. I'll miss the players, but it's not worth you getting involved. You need to let this go. You're risking your position at the hospital, too."

"My dad is a horrible human for everything he's done. What did you mean last night when you said he made you leave before? What did he do?"

He winces. "I don't want to talk about it right now."

"We need to talk about this later," I say calmly. "I love you, and we'll work this out. I have to go to work. I'll see you tonight, and we can talk more." I lean up to kiss his cheek and pull him in for a big hug. We stay like that for a few minutes.

He says nothing as I leave, and it makes me sad. SJ needs to see what we see. The man he is and the man this town needs. And God help anyone who gets in my way of showing him this.

CHAPTER 26

NOW

"We're not giving up, and neither will you." Evan crosses his arms and says to me the next day outside my dad's auto body shop.

"What can we do?" I look over at Evan as he leans up against his truck. I feel terrible about getting so drunk last night and having Callie see that. I never want her to think that I'm like her parents, but I hope it's clear she knows that. We went through it together all those years, the abuse and neglect. It was the first time in a long time that I felt relaxed enough with friends to let my guard down and really have a minute to deal with the bullshit that's been going on with this coaching position. It feels good to have Evan in my corner, advocating for me, as he knows I would do for him.

"I've already met with several other business owners and townspeople who are also sick of Hamilton's shit. We called an emergency board meeting for tonight. Locals will be demanding for the board to explain their reasoning for not hiring you. I think you should come. It'll be hard for them to bullshit anything when you're sitting right there," Evan says, crossing his arms.

"What time?" I ask.

"Six.

"I'll be there." I don't know if this will work, but I'm grateful he has my back again.

"This is going to end. We're done with Hamilton and his bullshit," Evan adds. "This is for you and for what he tried to do to the inn."

I feel like I've spent my whole life fighting. Fighting was my job in the Army, and then I came home and am expected to fight for another job. But it's hard to give up when they're fighting for me. But if it was reversed? I'd fight for them, too. Sometimes I guess we have to fight for what we want even when we're tired because people like Hamilton count on us getting tired and giving up. This time, I'm not giving up or walking away.

I wasn't sure what to expect when I walked into the high school auditorium and slid to the back to take everything in. Evan and about a dozen other business owners who I recognize stand with their arms crossed in front of the board at a long table at the front. The packed auditorium is standing room only. Allie, local attorney Preston, the bookstore owner Paige, and others. All looking like they're angry and staring at the board for answers.

Goldie's eyes light up when she looks back and spots me from across the room and waves. I nod and wave but stay in the back. Trying to blend in is hard when people are there for me, and I feel like the elephant in the room.

"Let's get started," Evan says firmly to the crowd. "I've gathered our community members who have questions about the way the school board has handled the recent hiring decision of SJ Reid. We intend to have a peaceful meeting and get answers with a resolution," he says as he looks across to all the members sitting behind a table. A long table is set up with Hamilton in the middle and the remaining board members sitting on either side of him, all looking like they'd rather be anywhere but here right now. I don't recognize most of them, which is interesting because this means that the decision of whether I got the job was decided by people who don't even know me.

"The board doesn't owe you an explanation, Harper. What you're doing here is uncalled for and a waste of everyone's time," Hamilton interjects. "I don't even know why you think you have the authority to call a meeting in the first place."

"It's not just me. It's the concerned citizens of Freedom Valley who have called this meeting for accountability. Are you going to tell all of us that we have no authority over our town? I have no idea how you've been able to maintain a position on the board after you got fired from the bank last year. You should have been removed from this position last year."

"You are out of line!" Hamilton fires, spitting angrily as he speaks.

Someone slides in next to me, and I look up to see Callie. She smiles and scoots closer to me, reaching over to grab my hand. Her smile is so beautiful that my heart drops at the sight of it. Everyone's eyes shift to us. This is probably wild to all of them, seeing us together and going up against her father.

I look up to see Hamilton staring at us with his eyes narrowed. And as right as I feel with Callie, there's nothing he can do to tear us apart again. I won't let it happen.

Evan continues, "Some people would like to say a few things. And we hope the board listens and considers what they have to say."

I look over, and all the players file in and line up in front of the board wearing their jerseys. My chest gets tighter as I see them arrive. *For me.*

Our QB Matthews steps up and says, "Good evening. The team has showed up in support of Coach Reid because he has showed up for us."

Soft murmurs go through the crowd, and another woman steps up.

"I want to tell everyone what Coach Reid has done for my son," the younger woman says, and the crowd goes quiet. I look over and see one of our players step to her side. My heart warms as he smiles proudly at me.

"My family is new here to Freedom Valley. I'm a single mom working two jobs, and this is my son Charlie's first season playing football. Football has helped him make new friends and fit in at his new school. My son is doing great in school and is happy for the first time in years. Coach Reid has been a big part of his success here, and he's helped him on and off the field by encouraging him and mentoring him. He's been an excellent role model for these players."

"That's nice, ma'am," Hamilton dismisses her with a wave of his hand. "But we require more than that to be a coach here."

"What are you looking for that Coach Reid doesn't have to offer?" Evan asks, crossing his arms and waiting for Hamilton to respond.

"That's none of your business," Hamilton snaps, his voice

rising significantly. "We don't owe explanations for what we decide."

"That's the thing. You do," Evan reminds him. "You are voting as a board member on behalf of our town, and we have a right to know why you think he's not a good fit for the position. Especially if we feel like you have been using your position to manipulate this town for your own benefit."

"You have no proof!" Hamilton says. "I have not done that." He looks nervously at the other board members, who do not look happy right now, and a few are looking at him in dismay.

"I have something to add," another man says, and I recognize him as another player's dad. "I'm Malcom Morrelli's father, also the head of the janitorial staff over at the high school. I have seen Coach Reid volunteer his time for months now in the hope that he will be able to get this position. How many people do you know who would volunteer their time for a job they aren't getting paid for? That level of dedication and support to our kids is impressive. I think he needs to be back paid for his time and awarded the assistant position effective immediately," he demands, turning to look at the crowd for support.

The crowd erupts in applause, and several dozen stand and clap approvingly.

"Now, Mr. Morelli, you are out of line," Hamilton scolds him. "I'm sure you wouldn't want this town to take a good look at your position in the Freedom Valley school district with such insolate behavior here tonight."

"Are you threatening my job, McGraw?" Morelli angrily questions. "Do you all hear this?" he asks the crowd, turning to address the auditorium. "How long are we going to let this man and his cronies bully this town? Who else is sick of this?"

The crowd erupts in applause and chatter of discussion, and a few people cheer.

"Calm down. No one is bullying anyone," Hamilton declares.

"Oh yeah? What do you call it when you threaten people's businesses and livelihoods if they don't do what you want?" someone else calls out.

"We demand your resignation effective immediately!" another man yells, and the auditorium breaks into more applause and cheering.

"This meeting is over," Hamilton announces as he stands.

"No, it's not," an authoritative voice calls out from the front of the room. It's Goldie, and she looks madder than a hornet. "I've sat here and watched you divide this town for decades, Hamilton, and it must stop. When Coach Reid started volunteer coaching this fall, these boys started winning games. Football in Freedom Valley has brought people closer in this community again. And what you've done here to Coach Reid and to others for all these years is unconscionable."

The crowd is silent now, hanging on her every word.

"You're hurting people. I'm moving to disband the board effective immediately and vote for new members to be voted in who care about this town and the people in it and not about boosting their own agendas. Who is with me?" she asks the crowd, and the auditorium erupts in applause again.

She turns and looks at the board. "The town has spoken." More applause and cheering.

Warmth fills me when I look around and realize that they are fighting and cheering on behalf of myself and other people who have been taken advantage of by Hamilton. Freedom Valley is finally feeling like the community I always needed it to be for me.

Goldie addresses the auditorium. "We have some work to do. Who objects to hiring Coach Reid as coach?"

The crowd is quiet, and Hamilton says loudly, "None of you will get away with this. You're out of line, Goldie."

"Mrs. Winters to you. My friends call me Goldie. And you're no friend of mine, Hamilton McGraw." She glares at him over her glasses, then she turns and walks to the back and stands next to me, her arm around me. The crowd erupts in applause, and all eyes turn to Goldie and me.

The applause gets louder. She turns to me and says, "Well, what do you say, Coach? You in?"

I nod and pull her into a hug. "Thanks, Goldie."

"This town needs you. You deserve this."

Hamilton and the rest of the board members gather their things and stand, not looking happy.

Evan raises his hand and says, "Okay, now we start assembling a new board. Who is interested? Let's build a team motivated to make this school the best it can be and look out for our community."

Beth joins him, and he turns to talk to a few other business members at the front. The focus is now on Evan, and I'm grateful because this has been overwhelming.

Callie and I lock hands, and I feel better with her at my side. She goes stiff next to me, and I look to see her parents heading our way.

"Crap on a cracker," she whispers, squeezing my hand harder.

Her parents stop in front of us, and Cheryl glares at Callie. "I hope you're happy, you ungrateful brat. Look what you've done, costing your dad his position."

There are so many things that I want to say. But I know Callie must make hard decisions about her family, and for this to stop, she'll have to handle this. But I'm not leaving her side.

"I love SJ, and I'm happy he'll be the coach. He deserves it. And Dad did that to himself," she says firmly, staring at her mother.

Her mom's hand comes up so fast and slaps Callie across the face, and a hush clears through the crowd as people stop and stare. Callie reaches up and holds her face. My body has gone rigid. I look over at Hamilton, and I see pleasure cross his face as he watched his wife strike his daughter, humiliating her in public. This is when I decide that she's done with them. Forever.

"You will be nothing if you're with him!" Cheryl hisses as she glares at both of us.

"Don't ask me for anything, Callie. You've thrown everything away that we did for you," Hamilton spits out, looking disgusted.

"You never helped me a day in your lives, and I've never asked you for anything. Sam, SJ, the club, and Goldie are my family. They fed me, cared for me, and made sure I was safe and looked after. I put myself through college and med school and became who I am today. All you've done is drink, scheme, and make yourselves miserable with every one of your wicked choices. You willingly hurt people, and that's going to stop. We're done. You're not my family, and you never have been. Stay the hell away from us," Callie says, not backing down. I'm so proud of her.

Cheryl's hand reaches up again, and I grab it midair and hold it firmly. "Touch her again, and I'll lay you out. Right here. I don't care who you are," I grit out.

"You're threatening me?" Cheryl shakes her hand out of mine and slinks back next to Hamilton. An evil look crosses her face and a smirk. "I knew you were trash. Now the rest of this town knows it, too."

"Why, because I won't let you abuse your daughter anymore?" I add, "We all know the truth. You won't be hurting my family anymore. And Callie is my family."

Cheryl and Hamilton glance nervously around them. People have crossed their arms, standing in solidarity next to us, and are glaring at the McGraws. "You don't deserve our last name," Hamilton says to her.

"That's okay, she can have mine," I say calmly.

Cheryl and Hamilton, both red and looking angry, turn and hurry away while glaring back at us.

Callie has tears in her eyes, but she's glued to my side. She's pulling her phone out of her pocket and reading a text, and her face grows serious.

My phone buzzes in my pocket, and I pull it out and click the ignore button. It immediately rings again, and a text message comes up. I look at it, and I freeze with what I see.

Axel: Answer now. Emergency.

I put the phone to my ear. "Axel?"

"Meet me at the hospital!" Axel yells over loud noise and sirens.

"What happened?" I demand.

"Bear and Sam. There was an accident. Meet me at Freedom Valley Memorial."

My heart drops, fearing the worst. Dizziness and nausea

rush through me. "Are they alive?"

"Yes. I'll explain when you get here."

At the same time, Callie says, "They need me back at the hospital."

"I'm on my way," I clip as I slide the phone back into my pocket, then turn and run to my truck.

"It's my dad and Bear," I choke out as we get into my truck.

"I know," she says. "I'll do everything I can, I promise, just get me there." Her fingers fly over her phone as I drive.

We pull up, and I barely remember parking before sprinting across the parking lot as an ambulance pulls away. We run in, and it's chaos. Callie sprints to the back. The waiting room is full of bikers from the club, looking pissed in their black leather vests with their arms crossed as they wait. The front desk lady is doing her best to field their questions, and everyone seems on edge. I scan the room and don't see Axel, so I head down the hall to find even more chaos. I see Callie, and she's yelling out orders completely in her element. She's wearing a yellow paper gown, and she's covered in blood. My stomach seizes. This is not a scene I haven't seen before. After engaging in combat on and off for over a decade, I've lost people and watched a lot of field surgeries. The outcome wasn't usually great. But this time it's at home, and I feel dizzy and sick. This wasn't supposed to happen here. This is home.

Callie doesn't see me. She's in motion and never stops.

She calls out orders calmly and moves from both bays where the curtains are drawn and where I'm assuming they're working on my dad and Bear. I scan the large area for Axel and finally see him in the back corner, his arms crossed, his eyes red, looking worried. He sees me and moves to my side.

"What happened?"

He runs a hand over his face. "The club was on a ride headed north of town when a car tried to pass in a no passing lane and took out Bear and Sam in the front."

"Did they have helmets on?" I ask, pleading that he'll say yes.

He nods. "Yes."

"Where's the driver?" I ask, looking around. Who the hell hits two bikers? I'm livid.

"It was a silver Corvette going way too fast. After the wreck, it took off. They don't know who it was."

I'm so angry I can barely see straight. "What are they saying?" I start pacing back and forth, my hand over my mouth.

"I don't know, but they're both alive. They got them here quickly. Callie's been going back and forth between them."

"What are they doing to find the driver?" I demand.

"I don't know." He looks angry as well but still shaken up.

"This one's going back to surgery!" she commands as she's running next to the gurney through doors. I can't tell who it was. Too many people were in the way working on the patient.

I start shaking and cross my arms, and Axel stands beside me.

"They're tough. They're going to be okay," I say, trying to convince myself.

The nurses come out and throw away their gloves, and Axel peeks behind the curtain. "That's Bear."

So my dad was taken back to surgery. I swallow and go in, and Bear is hooked up to a bunch of machines. His eyes are half open. He looks up at me, and the nurse pokes her head back in. "What are you doing back here?" she asks, looking at Axel and me.

"That's my uncle." I move to stand by him.

"That's my brother," Axel says at the same time, standing next to me.

"Okay, so you're all family, got it," she says dryly, clearly not believing us.

"You can stay back here, but only family," she says as her eyes cut to Axel, and he nods to her, and she leaves.

"Wait!" I call as she turns.

"How's Sam? The other guy." I nod to where they took him back.

"Are you family?" she asks.

"He's my dad."

She purses her lips like she doesn't believe me again, but her face softens. "He's in emergency surgery right now. Dr.

McGraw will update you as soon as she can."

"Will he make it?" I plead with her to say yes with my eyes.

"I don't know. But he's in the best hands possible with her. I'm sorry," she says as she runs to another patient.

I hang my head and pull a chair up to Bear's side. I'm not leaving him.

"I'm here, Bear," I tell him.

"I'm okay, kid," he says gravelly. I pat his arm, relieved to hear his voice.

I look up to see a New Hampshire state patrol officer at the foot of the bed. "Mr. Reid? Can I ask you a few questions?"

I nod as he steps into the room.

"Were you at the scene of the accident? We're trying to figure out what happened, but, uh...the club is not cooperating with information." I'm not surprised. The club hasn't been known to cooperate much with cops. For the past few decades, the club has had a lot of run-ins with dirty cops who have pursued the same agenda as the kind of men we stood up against in the auditorium tonight. They're not going to tell these cops anything, being members of the Eastern Bones. While I'm not an official club member, my loyalty will always be to the club. Bear and Dad are my family. I want this driver found and arrested. Whoever the driver is, they'd better hope the cops get to them before the club or I do. It can't hurt to have all hands on deck looking for this person who left two people badly injured on the side of the road and drove off. I'd like to know what kind of person does that.

"Axel," I call to the other chair where Axel has fallen asleep with his face on his hand. "Yeah," he says quickly, startled awake.

"Tell him what you saw." I jerk my thumb at the state trooper.

Axel looks at the officer, and his eyes narrow slightly. He looks over at me, and I nod to reassure him. He says, "Silver Corvette crossed in a no crossing and hit the first two bikers in the front of the pack. Driver took off."

"This is very helpful. Can you come with me?" he asks.

Axel looks hesitant but looks back at Bear and then follows him out. I can tell he's angry and anxious to find out who did this as well.

Bear, who has been sleeping, opens his eyes. I turn to him and ask quietly. "Did you recognize the car or driver?" I ask Bear, whose eyes are on mine.

"It happened fast, and I didn't see, but only one person in this town owns a silver Stingray," he mutters and drifts off again. Dammit.

I don't know who drives the silver Stingray, but I'll find out.

"Did you say a silver Stingray?" Callie calls from the doorway. Her eyes are wide, and she's staring at me, waiting for an answer.

I ignore her question, focused on my dad. "How's Dad?" She looks exhausted. She's wearing a cloth cap over her hair tied back, her braid tucked into it from surgery.

"He'll be okay," she says, and my chest heaves a sigh of relief.

She puts her hand over mine and one over Bear's. "You scared me to death," she says to Bear.

"Who would have thought that you'd grow up to save my life someday?" he says and coughs as he tries to laugh.

"Someone's got to keep you alive," she jokes with a smile. "I love you, Bear."

"Love you too, Callie."

"Get some rest. I'm going to step out and talk to SJ for a minute," she says as she guides me into the hall.

She turns and looks at me, taking my hands, the same hands that just saved my dad and Bear.

"He had a collapsed lung. We were able to fix it quickly, and he's stabilized now. He'll need time to recover, but he will be okay. He's young and strong."

"When can I see him?"

"He's still recovering. Tonight, I can get you back there," she promises.

I hang my head with worry. I can tell she's trying to be

there for me.

"He'll make a full recovery," she says, pulling me into a hug.

Relief fills me.

"They were both very lucky."

"Thank you."

She squeezes my hand, and we walk back to the middle of the ER.

All of a sudden, the hospital feels freezing, and I'm exhausted. And this is why I left her all those years ago. Because if I hadn't, she wouldn't have become the doctor that she is today and saved my dad and Bear's life.

"Who do you know that drives a silver Corvette?" I ask, remembering our earlier conversation.

Her face darkens, and she leans over and whispers, "Dr. Douchet."

"Is he here?" I grit my teeth. Seething rage, uncontrollable anger surge through my body right now, causing me to pace back and forth, trying to maintain my composure and not barrel through the hospital looking for this piece of shit.

"No. He was on call tonight, and we have tried getting ahold of him all night, and he's not answering," she says. "What are the police saying?"

"I don't know. They're talking to Axel now." I shake my head angrily.

This guy has not only messed with Callie, but he could

have killed my dad and Bear. He's going to pay for this.

CHAPTER 27

~

Callie

THEN

"It's cold out here." Shivering, I pull the heavy plaid blanket around our shoulders as we sit at our lookout spot.

SJ says nothing, and I look over at him. He looks worried and lost in thought. I stare at him for a while, and he looks like he has the weight of the world on his shoulders.

"What are you thinking about?" I slide my hand into his.

He turns and looks at me and smiles, but it looks sad. "You."

"Why do you look so sad?"

"I'm not sad," he says.

"Then what's wrong?" I nudge his shoulder and lay my head on his arm.

"The biggest problem I have right now is that I only have one lifetime, Callie. And that's not nearly long enough time to be with you. You're my forever."

"SJ, I'm not going anywhere," I assure him. *"We'll be together forever."*

NOW

"Where were you?" I demand as I stare at Thad incredulously. This monster just casually waltzed into the ER as if he didn't just try to kill my family. He was on call yesterday and left us hanging when we had multiple traumas. Because we both know where he was.

He glares at me with disdain. "I don't have to answer to you, Callie. I'm the attending here. You're...temporary," he says with a smirk. "*Very* temporary."

"Where were you?" I continue as I follow him, demanding an answer. Because I know where he was. And this time I won't back down. Nobody messes with my family. And by family, I mean SJ, Sam, and the club. All of them.

"Stop talking." He rolls his eyes in annoyance and waves me off with his hand like I'm a fly.

No one is near, so I continue to question him, not even caring about the consequences because I am so angry that I can barely see straight.

"Were you involved in the accident?" I demand. I know I'm crossing the line now by directly accusing him, and there's no going back. My body radiates with anger and defiance. "Where's your car, Thad?"

Spinning, he gets in my face and pushes me up against a wall. "And if I was? What are you going to do about it?" He glares at me, his face inches from mine. "Tell the hospital on me? I don't think so," he says smugly, his pupils dilated. He's high on something. I can see it now. God, why couldn't I have seen it before? How many patients has he treated high? How many times has he driven under the influence? How many people has he almost killed? Bear and Sam could be dead right now because of him.

I don't back down. "The police said a silver Corvette hit two of my patients last night. When the cops find your car, they will compare it with paint chips from Bear and Sam's bikes and easily identify you. You had better hope the police get you before the club does. You might just be safer in jail at this point. You won't get away with this." I glare at him with satisfaction, knowing the hellfire that will rain down on him.

His eyes flare angrily. "Nobody cares about your scooter trash." He squeezes my shoulders roughly, and I wince and turn my head, his face too close to mine. "Plus, they'll never find my car," he whispers.

"Are you high?" I demand, glaring at him, and he squeezes harder.

"What's going on here?" Ramie demands. He releases me, and I slink down, wincing in pain from where he roughly squeezed me.

"Get back to work," he seethes at Ramie, whose eyes are

wide with alarm and anger. "And you." He turns to me and smiles eerily like nothing just happened. "Your days are numbered here." He gives me a big cocky smile before he turns and saunters out of the room, straightening his white coat.

Ramie's on me as soon as he's gone. "Are you okay?"

I shake my head, angry tears in my eyes. "No, I'm not."

"We need to report this, Callie."

"I'll make a few calls," I say as I swipe the angry tears from my eyes. A part of me wants the club to handle this before the police do. Thad may think he has the upper hand here, but he has no idea the pile of shit he's just stepped in. I won't get SJ involved because he just got the coaching position, and I want him to stay out of it. But I know the club will handle this. This is what family does, I remind myself. We take care of our own. And the club is my family, too.

THEN

"It would be a shame for your dad to lose all of this, son," a voice calls from the shop door.

My head snaps over, and I see Callie's dad standing in his pleated khaki pants and buttoned-down shirt glaring at me. He looks surprisingly...sober. He looks tired, older, and beaten down. I don't feel sorry for him. He hurts the person who I love, and that makes me despise him. He destroyed my family.

"You have no right coming here." I shut the hood and wipe the sweat from my forehead, probably smearing grease across it. I'm exhausted. I have work here to finish up for my dad, and I

don't have time for him today—or any other day for that matter.

"You know what needs to be done, kid." He walks around the equipment and runs his hands over the car my dad is restoring for a customer. "This one's a beauty." I don't want him in here touching our stuff. He has a lot of nerve coming here.

I sigh, getting even more frustrated. "Don't touch our stuff." I glare at him. "What do you want?"

"You need to leave town. Leave Callie and go."

I roll my eyes and grab a grease rag and a few tools to put away. "Whatever," I mumble. "You think you can just run everyone off, Hamilton? Like your daughter?"

"My daughter is going to college. Without you," he says flatly.

I shut the hood of the car. "No, your other daughter," I say as the color drains from his face.

"We had a deal. She was supposed to keep quiet."

I glare and shake my head at him. "You're a piece of work."

"I will destroy her," he says flatly. "Just like I did your mother and sister. I won't stop, and I'll make everything worse for everyone you care about if you don't leave. I'll start with Callie, and I'll cut her off. She'll have nothing. Be nothing. All because of you. Is that what you want? You want to see Callie fail and not become a doctor? It'll be your fault, you know."

Anger fills me to almost a boiling point as I glare at him. "My dad has been more of a dad to her than you have. And the fact that he still cares about your daughter after what you did to him and our family shows the kind of man he is versus what you are.

You don't deserve Callie."

His face reddens and he glares at me. "I will make sure she fails if you don't leave. I will ruin her. Then I will ruin your dad. I won't stop until I destroy everything you love and care about. Are you ready for this fight? Because it will only end with everything you love destroyed."

I stare at him in disbelief. "You would destroy your own daughter just to spite me?"

"I did it once already with your mother." He shrugs. "You have no idea what I would do to make sure she doesn't end up with you," he says with a smile that makes my stomach curdle.

Jesus. I hate him even more.

"I will ruin this shop," he continues. "Your dad will have nothing by the time I'm done. Everything he's built here will be gone. Then I'll go after the club. I'll ruin every single member of the Eastern Bones. I'll destroy their jobs. I'll get all the cops that I have in my back pocket to put every single one of them in prison for a long time, starting with your piece of trash dad. You want that on your conscience? You really want this war on your hands? Because it will be all your fault. I will destroy everyone. I'll enjoy it, too."

"Get out. Get away from me."

I'm shaking because I'm so angry right now. I hate this man with every fiber of my being. He's the reason I don't have a mom or a sister. He's the reason that Callie has struggled. I just want her to get away from them.

"I'm never going away. I won't stop. Ever. You remember that. But if you leave, I won't hurt Callie. She'll become a doctor," he says coldly as he leaves, not looking back.

I sit on the rolling stool and place my face in my hands. I'm so tired. Tired of fighting to belong. I just want it all to go away. I want Callie to be safe and to get out of here. If I keep her from going off to school, what kind of person does that make me? I'm selfish if I don't do what he says, and she can't go to school. She's worked so hard for this and prepared for this for as long as I've known her. I just want her to be happy, no matter what. And maybe that's not with me. Maybe I'm in the way.

I know my dad would fight him back. But would he win? Would it be worth it? My dad doesn't deserve any of this. Neither does the club. If I leave, then they will all be safe. I'm the problem here. I'm the one who should just go, then they will all be safe.

I love Callie so much. Too much. Enough to let her go so that she can pursue her dreams. I would never want to hold her back. I've always known that Callie is probably too good for me. And she's too good for her shitty family. If I leave her, I know Mrs. Winters will watch over her.

I know what I need to do will hurt a lot of people. But I have to do it.

NOW

I knock softly on the door. My dad stirs in his hospital bed, and his eyes flicker open. He tries to sit up, pain washing over his face, but he's tangled with the wires and occasionally there are a few chirps from the machine monitoring his vitals. My heart drops seeing my usually healthy dad in this state.

"Don't sit up." I pull a chair close to his bed and lean forward.

"Don't give me that look," he grunts. "I'm fine."

"Fine is not the word that I would use to describe you right now, but I'm relieved to hear that you'll be okay."

"Callie fixed us both up." He coughs and winces.

I nod my head, relieved. "Do you know who the driver was?"

He grimaces in pain and nods. "Yes."

"You're sure?"

"That doctor here at the hospital. The one Callie knows."

I close my eyes, relieved at the confirmation. This guy is screwed.

"Yes, but I'm not sure they'll do anything. That guy has connections and deep pockets around town. Police asked us a bunch of questions; we'll see what they do."

"Is the club going to handle it?"

He just gives me a look, and his mouth turns up. "You

don't have to worry about club business. We'll be back on our bikes by next week." Dad never discusses the club with me. He knows I'm not really interested in being a part of it. But I hear things around the shop. I know that they handle things around town when they're needed. And it's not usually above board. But the club is who you call when you need things handled.

I grimace at that. "No, you won't, but nice try. Callie says you need several weeks to heal."

"We'll see. How are you and Doc doing?" he asks, obviously trying to change the subject.

"We're good. Just worried about you."

"She finally scrape off her parents?"

"No," I say.

His eyes darken. "You want your girl? Don't let anyone get in the way again."

I nod. "I'm not."

"She never had a father. A girl who's never had a father's love and affection has a harder time feeling what it's like to be loved by a good man. That's why you have to continually show her. Just always be there for her. Callie's a special girl."

"Where did you get all this wisdom?" I grunt in affection.

"I'm your dad. It's my job to be wise," he jokes.

I look away and blink to keep it together. My dad is all I've had all these years. He's too young for me to lose him. I need him and moments like these.

"It's going to be alright." He assures me, "I'll be busting out of this joint soon."

I stand and say," I'll be back, Dad." I need a minute before I completely lose it and take out Dr. Douche for putting my dad in this hospital bed in the first place.

I've already decided how I'm going to take care of Dr. Douche. I pause outside of my dad's door with two cups of coffee when I hear voices and stand to wait, not meaning to listen, but I can't help it.

"I don't know what I'd do if anything happened to you," Callie says quietly. "You've been more like a dad to me than my own dad, and I've never forgotten that."

"I suppose I owe you now for saving my ass," my dad jokes.

"Don't you dare scare me like that ever again," she warns, but her voice is soft.

"I'll see what I can do." He winces. "When can I get back on my bike?"

Her tone changes, and she gives him shit, "Well, let's see, Sam. You and I got in a knife fight. And I won. Because you were sleeping through the whole thing. It will be a while before you're back on your bike. But I have no doubt you'll be back to your old self before you know it as long as you give yourself plenty of time to rest," she says.

"You always were a funny kid," he says gruffly.

"I'll check back in on you later," she says as she hits the door and practically runs into me.

I hold out a cup of coffee, and she takes it with a grateful smile. "Thanks."

She leans in to kiss my cheek. "How are you doing?" she asks, her eyes on mine, softening.

"Better now," I say as I kiss her softly.

She kisses me and then looks around and back at me. "I know it was Thad. He pretty much admitted to it."

I nod. "Dad identified him, too."

"I confronted him."

"What? Callie!" I pull her down the hall and duck into a supply closet and pull it closed behind us so no one can hear us. "Why would you do that? Alone? This motherfucker is dangerous."

She winces where my hands hold her, and I gently pull back her scrub top and see red marks turning to purple bruises. "This is what he did to me."

"Where is he right now?" I take a few deep breaths, trying to compose myself. I'm almost past the point of feeling livid and entering murderous. Thad marked my woman in violence. My jaw is clenched, my entire body riddled with tension. My fist clenches so hard, and I'm rethinking of just exactly how I'm going to handle him now.

"I called Axel. He says the club is handling it." She shrugs. "I didn't want to bother you. I also don't want you doing anything that will jeopardize your coaching position."

I stare at the ceiling in frustration. Jesus. "He put his

hands on you. And you called *Axel*? Not me?"

She tilts her head. "I thought about calling the cops. I want to trust the cops in this town, but let's be honest. Thad probably golfs with them, not to mention my dad. I figured the club should have first dibs."

"Callie." I let out a deep breath in frustration.

"What?" She shrugs.

"Be careful, okay? The club isn't anything to mess around with. You have to stay out of the club stuff." I set my cup down and look at her and shake my head. "Stay away from this guy."

She nods. "Oh, I know what I did. You think I wasn't raised around the club just like you were? I'm sick and tired of people bullying and manipulating this town. It stops now. And if the club has to make an example out of my dad and Thad, then so be it. It's time we take it back."

"I am over it, too, believe me. But you have to know that when you put the club on something, it won't be handled above board."

"I don't care how it gets handled." She tilts her chin up in defiance. Her face is so innocent and beautiful yet so determined.

"Callie." I exhale a deep breath and stare up at the ceiling. "Stay away from club business." She may not see it, but I'm trying to protect her. Plus, I've already got plans for Dr. Douche.

"Okay," she says, wrapping her arms around my neck and pulling me close to kiss me, her lips soft and sweet on mine. And this is exactly why I don't want her near the club when they handle club business. She needs to stay sweet. Let the club take out the trash. That's what they've done for decades here in this town. Not many people realize how much the club does to look out for people. They don't need to be on anyone's radar or for this town to see what they do. Hamilton McGraw had a pass for a long time, I think from my dad protecting Callie, but now his pass has expired, and I think the club will be handling him, too.

"Dinner later? I can pick up something." She lays her hand on my chest.

Relieved that she's changed the subject, I let out a deep breath. Despite her frustrating me, I love that we get to do life together now. Everyday stuff. She's mine, and nothing will get in the way.

"That would be good. I mean it, though. Stay out of it. Promise me."

She nods. "Okay, fine."

"I love you, Callie."

"Love you, too," she says, kissing me. "I better get back to work and finish up so I can come home."

Home. I love hearing her call our place that.

It's dark, and I'm at home with Harley on the porch. I hear a car and a door slam and look over, and it's Callie. I stand and make my way to her, wrapping my arms around her, pulling her close until her breasts press into my chest, her hair tickling my cheek. "How was the rest of your shift?"

"I might not have a job anymore," she murmurs as her arms band around me, holding me tight.

"What happened?" I pull her over to the outdoor sectional, the shadow from the fire in the firepit flickering across her face.

"I'm going to apply at a few other local hospitals. I just don't think it will work out here at Freedom Valley Memorial," she says with frustration and sadness.

"Why?"

"There's just so much drama with Thad and my parents at the hospital. I got called into HR today to talk about everything. That doesn't make for a good impression for getting the contract to work full time."

"Then they don't deserve you." I shake my head. "There are other hospitals where you can work."

"I know. I'm officially not in contact with my parents anymore. I can't do this anymore." I search her face as she says this, and she's calm.

"Are you sure that's what you really want?"

"Yes," she says firmly. "It's done."

"Okay."

"Okay?" She searches my face.

"We're family, Callie. I'll support you in whatever you want to do."

Her face softens. "Okay."

"Just a warning, though. Nobody messes with my family." I run my fingers down her braid. "Do we need to file a complaint with the hospital? What do you want me to do to make sure your parents stay away from you?"

"I've already filed two complaints with HR about Thad and a police report. It's his word against mine, and he's been there for a long time. Ramie saw him assault me, so that helps."

My jaw tightens with the reminder of him putting his hands on her.

"You're a great doctor, Callie. They see what kind of person he is. Plus, after they realize he was the driver who hit Bear and Sam, I doubt he'll have a job there much longer, anyway."

"It'll be hard to prove. He has friends at the hospital and the town chief of police. Plus, no one can locate the car."

"He'll be handled, Callie. This is my dad and Bear. And I can't have him putting his hands on you. It's not safe for you to work there until he's gone."

"I know," she says softly, laying her head on my shoulder. She breathes in deeply.

"Did you just smell me?" I tease.

"Yeah," she sighs. "You smell good."

"What do I smell like?"

"Like home."

I smile and pull her in closer to me. "Welcome home."

CHAPTER 29

Callie

THEN

"Home is not where you were born;
home is where all your attempts to escape cease."
Naguib Mahfouz

"One more week until graduation!" I say excitedly to SJ.

He smiles at me, but his smile doesn't reach his eyes. I've been really worried about him. He's been distant for the past week. I know it's probably just graduation stress.

"Hey, what are we doing for the summer? We should start looking for a place together right away in the city," I tell him as we walk down the school hall together, holding hands. "I don't want all the good places taken." I turn eighteen next month, and I can't wait to get out of here and live on our own far from my parents. SJ and I will finally be free.

"We'll figure it all out." He shrugs but doesn't look at me when he says it.

"Hey, are you okay?" I search his eyes, worried.

"Yeah, I'm fine," he assures me. "Think you'll be able to come to Evan's party this Friday out at the inn?"

"Definitely. Wouldn't miss it." Richard and Margie have a huge going away party planned for Evan. "It's going to be a good time," I say as we reach the end of the hall where our classes are across from each other.

"I'll see you later," he calls over his shoulder as he heads to his class.

"Bye!" I call after him, watching him go. I still can't shake the feeling that something is off with him.

He has his arm around me and doesn't venture far from me the whole night. He leans in and kisses me on the cheek when we're swinging in one of the hammock chairs, chatting with friends.

"You two are the perfect couple," Allie calls from across the firepit. "And you're both going off to college together. That's so sweet."

I smile at Evan's sister Allie, who is a few years behind us.

I've always liked her.

"Sweet isn't the word to describe it." I laugh. "It's relief. My parents have made our lives a living hell. We'll finally be free and starting our new life in college."

"I'm so excited for you guys." She hands me a red Solo cup with lemonade. "You're like legit high school sweethearts."

I look over and lean my head on SJ's chest. "Yeah, we are."

I squeeze his hand, and he squeezes back, but he's looking off into the distance.

"We have a future doctor in the crowd. What's everyone else doing to conquer the world?" Evan asks the group, strumming his guitar next to the firepit.

"You excited to be a badass Marine?" SJ asks Evan.

"Hell yeah! I ship out in eight days," Evan says. "I'm going to see the world before I come back to run the inn with my dad."

"Are you worried about him going off to the Marines?" I ask Allie as I nod to Evan, chatting with SJ.

She shrugs. "Mom is. She worries about everything, though. But there's no changing Evan's mind. He's wanted to be a Marine for as long as I can remember."

SJ leans into me and pulls me closer and whispers, "Want to head out?"

"Yeah." I wave to the group. "We're almost to the finish line, guys," I say to the group as we say our goodbyes. "See you guys at graduation!"

We stop at our lookout spot on the way home and make

out for a while. I'm so excited for this next chapter with SJ. We're going to make so many memories together on our new adventure. And no one will get in our way.

"I love you," I whisper to him.

"I love you more," he whispers back. But something is off.

NOW

A cold nose pushes me in the face, waking me up by nudging me continuously. I open my eyes to Harley, trying to get my attention. I sit up, and SJ tenses up next to me, and I reach for him. He's having a nightmare, and his body is rigid and stiff next to me. He calls out something I can't understand and sits up straight, breathing heavy. Harley runs to his side of the bed and climbs up at his feet, nudging him, doing what she's been trained to do. Get help when SJ needs help. My heart clenches. "Good girl, Harley."

"Hey, it's okay." I reach for him, and his arms protectively pull me into him. He's panting, shaking, and sweating.

"It's okay," I whisper, reaching over to turn on the lamp.

His chest heaves as he looks around wildly and swallows. Sweat runs down his face, and he scrubs his hand over his face as he looks around and sighs.

"I'm here," I call softly. Harley has jumped on the bed and lain across his outstretched legs.

He nods and looks over at me nervously. "I'm sorry."

I put my arms around him. "Nothing to be sorry for."

"I'm sorry I woke you up, and you have to work tomorrow," he says, throwing his legs over the side of the bed. Harley follows him and stares up at him.

"Where are you going?" I ask.

"To the couch. Just go back to sleep." He scrubs a hand over his face.

I stand and gather my pillow and a blanket and follow him.

"What are you doing?" He stops in the doorway and looks back at me.

"I go where you go. You sleep where I sleep now, SJ. Deal with it."

He looks up at the ceiling and back at me. "Fine, let's go back to bed," he says reluctantly.

We crawl back into bed, and he puts his arms around me, but I can tell he's still wound up. "I love you."

"I love you more," he whispers into my hair as his hand goes down to stroke Harley, who lies protectively at the foot of the bed.

"If you have a nightmare, we have a nightmare," I say. "We do this together."

"You don't deserve my bullshit, Callie."

"Well, I'm pretty sure I have my own truckload of bullshit I bring to the table, too. It comes in the form of manipulative parents and an ex-colleague who tried to kill your family.

You didn't ask for that either, now did you?" I remind him. "We all have stuff. And it's all heavy and hard. We do hard together."

"I wish I could go back in time and not leave you," he says softly. "I think about what I did almost every day."

"We can't go back and change the past," I whisper, looking into his eyes. "But we can change the future. We finally get to be together."

He nods, but I can tell something is on his mind. "What?" I ask.

He swallows. "I have my PTSD. It's a lot to make work," he admits. "What if we can't make it work?"

"Have you ever noticed that most of our current issues are my parents?" I ask. "Now that I've cut them out, things will get better for us. My dad won't be asking me for money all the time, threatening us, or messing up our jobs. I won't have to see them, and they'll have no place in our lives."

"They ask you for money?" he asks, confused. "Why?"

"I think they've always lived above their means and tried to keep up with everyone at the club. It's catching up to them. They've always looked at me as their investment. I guess they want to cash in now."

"Absolutely not. That's not right. Just because they paid for your college doesn't mean you owe them," he says. "You're not an investment. Jesus, Callie."

I laugh and shake my head. "They never paid for my

college. I have massive student loans. But he likes to tell everyone he put me through school. When, in reality, they never paid a dime for anything. In fact, he even asked if he could borrow money from me when I worked part time in school."

His jaw drops in disbelief. "He never helped you?"

"Not a penny. Never came to New York to visit me or attend either of my graduations. Goldie was there along with your dad." I shrug.

I open and close my mouth. I don't even know what to say. Unbelievable.

"Yeah, I'm telling you, it's all a facade." I shrug. "I have the people who mean the most to me in my life."

"How can I help?" he asks as he leans on his elbow.

"We could go somewhere else and start over fresh. Somewhere where no one knows us," I suggest. "Maybe it would be good for both of us."

He looks at me and shakes his head. "I don't want to leave. My dad and Goldie are here. We can make a good life here together."

I nod, relieved. "I don't really want to leave either. But sometimes running away sounds good."

"No running." He brings my hand to his mouth and kisses my wrist down my arm. He turns and covers my body and kisses me by my ear, and I melt into the bed and into him.

"SJ..." I whimper.

"I'm going to show you that I'm never leaving you again," he whispers into my ear, and I sigh with relief.

He kisses down my neck, and my shirt is up and over my head before I can even move.

I pull him closer and trace my fingers over the muscles of his back and kiss him deeper.

This man and I have a past, and now we have a present. But can we get past what's trying to keep us from having a future?

CHAPTER 30

THEN

I know what I need to do, and it's destroying me. I can't eat or sleep. I lie awake at night thinking about whether I can live with myself if Callie doesn't become the one thing she's ever dreamed of, and it's killing me. I just worry constantly whether I'm doing the right thing, but I know I have to do something. I will crush my own heart if it means saving the girl I love. The part that Hamilton said that stuck with me was that Callie won't be able to chase her dreams with me dragging her down. Hamilton's not wrong in that. What am I going to do, go to college with her and get in her way? College isn't for me right now. At least not the

college where she's going. And I don't want to live in New York City. But damn if breaking her heart isn't going to crush us.

I park and look up at the recruiting office. I had a long talk with Evan about the Marines, and I'm going to do it. If I can get out of the way and let Callie become who she is supposed to be, maybe she can forgive me someday. But I can't live with myself if I hold her back from her dreams. She already has her parents on her back enough. She doesn't need me weighing her down. I know that if I stay in Freedom Valley, she might stay too. I need her to go and be free.

"Are you coming in to talk to someone?" asks a guy in uniform with a coffee cup in his hand, holding the door.

"Yeah, the Marines," I say as I step inside a long hallway with offices of all the branches of the military displayed above the doors. I look at his uniform, and it says U.S. Army.

He looks me over and grins. "Come with me."

"I don't know…" I glance over at the Marines door.

"The Marines don't have what you need. I'll take care of you." He nods confidently to the Army office.

"I guess we could talk." I shrug. I'm nervous, but I am curious about what he has to say.

He hands me a cold bottle of water from a small drink fridge. "Alright, let's talk. Why do you want to join the military?"

"My buddy just joined up, so I was thinking I could, too," I say, realizing it probably sounds dumb.

"Let's get some information and get you in for the test to see

*where you're at. Can you take it today?" He turns his wrist over
to glance at his watch.*

I nod. "I guess. What's better about the Army?"

*"Bonuses. I can get you a sign-on bonus and, depending
upon your test score, your choice of jobs."*

*"That would be good. How soon could I leave for basic
training?" I ask.*

"A week if I had to guess?" he offers. "Is that too soon?"

"That'll work, actually."

NOW

We just had a little private meeting with Dr. Douche. I wish
I could be a fly on the wall when the cops arrive. In fact, in
about ten minutes, the cops will be in the driveway of his
gated community where his wrecked car sits in his garage
with the doors wide open. His confession is written out and
is on his kitchen counter signed, and he's still tied up in his
kitchen chair waiting for the cops. We also found all of his
drugs and laid them out for the cops to see, too. I would be
lying if I said I didn't enjoy taking this asshole down. But it's
done, and he's handled. A copy of that confession along with
a video of him confessing has already been anonymously
emailed to the hospital human resources director as well
as the local news stations. He knows that if he talks about
anything that went down tonight, the club is coming for him

next. And judging by the way he was scared, he won't be talking.

"Give it a week. This house will be on the market, and he'll be relocating," Evan hedges as we walk through the woods, almost to where we parked my truck on the other side of Dr. Douche's property. "Or the club will help relocate him," I say with a grin.

"Real ballsy of him to store that car in his garage," Ty says as he vaults over the fence.

"Who was he going to call for a tow? Not the guy he tried to kill." I roll my eyes.

"Thanks for your help, guys," I call as we all slide into my truck.

"Anytime." Evan grins.

Ty holds out a bag, and we all dump our gloves in it. "Piece of cake."

"If anyone asks, we were all at Logan's working out in his barn," Ty says as he slides in the back of the truck.

"It was a good workout." I shrug.

"It was," Evan confirms, cracking his neck and smiling.

I don't want to be the bad guy this town has tried to make me out to be, but I also won't sit back and let the people I love get hurt. That's why I dealt with that piece of shit Dr. Douche. I'm not the scared kid who left Freedom Valley years ago. I protect what's mine, and Callie's mine. And God help anyone who gets in the way of that.

I didn't like Callie seeing me after I had a nightmare the other night. I've done a good job to power through and not let anyone see me struggle. That's part of why I moved out here to the land and cabin. I needed to heal in peace. Having her here with me has been good, but I don't like her seeing me at my worst. It's hard to let people in.

When Callie told me that Hamilton didn't even help her with school, I was livid. That was what he threatened me with, and he didn't even end up helping her. She did it on her own, and I hate myself for this right now. I'm questioning every decision I made. Why was I so afraid of him? Why did I leave? I know I did the best I could back then, and it will all work out. I will make damn sure of it.

And I need to have a conversation with Callie. But the truth is, I'm ashamed, and I deeply regret leaving her now. She has every right to be angry with me. I was worried that if she knew about her dad, it would drive an even deeper wedge between them. And now? I don't care. They're done.

But deep down, I know I became the man I am now because of the Army. And she became the doctor she was meant to be. We were two scared kids who figured it out.

"Tell me something, SJ. What happened in the Army?" she asks softly as we sit on the outdoor swing on the deck covered in blankets in front of the firepit.

"What do you want to know?" I ask as I pull her legs over my lap and tuck the blanket tighter around her. These are the questions I dread her asking, but I know we need to have this talk.

"Well, why the Army?" she asks, the light of the fire dancing on her face.

"They offered me a better deal than the Marines," I admit. It's the truth. But the Army ended up being my home for over a decade, and I have no regrets.

"How many times were you deployed?" she asks curiously.

"Half a dozen," I say, swallowing. I wondered all of those times if I'd be coming back to her and whether we'd ever find our way to this spot together again. Sometimes the dream of being here in this place with her is what got me through.

"Why did you run away?" she asks softly, her face full of compassion instead of anger now when we talk about it.

"I left so you could focus and not have me in the way. I wish I could go back and write the past differently, but I can't. I let a bunch of what-ifs get into my head back then."

Her face softens. "I want to know everything, SJ. The good, the bad, and the ugly. All of it."

I nod. And I'll give that to her.

"It was good, and it was bad. I made lifelong friends. I saw some good things and some bad things. The Army made me strong and tough. It healed me from my past with my mom leaving me. I worked out a lot of things while I was gone. But it also broke me in ways that I probably can never be fixed. When I came back, I was bad for a while. I stayed up in the loft of the shop and didn't come down. I worked nights so I didn't have to face anyone. Evan helped me get sorted out, and coaching has helped me and given me a purpose. At first, it was a reason to get up every day. People needed me and relied on me. It felt good to be needed."

Her face softens as she listens to me. "Why didn't you want to go to college? I still think we could have gotten through anything together. I would have supported you if I'd have known you wanted to join the military."

"I did go to college and got my degree in education when I was in. I almost completed my master's, but I got injured and ended up getting out early before I could finish. We still did what we needed to do, Cal," I say softly, cupping her face. "Everything is working out."

"What injury?"

"My shoulder. I had surgery on it." I shrug. "I can't be on active duty anymore."

"How are you doing now with the PTSD?" she asks, looking into my eyes without judgment, only compassion and love.

"A lot better but I'll always be working on it," I answer honestly. Relief fills me when I think about how far I've come and worked for this moment. I'll never take being mentally and physically healthy for granted. Health is a gift.

"How can I help you?" she asks, her blue eyes looking into mine like she's trying to read me.

"You're helping me by being with me," I admit. And she is. Just having her here with me is like the missing puzzle piece I've been looking for all this time.

"I'm mad. We should have been together. We lost twelve years," she says, shaking her head.

"I know. And we're not losing anymore. Not another single day." I'm going to make sure of it. She's mine, and I'm not making sure a day goes by that she doesn't feel my life and support.

"I wish things had been different," she whispers.

I pull her to me. "We did the best we could. We were kids. But you're mine now," I murmur.

"There was never a time when I wasn't really yours, SJ. You've always had my whole heart."

CHAPTER 31

Callie

THEN

"Go out with that boy, and there will be consequences. For both of you," he threatens.

"What is that supposed to mean?" I ask. Why is he threatening SJ?

"It means you're not going out with him. You need to focus on school, young lady."

I roll my eyes. So it's going to be like this. It's summer now. I don't start school for months.

"Okay," I call out.

But it's not okay. I look for my suitcases. I'll just pack my *stuff and move out. I'm eighteen in a few days. What can they do to stop me?*

I call SJ, and it goes straight to voicemail. Weird.

I text him.

Me: Hey, things are imploding here. Can I come stay?

Waiting for him to respond, I pack up as much as I can and check my phone. No response. My parents have gone out for the night. I load up all my bags and drive to the shop. Hopefully, I can stay there until we figure things out.

I frown when I pull into the shop, and SJ's truck is parked out front. He must have been busy working and couldn't respond to my texts.

I head into the open bay, where rock music is playing softly. I scan and don't see him, but Sam stands and straightens and heads toward me. He has a grim look on his face.

"Hey, where's SJ?" I look around for him.

"He's gone, Callie," Sam says, looking uncomfortable.

I look over, and the tow truck is here, so he's not out on a tow. "Where is he?"

Sam turns and places a hand on my shoulder and says softer than I've ever heard him speak, "He's not coming back."

"What do you mean? Where'd he go?" I ask, confused. My heart is seizing in my chest, and it feels really hot in here. "What happened? Is he okay?" It's taking me a moment to realize what Sam is saying.

"He joined the Army and left for training."

I swallow, and time stops. I feel woozy. I see Sam but not very well because hot tears blind me.

"Why? He didn't say anything..." Utter disbelief and devastation fill me with what he's saying.

Sam nods. "He didn't tell me either until right before he left."

"Why?" I ask again, this time in a more demanding tone.

He shakes his head. "I didn't understand it either."

Sam looks at my bags, then back at me. "Are you going somewhere?"

Agony fills me when I realize I have nowhere to go, and no one to turn to. He's gone.

"I was going to ask to stay here. Things aren't good at home." I break out in a sob, realizing how stupid I sound right now.

"Come here." He pulls me to his coveralls, and I shake with sobs as I put my arms around him.

"I'm sorry..." I choke back another sob. "I better go."

"You're not going anywhere. Come on." He walks me to the stairs. "You can stay here. It'll be okay."

"Why did he leave me?"

He sighs and shrugs, looking defeated.

"Where's Evan? Does he know?" I wish this was a joke and they were all pranking me, but I know deep down that they're not.

"Evan shipped out this week, too."

My heart shatters. Maybe he'll realize he made a mistake,

and he'll come back for me. I'll just stick to the plan, and he'll come back, I reason.

"If I go to New York early, can I stay here until Goldie can take me?" I swipe my eyes with the back of my hand.

He nods. "We'll figure it out. I'll help you."

Maybe he'll call. He'll explain everything, and it'll all be a big misunderstanding. "Did he leave a note or anything for me?" I ask, as I continue to try to understand.

Sam just shakes his head.

This can't be happening. We had plans. We were going away together. He never said anything about joining the Army. This feels like a terrible joke.

NOW

"What's wrong?" I ask as I take the steps two at a time, wondering why Callie is at her cottage and not at our house, where she belongs.

Goldie waits for me on her porch. Her arms are across her chest, and she looks upset. She shakes her head, her bright eyes red and filling with tears. "I'm glad you're here. Callie's being ridiculous."

"What do you mean?" I ask, handing one of the bouquets I'm carrying to Goldie.

Her eyes soften as she reaches out to lay a hand on my

arm. "Thanks for the flowers. She got really upset today and thinks she needs to slow things down with you. She says she's the cause of Bear and Sam getting hurt and her dad keeping you from coaching."

I turn and find Callie sitting on the porch chair, looking upset, her face in her hands as if she's been crying.

"What's going on?" My mind processes things quickly, but I want to know all the facts before reacting.

"I feel like you were doing really good before I came back." She shakes her head. "And then because of the people of my family and Thad, you almost lost everything. Your dad and Bear," she whispers. "I don't know what I'd do if we lost them. I know it's not directly my fault, but by association, you seem to be almost losing everything that means the most to you, and that's not fair."

My eyes narrow and I say, "What are you talking about?"

She looks away, not answering.

"Callie, talk to me. Now." My heart races. We've come too far for this, and we won't let this town break us apart again.

"My family destroys everything that I love and hold near and dear to me. I can't put you all at risk anymore. Maybe we should slow it down." I know she doesn't mean this. She won't even look at me.

"No," I clip.

"Who is going to get hurt next?" She tries to reason, but there's no conviction in her voice, and she's wavering.

"No one." I cross my arms and stare at her. I'm not accepting this.

She shakes her head, still unable to look at me.

"What do you want, Callie?" I question, trying to get her to look at me.

She gazes off into the yard and whispers, "I want you to go."

I stare at her. This is not the Callie I've spent every moment with in the past few weeks. She's scared. She's cutting me off before something happens to us again. She's coming from a place of hurt. "What do you want, Callie?" I ask again, one more time.

She looks at me, tears in her eyes, and I can feel it. She doesn't want this. She's had a lot happen in the past week. More than most people could handle. And she's scared.

"Okay, Callie," I whisper, placing the flowers down on the chair and turning and walking back to her cottage. I open the door, and she follows me.

"What are you doing?" she asks, confused.

"I'm packing your shit. You're coming home." I turn and start opening the closets, looking for a bag.

Pushing by Callie, Goldie opens the hall closet and rolls a suitcase over to me. "Thanks," I say cheerfully, unzipping it and setting it on the bed.

"Goldie!" she huffs.

Goldie shrugs. "Just helping."

"You're not helping." Callie sighs, but I can see hope in her eyes for the first time. She wants to come home. She *needs* to be home. And home is with me.

Goldie helps me stuff clothes into the suitcase. "You're evicted, honey. You better go with him." She winks.

Callie has her arms folded over her chest, watching us. "You're not going to stop, are you?"

"Nope," I say as I grab an empty shopping bag on the counter. I head into her bathroom and begin dumping what's left of her hygiene products in it. I know she has stuff at my house, too. But we'll just make this move official and bring as much as we can.

"Fine, stop. I'll go. You two are ridiculous, you know?" she says, exasperated.

Goldie grins at me and pats my back as she turns to head out.

I walk over to her and pull her to me. "You don't get it, do you?"

She says nothing but lays her head on my forehead. "I'm just tired of us having to always fight to be together."

"Otters stay together. We fight together."

"I don't want anyone else getting hurt. If we were meant to be together, then why does everything stand in our way?"

"It won't always be this way, Callie. We're going to be okay. We're going to make it."

"I don't want anyone else to get hurt."

"You didn't hurt Bear and Sam. Dr. Douche did."

Her mouth quirks up at me calling him that.

"You said we do all of the hard stuff together. Remember?"

She nods.

"Look at me." I tip her chin up, and her blue eyes fall on mine.

"Let's go home. Harley's waiting in the truck."

"Okay," she whispers.

Callie

THEN

"It won't be so bad. I mean, one bathroom and six girls. You can make a schedule, right?" Goldie asks as she cuts into her waffle, trying to be positive and cheer me up. It turns out that New York City is the city that never sleeps. We can go out for waffles at midnight after catching a show. Goldie took vacation time to drive me down to the city. In just two weeks, she helped me find a room to rent in an apartment that I split with several other girls and a job at the local hospital as a nurse tech. I start my training classes for that on Monday. It'll be a great job while I'm in school. Things are working out, but this isn't *how I thought college life would go. It's damn near killing me not having SJ here with me living the life that we planned out together. But now that I'm here in New York City, I'm trying to picture SJ here, too, and I can't see it. Was he just supporting me all along? What did he really want? How did I not see this? I want to find him, fix things, and go somewhere else. Anything to have him back with me.*

It feels like SJ is a ghost now who never really existed. And now that I'm in a new place, I can't feel him anymore. He's not here and never will be.

But Goldie has helped me see that I'm not alone.

I shrug. "It'll be fine. I'll probably be so busy with school and my job that I won't be there much anyway."

"Hey, look at me," she says.

She tilts her head and smiles at me. "You can do this."

I nod but look away and blink back a few tears at her kindness.

"I heard from him," she says softly, cutting another piece of her waffle.

I shake my head. "I don't want to know." I'll just get mad because I haven't heard from him. He hasn't bothered to reach out to me.

She sits back and studies me. "Okay."

I look out the window over the city skyline and think about what it would have been like if he was here eating waffles with us.

"Have you heard from your parents at all?" she asks.

"No." I shake my head.

"I'll help you with anything you need. When school starts next month, you'll do great. And on your school breaks, you can come home and stay with me, or I'll come back down," she says happily. "Oh, we'll have so much fun!"

"Thank you for helping me, Goldie," I whisper.

"You're welcome, honey. Now, eat your waffle. I don't want to worry about you being hungry when I go home."

"You don't have to worry about me, Goldie."

"I'll always worry about you."

NOW

My parents made me feel like I always had to do everything on my own. SJ makes me feel like I can do anything by myself, but he won't let me. Whenever I try to return to my independent ways, he reminds me that he's here now. And I kind of like it. Okay, I like it a lot.

I was shocked last night when he packed up my stuff and took me home with him. I honestly thought he would just turn around and leave. But he didn't. When we got home, he made space for me in his closet and told me I'm home now. I feel like I can finally breathe. I have a real home with SJ, where we were always meant to be. Together forever.

Goldie's was the closest I ever felt at home. But here with

SJ feels right. My heart feels so full being here with him.

I glance down at my phone. It's been blowing up on and off with texts from my parents. I'm not answering them.

I sent a text to both in the same chat: Do not contact me anymore. I'm blocking you.

It's done. SJ's right. We fight together. When he's tired, I'll fight. When I'm tired, I guess he just moves me in with him.

Harley flops down next to me and lays her head on my leg.

"Hey, sweet girl. How are you?" I stroke her soft ears and notice she's a lot happier and calm now.

SJ leans down and kisses me. "Hi," he says.

"Hi," I say back and smile over at him.

"Feel better today?"

"Yeah, I let my parents know I blocked them. So be on the lookout for them popping up like mean little leprechauns."

"We'll handle whatever comes our way." He shrugs. "You work tomorrow?"

"Yeah, and I have a meeting with HR first so that should be interesting. I could be getting let go."

"You want to go by dad's shop and bring him lunch today? He's going stir-crazy now that he's finally home from the hospital but can't work. He could use a little reminder from his doctor that he needs to take it easy."

"Yeah, of course. I can do that," I agree.

"Do you want to keep Harley with you today?" he asks as he scratches her ears, and she leans into him.

"Yeah, I'd like that." I look at him and think about how good life feels when we do normal things together like eat, go to his games, and have Harley with us.

He scratches her ears. "She knows you need her."

"It's official, huh? When will you officially be head coach?" I stare at him, full of pride. I'm happy for him.

He nods, beaming with excitement. "We're telling the team tonight. Evan got the new board going, and everything is official." He smiles at me. He's a lot happier, and oh, how I missed this.

SJ: Can you check in with Dad and Bear? I'm finishing up some things and running behind.

I send him a text back letting him know I got it, and it's no problem.

I let myself into the shop, and Axel waves across the bay. He's been helping Sam out since he's been out. "Hey, Axel. Where's Bear and Sam?"

He nods upstairs and continues working. Before I can make it up the stairs, he calls, "Callie."

I turn, and he nods to the front of the bay he's working on. I see my parents' black SUV has pulled in and my parents are getting out. Great. I groan.

"Axel," I call, and he's beside me before I can finish asking him to come over.

They stroll in, and my mom looks around disdainfully like she's thinking she's going to need a shower after just stepping foot inside of a place that she deems is so beneath her. I roll my eyes.

"I told you to leave me alone," I clip. "You need to leave."

Axel tenses but still says nothing, his fist clenching next to me.

"You have no loyalty, young lady," my dad barks.

I just stare at them. "I'm done with both of you. Stay away from me."

"I'm your mother," she shrieks. "How can you choose these bikers over your own family?"

"You're not my family. You are abusive, toxic, and vile, and I will say it one last time. Stay away from me."

Her eyes get wider, and she steps closer to my dad who isn't saying anything either. I look behind me and Allie, Paige, and Beth are lined up behind us with their arms crossed. Wow. They're here for me. Warmth fills me when I think about my newfound family we've created here. Sometimes family isn't always blood.

Beth says, "You have about thirty seconds to get going."

Paige picks up a pipe in the corner and rests it on her shoulder, ready for what, I'm not sure, but my eyes are wide in surprise and shock.

Allie pipes in, "My turn to speak. Leave town. Sell your

house, whatever you need to do. But you better go. Don't come back, there's nothing here for you. If you do come back, we'll make your life a living hell. All of us. Get." She glares at them, and Allie is scary when she's mad.

"You can't make me leave town," my dad spits.

"Why not?" Paige asks smugly. "It sucks when someone bullies you so badly you have to leave, doesn't it?" She swings the pipe around, and he eyes it nervously.

"Ten seconds," Mellie says from behind me.

"I don't have to put up with this." He turns and stomps to his SUV. My mom follows, looking back to glare at me one last time as she gets in. Because that's it for me. I have my family now, and it's not them. It never was.

SJ walks in and takes my hand and pulls me toward him, looking around cautiously at what just happened.

"What's going on?" he asks as he takes in the scene.

Axel looks at all of us and says to SJ, "They are scary."

"Who's scary?" Beth asks innocently as she picks up a stack of pizzas and carries it to the break room. "We just brought pizza."

"Are we going to eat or what?" Mellie asks casually from behind us.

Allie smiles sweetly. "We brought dessert from the bakery."

SJ stops in front of me and asks again, "What just happened?"

"My parents stopped by. I told them to leave, and they did. With help from friends." I try to hide my smile.

"You okay?" he asks, looking at me, his whiskey eyes full of concern.

"I'm going to be fine." And for the first time, I believe this.

"Where's our dog?" he calls over his shoulder as he goes to check on his dad.

"Upstairs with her grandpa," I call back, and he laughs and shakes his head. "I'd love to see his face when you call him that."

After everyone has eaten, caught up on everything going on, and given hugs and left, I watch SJ working on a car. I finally ask him the million-dollar question. "Why didn't you just tell me that my dad threatened you and made you leave?"

He stops sanding down the car and comes over to stand in front of me. "I didn't want to see you hurt again, and I was ashamed I let him get to me like that. Also, I was a kid," he says. "I believed it when he said he would hurt you and everyone else."

"I wish you'd told me."

"See this car right here? You and me? We're the car. We got sanded down, polished, and made new again. Your parents?" He holds up the sander. "They're useless like this sandpaper." And he rips the sandpaper off and tosses it into the trash can.

I hold my breath while he continues. The air feels electric between us.

"A fresh start," he says. "Their part of your story is finished. They won't get to be a part of our happily ever after."

"From now on, it's no longer us against the world. You are my whole world. You're my forever, Callie."

I cross the bay and kiss him, closing my eyes and savoring this moment, holding him close.

CHAPTER 34

Callie

NOW

I cross my legs and uncross them nervously, tapping my foot and trying to relax. If they're going to let me know, I'd just rather know so I can go home. Not knowing is driving me nuts.

Finally, the door to the human resources office opens, and a tiny woman with a huge pregnant belly steps out. "Dr. McGraw?" She smiles sweetly.

I stand and follow her into her office, and she reaches over to shake my hand. "I'm Whitney."

"Hi." I shake her hand and sit and wait.

"First, I want to apologize on behalf of the hospital for what happened with Dr. Douchet. I want you to know that he's no longer employed here. We are conducting a full investigation. I'm not able to give you any details currently, but I am very sorry."

I breathe a sigh of relief. "He's gone?"

She nods. "Yes."

"Am I being fired?"

She laughs. "No, you're being hired." She slides a packet of papers across her table to me. "I also asked for a ten percent increase in your base salary for what you've been through. And we've also enrolled you in our bonus program to compensate your student loan payments while you're employed here."

I smile and laugh nervously. "Really? Thank you." Relief fills me, and I finally exhale. I hadn't realized I'd been holding my breath.

"Really. You're a great physician. Everyone has such lovely things to say about you, and we're lucky to have you here. Welcome aboard, officially." She smiles warmly at me.

I nod. "Thanks, I'll look over all of this."

"Yes, and let me know by Monday if everything is good to go. See you around, Dr. McGraw," she says as she returns to her computer.

I step out into the hall and text SJ that I got the job. He immediately texts back.

SJ: Yes! You deserve this! Love you! Now get home so I can show you how much.

CHAPTER 35

NOW

"Good game, Coach."

"Thanks," I call back to someone already lost in the crowd since our game has ended. There's still a rush of energy in the stadium.

This was the last game of the season, and while we didn't get to the state championship this year, we played a great season. I have a feeling that next season will be even stronger.

It's been a helluva season. A few people in this town figured out that the high school kid who let people bully him is gone. Now I'm a strong coach who doesn't take shit from anyone. They wanted to make me out to be the bad kid? Didn't work. But I'm still here, and I'm going to make damn sure that no other kid gets bullied and pushed around like I was. Not on my watch. Goldie taught me well. Take care of your community and look out for others. I'm taking a page from her playbook.

After making sure all the players headed out safely for the night, I lock up and turn and see them waiting for me. *My family.*

When I came back, I couldn't have imagined that this was how things would go. I always felt Callie and I would find our way back to each other, but this was worth all the struggles and years apart. Because she was meant to be mine.

"Good game, Coach," she echoes from across the parking lot. She's sitting on the tailgate of my truck, bundled up in a blanket. Harley sits next to her wearing a sweater, tongue hanging out. Her tail wags as I approach the truck, and I scratch her ears as I lean in to kiss Callie.

"Hey, beautiful. You didn't have to wait for me." I pull her into a hug. I know she has to be tired after her long shift at the hospital and then coming to the game.

"Of course, I did." She pats the tailgate next to her, and I slide in. "I'm so proud of you."

Slipping my arm around her, I pull her closer to me. I reach into my pocket to pull out the ring and hold it up to her.

"SJ…" she breathes. Her eyes soften, and her hand goes over her mouth.

I gently pick up her hand and say, "I've been waiting for the perfect moment for this. But this feels like the perfect moment. You, me, and Harley. Callie, will you marry me?"

Yes," she says with a huge smile as I pull her hand toward me and slide the ring that Beth, Allie, Mellie, and Paige all conspired to help me pick out quickly from a local jeweler. How they kept this a secret is beyond me. I've wanted to give it to her for over a week now.

"It feels good to have you both here with me. My family."

"Nowhere else we'd rather be." She leans toward me and wraps her hands around my neck, pulling me close to kiss her.

"Let's go home."

Callie

"Five minutes!" Mellie calls.

"There," Beth says as she fixes my hair and sets down the curling iron. "Perfect."

"Here's your bouquet." Allie hands me a beautiful bundle of yellow roses. Simple yet beautiful.

"How do I look?" I stand and straighten my dress. I look up to see Paige, Mellie, Beth, and Allie staring at me in adoration. Beth wipes her eyes.

"What?" I look between them all, confused. Nerves fill me as I think about seeing SJ and his reaction to me in my dress.

"You look so beautiful," Paige breathes.

"Thank you." I put my hand to my face and fan it, hoping

I don't cry and mess up my makeup. I'm so happy and nervous; all the emotions are rolling through me.

"Ready to become Mrs. Reid? Or Dr. Reid?" Allie asks, linking her arm in mine and guiding me to the doorway.

"Absolutely ready." I smile.

Evan plays guitar outside, and Sam waits inside the doorway for me, ready to walk me down the aisle and give me away. He smiles at me, looking handsome in his suit.

I take his hand, and he guides me outside to the beautiful aisle set up in ivory down the backyard. It's lined on each side with lanterns containing burning candles. The sun is going down, giving us a beautiful sunset view of our lookout. A spot we get to share with our family and friends. White lights are strung everywhere and wrapped around trees. Chairs are set up on both sides of the candlelit aisle. There are no his and her sides. It's a beautiful mixture of familiar faces who love and support us—friends from the hospital, the Eastern Bones members, SJ's Army friends, and people from the town we love. I cherish all of these people so much.

Goldie joins Sam and me. I smile at both, and they join me on either side. "Ready?" Goldie whispers. I couldn't decide who would walk me down the aisle, so I asked them both.

"Let's do this," I say as we walk down the aisle, and my breath hitches when I see him waiting for me. He's in a black suit with a red tie. He smiles and looks up at Evan and back at me, looking proud.

When we get closer to him, my heart beats faster. He walks over, and Sam tucks me in next to SJ. Goldie kisses my cheek and says, "I love you." Goldie and Sam take a seat next to each other in the front. I turn to face SJ.

"We made it," SJ whispers loudly with a relieved sigh, and a few people in the front laugh.

Bear smiles. "Welcome, everyone. I've known SJ and Callie for a very long time. And there's no love like the love these two have for each other. Even when they were lost, they still found their way back to each other. Because they are meant to be."

Bear looks at SJ. "Go ahead with your vows."

SJ turns and looks at me, taking my hands, his shaking nervously in mine. "Callie, I promise to love you forever. I promise to make you laugh no matter what and do anything to make you happy. I promise that we will be a family forever. I love you."

"SJ, I have spent the past twelve years with a part of me missing that I never thought I'd find again. You are the person I want to spend forever with. I promise that from this day forward, I will never stop loving you. Nothing can ever divide us again because I know that with our love, we will be stronger together. Forever."

"There's my wife," SJ murmurs as he wraps his arms around me and nuzzles my neck, stealing me away from a few of my friends from the hospital I was talking with.

"Yes, husband?" I tease as he pulls me in and wraps his arms around my waist.

"Just missed you."

"It's only been about five minutes since I last saw you." I chuckle.

"Too long." He grins. "Plus, I want to cut our cake."

"I love you, Mr. Reid."

"I love you, Dr. Reid," he whispers as he pulls me in to dance, resting his forehead on mine.

"Ready for forever?"

The end.

FREEDOM VALLEY SERIES

Falling Inn Love

Baked Inn Love

All Inn Thyme

All Inn Books

Forever Inn Love

Snowed Inn

NON-FICTION

Writers Inspiring Writers with Jennifer Probst

Erin Branscom has read everything she can get her hands on for as long as she can remember. To this day, her favorite place is still the library. In 2021, after a decade of writing novels just for fun, she finally decided to finish a book series and has found writing novels to be her greatest escape. Erin is a passionate author's advocate and loves sharing books on all of her platforms. She lives in Oklahoma and loves gardening, traveling, and spending time with her husband, four kids, and best friend Molly, a Boston Terrier mix.

Website: Erinbranscom.com

Mailing list: bit.ly/3Z0QbV2

TikTok: @mylevel10life

Bookbub: @erinbranscom

Goodreads: www.goodreads.com/mylevel10life

Facebook: @erinbranscomauthor

Facebook Reader Group: Erin's Reading Nook

Instagram: @mylevel10life

Email: erin.branscom@gmail.com

ACKNOWLEDGEMENTS

Dusty, Kameron, Ethan, Audrey, and Charlotte, thank you for being the best family I could ever ask for. Thank you for always supporting me on my crazy adventures. I love you all so much!

Avi, you're a great kid and I'm so glad we get to have you in our lives.

Mom, thanks for reading my books and encouraging me. You're the best mom.

Dad and Michael in heaven, I miss you both so much. Every day. It's not fair. I wish you were here. I hope I've made you proud.

Julie and Elizabeth, thanks for being great sisters. We've been through so much in the past few years. Our family is still standing strong.

Auntie Susan and Auntie Paula, you are the best aunts anyone could ever ask for. I love you both so much.

Molly, you are my best friend in the entire world. Thanks for listening to me talk about all this book stuff and for always keeping me warm in my chair. You deserve all the bones and snuggles. I'm so sorry I keep bringing home more dogs. You know you're always my #1.

Brianna, I couldn't do it all without you! Thank you so much!

Erica, you're my favorite human. Period.

Kristi, your taco dates, and brainstorming sessions mean the world to me. I'm so thankful for you and your friendship. Also, your success is so inspiring. You work harder than anyone I know!

Nicole and Jenny, thank you for making this book the best that it could be!

Enni (Yummy Book Covers), thank you for bringing Freedom Valley to life. I love all these covers so much! Thank you for all that you do!

Laura, thank you for being the best alpha reader and giving me real feedback that challenges me to always do better.

To my beta readers, thank you so much for all your support and help!

To everyone reading this... Thank you for taking a chance on me and my Freedom Valley world.

www.ingramcontent.com/pod-product-compliance
Lightning Source LLC
Chambersburg PA
CBHW070559300726